EREV

EREV

ELYA SCHECHTMAN

TRANSLATED FROM THE YIDDISH BY

JOSEPH SINGER

CROWN PUBLISHERS, INC., NEW YORK

© 1967, by Crown Publishers, Inc.

LIBRARY OF CONGRESS CATALOG CARD NUMBER: 67–17706

PRINTED IN THE UNITED STATES OF AMERICA

BOOK ONE

BOOK ONE

1

AND AS THE STUBBORNNESS MOUNTED, his waning powers flickered and grew consumed within him.

Finally, unable to push himself any further, he stopped. He felt the game left leg that was bent at the knee burn mercilessly and draw. The eyes—those solitary windows of light and life—flooded over with tears of pain. His heart pounded.

He stood there in the middle of one of the longest, most turbulent, autumn nights of the year and if not for the crutches that supported him he would have fallen face first in the sand.

From somewhere behind the silvery-green ponds of the distant, frigid yet thickly starred sky, a large, nearly full moon suddenly came floating out over the forest.

He wipes his eyes on his sleeve and looks directly at the moon. His thoughts are blank. It merely occurs to him that the glistening-wet moon is trembling on the wind. . . . Long red drops fall onto the earth. A few even find the corners of his mouth. He licks them with his dry tongue. How very salty they taste. . . .

He breathes heavily and noisily, his mouth agape. A stray, forgotten whiff of a leaf burned by the sun comes drifting on the wind. The earth already smells of snow.

*   *   *

Earlier, before he had found his sister lying in her own blood on the threshold, long before that, he had already lost count of the days and even of the weeks.

3

Through cities and towns, down roads and wayward paths he wandered, half-starved. He would not even stretch his hand out but waited until others would guess his needs. And when they gave him something, he felt insulted, humiliated. Through sweltering days and cold rainy nights he hobbled along on his crutches, the soldier coming home from the Russo-Japanese War.

He knew that this was his only solace, the source that fed and nourished his courage and his will—home. Wherever he might be, whatever the occasion, it lingered there before his eyes. He could see his father on the ladder picking the rotting apples from the trees and laying them carefully in the basket. Friday evenings after work, he would sit on the mound of earth beneath the crooked windows of their house and smoke the last pipe before the Sabbath. His head would be bent toward his shoulder and he would be snapping the fingers of his left hand. And Mother . . . the white kerchief tucked behind the ears, walks heavily but quietly from the stall carrying in her veiny hands the milkpail with the two, newly banded wooden hoops. In the family, she is known as "the Quiet Summer." And beneath the old, low-set, thickly branched pear tree stands his brother, Daniel, with the green, woolen scarf over his shoulders, his hair gray as a dove, a paint brush in hand. He always looks off somewhere into the distance, then makes a brushstroke. His wife, Malka, refers to him as "My ornament, my crown, my worry. . . ."

But the clearer the soldier saw them the sharper his feeling—*I have no home. It's nothing more than a lovely dream . . . an illusion.* And he felt miserable and alone. And even if such a home did exist in some faraway place, he, Avrom Boyar, would never find his way there.

He had seen the summer die before his eyes. The last of the hot days had smoldered. The wormwood had already bloomed along the roads. Everything everywhere was withering. High in the sky the storks noisily arranged their long migrations. Wild ducks were strung out in long snaky trails.

4

Below, alongside the river, the woodcocks flew. Waxen-yellow leaves fell from trees. Only the service-tree still wore its fiery crown.

Heavy was the soldier's heart. But as soon as he reached the Polesian swamps overgrown with bright moss, with reeds and osiers; as soon as he saw the wooden shacks with the yellow pumpkins on the black thatch roofs; the flax; the earthen jugs on the twig-woven fences, and the sunflowers in the gardens—those large, end-of-summer eyes with the thick, golden lids—all this made Avrom Boyar tremble with joy for the first time after all his trials and suffering.

He stood there as if rooted, disbelieving his eyes, still afraid that this familiar, pointy leafed maple; the old stunted willows in the dank, dark valley; the lofty pines whose roots showed above ground with the warm, sharp odor of pitch still clinging to them; the scattered white-striped birches; even the rolling white sands that stretched for miles—he was afraid that all these were nothing more than a beautiful dream, a magical fantasy.

And in order to convince himself, the soldier closed his eyes and waited a moment before opening his dust-covered lids. No, he hadn't deceived himself. Everything for which he had been pining so desperately for months lay before him so lifelike and true.

And suddenly beneath his one good foot he felt the Polesian earth—the earth on which he had been born and raised.

Made it, have you? he asked himself. *Well, Avrom, take heart. . . . It's no longer far. . . . You'll rest up a day at Rochel's where you'll be royally greeted. . . . Ah, it'll be good to be a guest. . . . And later—home.*

And with a kind of drunken joy he drove the crutch against the ground and cried out: "Mama!" And then with pride because he had survived, had endured everything and not buckled under, he added to himself very softly, "I'm coming home, Mama, I'm coming home."

5

Emaciated, merely skin and bones; a shadow with half-closed eyes, a scraggly, curly beard and white, cracked, dried-out lips; a dust-covered phantom with a cockade on the lambskin hat and wearing a short, shrunken, military greatcoat, the discharged soldier hopped on his crutches half-barefoot, ever nearer and nearer to home, where his parents each morning and night in their small alcove uttered the prayer for the dead over him.

But it was still a far distance to his parents' home deep there somewhere in the Polesian forests. In fact, he still had a way to go to reach his sister Rochel's house.

And day by day the soldier hobbled ever farther into autumn. At first, the roads were livelier. Peasants tilled the land, sowed the winter grain, dug and carted away wagon-loads of potatoes. Tethered cattle grazed on the meadows. In the valley, cowherds sat around flickering bonfires.

Frequently, a wagon would ride by. Every peasant was glad to give a soldier a lift—every shack was good for a bit of food or a night's lodgings.

Lying there in the fresh hay in the evenings, bone-weary, he would listen to the dear, familiar song float up to the sky:

> "Something rustled in the woods
> The sun turned to the wind,
> Wind, you wind
> Don't you break, don't you bend
> My plants along the road. . . ."

And tears would fill the soldier's eyes as he listened to the song fade off into the night and be borne by the wind into the forest. And the trees all around would rustle, rustle. He could not explain why the song made him cry. His soul would be filled with sadness.

But soon somewhere nearby, apparently among the shocks of corn, many strings would strum beneath someone's fingers and a warm voice would begin to sing:

> "Oh, be well my black-browed love
> Please do not forget me. . . ."

6

The soldier would smile through his tears. *No,* he would say to himself with assurance, *Dobche has not forgotten me.* . . . He would fold his arms behind his head and begin to sing softly:

> "What did you do to me, dear life of mine,
> That I am so drawn to you?
> You did nothing to me, dear life of mine,
> I simply fell in love with you. . . ."

And then the whole night through he would dream of the girl with the black eyes and the long blonde braids. In his dream he would hold her and ask: "Couldn't you guess, couldn't you see that I'm in love with you? As soon as you came to your Uncle Zachariah's, actually, as soon as you stepped off the wagon, you planted both your feet deep in my heart. . . ."

HE DID NOT REST UP AT HIS SISTER'S as he had hoped, nor was
he an honored guest at anyone's house. He had hopped into
the village a half day after the massacre and had found her
lying in her blood across the threshold. That very night, by
the light of a dozen lanterns, she was buried in the Jewish
cemetery.

At first, no one knew who he was, the bearded soldier
in the fur cap with the cockade, who kept pushing close to
the coffin, trying to put his shoulder under it. But one told another and soon they all knew.

"It's a brother. . . ."

"Home from the war. . . ."

"Come to visit his sister. . . ."

"Woe is us, woe is unto us. . . ." And a fresh lament
erupted in the night and rose up to the sky.

That same night, right after the dirt had been flung on
the grave, he let no one detain him and rapidly detaching
himself from the crowd resumed his journey. Now he was
even more anxious to get home. Maybe they were all lying
there stretched out across the threshold?

And with each passing day Avrom Boyar grew more and
more like the autumnal forest—blacker and more silent. He
did not even stop for the nights. He had entered that part
of Polesie where people are few—and the swamps many. Seldom did he come across a village there, and miles of forests
separated the isolated farmhouses.

And the days were very short. Just now, another had

ended. A kind of ominous silence hung over everything despite the rustling of the wind. Seldom was heard now the chuck of a woodpecker pecking at a dried-out trunk or the song of the bluethroats at the end of the day.

The wind carries to him the smell of water—somewhere nearby flows a river. His satchel holds a few potatoes, a small head of cabbage, two onions, and a pinch of salt. He will go down to the river bank, build a fire and cook for himself a meal. The hunger gnaws at him until he feels faint.

And although he is starving, still (a habit) he works slowly, deliberately, earnestly and with devotion, as if he were doing all this not for himself but for someone gravely ill—for whom the food can mean salvation.

Onto the stiff skirt of his greatcoat he peels potatoes, shreds cabbage, and slices a pile of onions. Then he sweeps it all into the smoke-blackened, brass military kettle and with one crutch works his way down the steep, sandy bank to the water. The river is still running but it is icy cold, on the verge of freezing over. The dense, leaden waters barely reflect the low setting sun. First he washes his hands, then his face, and only afterward rinses the food in the kettle. At the same time he speaks to his mother: "I'm coming, Mama, I'm coming!"

In the dense, leaden-gray waters that do not reflect the sinking sun he suddenly sees burning lanterns and hears the first spadeful of dirt hit the grave of his slain sister. He gets up quickly—the water draws him to itself. . . .

It is very hard for him to scramble up the steep bank carrying the full kettle. His foot keeps sliding in the shifting sand as if the ground were being pulled out from under it.

Sweating, his one good leg barely supporting him, he claws his way up to where his greatcoat, his satchel, and his other crutch are lying. He catches his breath and with his hands digs out a shallow pit in which to build a fire.

Having arranged the twigs and the dried cones—those that were handy—on top, he reaches into his pocket for the

9

matches, but his face suddenly grows even darker and the eyes drier and more glazed. He searches, taps, shakes, turns all his pockets and the satchel inside out. No matches.

He retraces his steps down to the river, searches there and rummages. He remains sitting by the water and stares into the rushing current. The sun goes down. A crow sharpens his beak on a pine bough. It seems to the soldier that he is the only human being on earth. And the river calls to him again.

He quickly scrambles up the bank on all fours and lies there with his eyes closed. He can almost taste the hot potatoes and smell the salty sweetness of the mushroom soup. He leaps to his feet and angrily strikes the crutch against the kettle and everything goes flying. The kettle itself rolls clanging down the bank and falls into the water.

The soldier looks down at the river. The kettle hasn't sunk to the bottom. It has half filled with water and goes floating with the stream. And the current carries it between the sandbars to an island where a solitary pine sways over the water. Apparently as long ago as the spring it had been torn loose from a raft.

Avrom Boyar takes to the road again, following the sunset. Silvery-white rays shimmer in the west. The woodsman knows—it is a portent of frost. The blustery night winds tear the stars loose from the sky. Such winds bring blizzards.

And the soldier, drenched in the sweat of anxiety again, stumbles down roads and paths along the deserted black forests, and mumbles: "I'm coming, Mama, I'm coming. . . ."

The night presses upward from the earth and down from the sky. It is starry, this end-of-autumn night, yet black and extremely long—on the eve of winter. The crutches sink into the sand and refuse to withdraw. The strain makes the wounded leg swell and suppurate. The pain travels even higher in the body, courses through all the veins up to the neck and begins to pound at the head and eyes. And as the

10

stubbornness mounts, his waning powers flicker and grow consumed within him.

*   *   *

Avrom stands there in the middle of the night on the sandy road neither asleep nor awake, his face cinder red, his eyes flooded with tears of pain, his heart pounding. A tremor goes through him and if not for the crutches that support him he would long ago have fallen with his face in the sand.

And the wet moon still trembles on the wind. . . . Strangely long, thin, crooked shadows creep over the piles of sand. They rise, sway, and fall again. Avrom feels that someone is following him, dogging his steps. He even hears dry twigs break under somebody's feet.

"Rochel," he stammers, "Rochel, where are you?" And suddenly he begins to scream: "What do you want? What do you want of me?" No one answers and his voice sinks in the swamp. And somewhere there in the marshes a sick bird cries out. Avrom listens to the sharp, chopped-off cry issuing from the drowning gullet and he forgets about everything else. He has only one passionate urge now—to go into the swamp and find the sick bird. *Who else will help him?* he wonders as he moves on. But again someone is following him. The other springs down from the sandhill, also on one leg, and silently pulls the crutches out from under the soldier's arms. The moon tears from the sky and strikes against a treetop and the earth becomes covered with sparks.

The soldier lies in the road while the tall, thick forest growths entwine themselves around him. A white egret with long, black legs springs from his one shoulder to the other and with its yellow-green beak pecks at his temples. He cannot defend himself against the bird. With its bony beak it will soon bore through and shatter his skull. A black birch aglow with fire roams through the forest. Blazing, moist earth creeps into the soldier's eyes. . . . He is astride a sweat-

11

ing horse, his sword unsheathed. With thousands of others around him he shouts: "For the Tsar!"

Suddenly the horse rears back on its hind legs, almost dislodging its rider. A black stream of blood gushes from its mouth. Kicking its front legs in the air the horse begins to slide down from the sap. . . . Avrom Boyar tries to dismount when suddenly he feels something thin and dull, but terribly hot, pierce his upraised knee with a murderous rage. . . .

3

DOWN THE SAME SANDY POLESIAN ROAD on which the soldier lay unconscious rolled a wagon bearing four passengers.

The two younger men, having waged a long and heated debate about the individual, the masses, personality, and the rabble, had dropped off into a contented sleep.

The third man, well along in years already but still called Lazar the Ashmedai by fellow coachmen because of his strength, sat in front on the driving box. His body, quite broad at the bottom, tapered to a narrow top. His hareskin cap was pulled well down over his face, his head dangled on his chest, his eyes were closed and he seemed to be sleeping. He was merely dozing, however, as was his custom at any time when no one disturbed him.

The fourth passenger, a woman, had not dozed off, nor slept the whole night, nor uttered a single word during the entire long journey. She just sat there, her back stooped, her head in her hands, her eyes staring as if convinced that on this windy, starry, moonlit night in this very forest she would yet meet that individual who would help her, advise her, show her how to put an end to her existence, and how to cut the noose she had worn secretly around her neck for nearly a decade. *You've lived a shameful life, Yeva,* she told herself, *a shameful life. . . .*

The deeper the wagon penetrated into the forest the more she was seized with a feeling of inner coldness and despair.

Her husband lay sprawled the whole length of the wagon,

13

wrapped from head to foot in a black fur-lined coat—he kept talking in his sleep. She smiled contemptuously. *Giving a report to his Mommy again . . .*

The other man, the Doctor, lay at her feet, his head pillowed on a sack of oats. His handsome black beard swayed with every motion of the wagon and the large eyeglasses reflected the light of the moon.

It was years already since her husband had stirred a human emotion within her. Even his baiting wiles, which had been so provocative in the past, no longer incited her. Lately, she had fallen victim to one of life's worst afflictions—indifference. Everything and everyone with whom she came into contact left her with the same reaction—*who cares?*

True, she never could forgive nor less forget the crimes he had committed against her as a human being and as a wife. Time, however, had dissipated all enmity and hatred and relegated him to the position held by the other inhabitants of the four-story building that was their home: his father, Reb Nossan Lande, the former rabbi and now a kind of hermit saint; his mother, with her triple chins and dangling earrings, the forceful businesswoman who confided in no one and personally visited the annual fairs in Leipzig; his two arrogant sisters; their husbands; or even the household furnishings that required nothing more from her but some daily maintenance.

But as the wagon pushed deeper and deeper into the forest, and nearer to that place from which she had been so violently torn, the smoldering wounds, resentments, and sorrows were once more stirred within her. And her husband's moralizations about the superiority of the individual, his remark that "only a personality can guide the masses," had galled her beyond endurance. Until now, his words would have had no effect upon her but for an occasional bitter smile at the thought that he prided himself on being one of the "individuals."

But now, rumbling along in this wagon that seemed

14

about to shake loose her very soul, she suddenly felt deeply insulted. Ever since she'd known him he had never even remotely thought of her as an individual too. . . .

And now that she was fast approaching the place where the greatest tragedy of her life had occurred, those thoughts that had never allowed her a moment of peace began to torment her with renewed fury.

And he, who from mere lust and caprice had taken her by force, and fathered her child . . . he, Alexander Lande, the absolute master of a hundred looms and a beautiful young wife, now lay sprawled in the wagon under his fur coat—lest, God forbid, he catch cold—and mumbled in his sleep. She had a sudden urge to shake him by the shoulders and to cry: "Listen here, Alexander, an end to this game! They know I'm not going there because of a sick mother. It's on account of Daniel that I came—it's for him that I'm bringing the Doctor!"

Suddenly, a terrible thought struck her: *No, it isn't because of Daniel at all. . . . I've come to visit the graveyard of my love. . . .*

And she sat there, stooped, and staring into the night, waiting for that something . . . that someone . . .

And the moon floated over the Polesian forest and the earth was blanketed beneath a gleaming hoarfrost and somewhere within the swamp the sick bird kept crying. The cold and the glistening stars gave portent that day was about to break.

Suddenly, the horses jerked the wagon. It may have seemed that Ashmedai had shirked his duties and allowed them to stray onto a strange path in the darkness, but the moment it happened the coachman came instantly awake and looked up with alertness. "So, that's the way it is?" he growled, drawing the reins taut. "Going downhill you'd malinger, would you? Go on with you, not with me will you creep like a prince after a sweatbath. Gee up!"

The early morning breeze carried off his voice, and Yeva

could not hear what he said to the team. She felt like begging him, *Don't push the horses so hard.* . . . *It's more than I can take to come back to the place from which I was so cruelly driven.*

She moved closer to Ashmedai and yelled to him over his shoulder: "Don't be in such a hurry, man! I'm not up to meeting Daniel—or my mother just yet. She is my worst enemy. . . . If not for her and her brother, Abushl, none of this would have happened. . . . She hated me ever since I was in the cradle. She hated everyone, but me most of all. . . . The only daughter, and so much hate. . . . But why?"

The wind flung Ashmedai's great beard into her face but she did not even feel it. Only after he had leaned toward her and shouted, "Madam, hold on to the side!" did she realize that she was kneeling with both her hands on his shoulder. *Had she actually said these things to him? No, it could not be.* . . .

"Did I say anything to you?" she asked him, amazed at herself.

But just then Ashmedai leaped to his feet and bellowed so that the whole forest shook: "Whoa now!" And he sprung from the wagon. Before she could grasp what was happening, the wagon was on its side and she lay in Ashmedai's arms watching a wheel spin overhead.

"Lucky!" he grunted.

She scrambled out of his arms and stood up. "We could have been killed!"

"I couldn't hit him, after all."

"Hit whom?"

"There," he pointed with his whip handle, "someone's lying in the road."

The noise and commotion, the cries of fear from beneath the capsized wagon added to Ashmedai's roars not only disrupted the forest but temporarily revived the soldier too.

He opened his eyes and looked up at the trees. In front of him—a wagon on its side, people, horses with heads thrown back, a thill pointing up into the sky. . . . And close to the earth, reclining against a tree—the moon, so drawn-out and pale. . . . No, no, it could not be the moon! Hadn't it just shattered, crumbled into little bits and been strewn all over? No, it wasn't the moon but a slice of bread. . . .

And now he saw his sister crawling out from her grave. Her head was not visible, only her bare arms, bloody to the elbows. These blood-stained hands swayed over the mound of sand and with grasping, talon-like fingers clawed at the slice of bread. The soldier's mouth grew even more bitter inside and his throat more parched. "Rochel!" he pleaded. "Rochel, don't take it all, leave a crumb for me too!"

And the long-legged egret began to peck at his temples with its yellow-green beak again, until he felt himself going mad. . . .

But soon everything dissolved into blackness—the wagon, the people, the bloody arms, the crust of bread—it all vanished from sight. . . .

Yeva was secretly pleased that the wagon had turned over. Whatever happened, the journey would be extended . . . the dreaded homecoming delayed.

Her husband, still terrified by being so rudely roused, came running at the Doctor, waving his arms madly and screaming in a thin, lunatic voice. How many highwaymen had actually attacked and would Ashmedai be able to hold them off? After all, the teamsters considered him a champion. . . .

"I'll buy him a horse if he saves us! Tell him that I'll buy him—"

"You'd better shut up, Mr. 'Individual,' " his wife exclaimed. "No one has attacked us. You're even a bigger coward than I thought."

She helped the Doctor to his feet. "Come, there is a man lying in the road."

The Doctor, who had little experience in such matters, spread his hands helplessly and blinked. He had lost his

17

glasses and could see little now beyond the strong moonlight.

Alexander took a step toward him.

"What do you think, is he faking?" he asked with impatience.

The Doctor sighed. "No, he's not faking. Take his hand and you'll see for yourself. This man is on fire. . . ." Desperate to help but unable to do so, his suffering seemed more acute than the victim's. "A terrible accident, indeed. Look here, the leg is all swollen. It could be anything, even a gas inflammation. It's entirely possible. Here, Alexander Natanovitch, take hold of his leg. You'll see for yourself."

Alexander Natanovitch went off to put on his fur-lined coat.

"What do you think of this weather?" he asked, pacing alongside the wagon. "Illya Illitch, find out from him who he is."

"Find out who he is? Some trifle *that* is! That's the hardest thing of all." He stooped again to take the soldier's pulse. "The one who always suffers most from war is the common man. It's disgraceful! I haven't the slightest doubt that this man was discharged from the hospital before he was cured."

"Illya Illitch, let us waste no more time," Yeva said. "Can you find out anything from this man in his condition?"

"Absolutely not. But at this time it seems to me that it isn't too important who this man is and where he is going. We've got some twenty versts yet to go, wouldn't you say?"

"Just about." She turned to the coachman, who was harnessing the horses. "Please take out the side of the wagon and bring it around here, Reb Lazar."

"What for? I'll carry him to the wagon."

"No, Reb Lazar, bring the wagon-side here." She looked at her husband. "We'll take him along with us. Once we get there, we'll decide further what to do with him."

The Doctor, a bachelor, listened with eyes closed. He had

18

heard something new in her voice, something unusual here in the cold, moonlit, eve-of-winter forest.

"Do you agree?" she asked her husband.

"God bless you. Of course, I agree."

Alexander Lande stood by the side of the wagon completely bathed in moonlight. The whole journey had distressed him. His lips were twisted. He was suspicious of everything and everybody. Wherever he looked he sensed a plot against him. . . . They wanted him dead. He was convinced that Ashmedai had capsized the wagon intentionally, that the soldier had purposely lain down in the road. He was a fake soldier anyhow and nothing good would come of the whole thing. . . . The old pains in the stomach came surging back.

"Why are you just standing there, Alexander?"

"What can I do to help him?" And as was his wont whenever he witnessed a tragedy he put his hand inside his pocket to give a donation to the victim.

His wife came up very close to him: "Alexander, the soldier must be transferred into the wagon," she said quietly. "It's just possible that he's an individual too."

He had trouble recognizing her voice, so full was it of bitterness and contempt.

4

THE STARS BEGAN TO FLICKER OUT, the moon cast a silvery grayness, day was dawning. The cold wind grew stronger still and chilled the bones. The sun was about to rise. The weary, foam-flecked horses plodded along with effort, making the wagon wheels creak.

Ashmedai dozed on. It had never occurred to him that these fine people should thank him or even mention his self-sacrifice. If he had not jumped out of the wagon in time and broken its fall with his body they would have surely all been crushed.

Yeva had settled herself at the feet of the soldier, who lay there still dazed and quiet and only from time to time took rapid, noisy breaths. Smiling, she watched the Doctor trail the wagon, his hands folded behind his back, his head erect. He walked with an odd, highstepping stride, his beard bisected by the wind, and whistled the tune of a favorite song.

> I sieved my sieve through,
> It scattered everywhere,
> Scattered everywhere,
> My shoes were torn
> So I dance in my stockings—

And when he came to the refrain, "dance, dance, come dance with me—" he began to whistle with youthful abandon and raised his feet even higher. *What a sweet man,* she thought, *he lives only for others. For the fifth year in a row he can be seen every night in his low, two-wheeled britzska, a tall, bony, yellow horse between the crooked thills. Every night he rides there through the narrow little streets among the crooked little houses. It's even said that he moved to this provincial town just because so many paupers lived there. . . . He doesn't even wait to be called but comes on his own—and like a friend, a member of the family. . . . And these paupers are not ashamed before him, neither with their ailments nor their poverty. . . .* Yes, he certainly was an idealist and she was terribly grateful to him that he had left everything behind and agreed to accompany her on such a tedious journey. But his goodness, devotion, and willingness to do everything for her had also created a terrible problem, and she knew that she had to free herself of him before she grew too deeply indebted.

Her husband had withdrawn his head inside his raised collar to avoid inhaling the steam that exuded from the overheated horses. He sat alongside the coachman, puffed on his Turkish cigar, and gloated over the fact that his workers had announced a strike at the exact time when the market was glutted with goods and his warehouses were bursting. *Let them enjoy their speeches on empty stomachs,* he thought with spiteful relish. He, Alexander Natanovitch Lande, had locked them out of his factory and gone off with his wife to pay a sick call on her mother. Actually, he was going more to speak with Yeva's father, old Gavril Boyar, who was filthy rich and might be enticed into a partnership.

Seeing him so pleased and smug up there enjoying his cigar, Yeva innocently remarked, "Alexander, suppose the soldier dies on us?"

He rose to the bait. "That's all I need at a time like this!"

"How come you're so afraid of everything? You were such a big hero when it came to me."

"Yeva, what's wrong with you today?"

"I want to be just like you, Alexander—an individual too."

21

He did not answer. The less one spoke with one's wife the better.

"Keep those horses moving and stay awake." He nudged the coachman. "All the man does is sleep. . . ."

Ashmedai did not even open his eyes but scratched himself behind the ear with the whip handle.

"Enough now! The horses are going uphill. . . ."

"Since when do you spare strangers' horses? Whip them! Whip them! The patient must be taken inside! I mean, we'll take him into the first house we come to, Yeva. After all, we did all we could for him. In the long run, one dares not—"

I know! I know! she yearned to say to him, *you've bought off your conscience already*. . . . But just then she noticed the soldier throw off his cover and raise himself to his elbows. His eyes were still closed but his neck was straining, extended, and his coated tongue licked the dry lips. She ordered the wagon stopped, drew the tin kettle, pillowed his head in her lap and without waiting for the Doctor's approval began slaking his thirst.

The soldier gulped noisily and choked on the water. His chin trembled and his teeth chattered against the tin vessel while great drops of sweat broke out over his forehead. And the eagerness with which he drank, combined with the trembling of his body, made her feel terribly worried and afraid for him. But disregarding any ill effects this might have had upon his condition she continued to assuage his terrible thirst. Yet the more she strove to do so the harder it became, and the kettle almost dropped from her fingers and dripped water down his jowl, beard, and greatcoat.

"That's enough, enough!" the Doctor shouted running up. "God have mercy on you, such a cold drink on top of such a high fever!" He wanted to arrange his eyeglasses but they weren't in their usual place—actually they hadn't turned up yet. He took the sick man's pulse again, first lowered, then raised his eyebrows. "Hm—yes . . . it might be beneficial to give him a sip of wine."

22

"It's there where it should be," Ashmedai grunted, then quickly added, "A bit of wine wouldn't hurt a healthy man either."

Yeva, glad that the wine could rectify her error of judgment, turned to her husband. "Alexander, give me a bottle of wine. He won't use up too much of it and even if he should and Mother needs more, we'll—"

"What is there to talk about? Let him drink all he wants! I think he's saying something. When will it be possible to find out who he is?"

"Not one clear word," the Doctor said, pouring a little wine into the kettle lid. "You won't get a single clear word out of him, Yeva Gavrilovna," he said, handing the lid up to her.

He watched with envy as she gave the sick man a drink, covered him, then brushed the hair out of his eyes—and he observed with near anger: "You'd make a marvelous nurse."

"I, a nurse? . . . Yes."

He sighed softly and without waiting for the wagon to start up began to walk on ahead along the side of the road.

Someone extinguished the last star in the sky.

The wagon began to wend its way uphill again as dawn broke over the still, still forest. A joyous chirping heralded the sun, seen again after so many cloudy days. Ashmedai opened his eyes, looked up, and began to urge the horses to a faster pace. The higher the wagon climbed the more expansive and fiery grew the sky.

Yeva sat with her eyes cast down. It was ten years since she had last seen the sun come up but she only glanced at it through her lowered lids. Her husband and the Doctor were saying something to her but she was somewhere else now, far in the distant past. . . . Another dawn on the very verge of summer. In order to avoid her mother, brothers, and sisters-in-law she has run away to be with him, with Daniel, there in back of the village. . . . She never has been able to be the first to come, she always has to find him already waiting. . . . She sees him now, his fingers entwined in the wild mop of hair. . . . He does not even turn toward her. . . . Apparently he hasn't yet noticed her arrival. . . . But as soon as she sits down quietly near him he slips his hand around her neck and whispers: "I searched for my beloved all night and could not find her."

She presses her head against his shoulder, they kiss, and she says: "I came to you, my beloved, in the field. . . . I rose before the sun. . . . Let us go out to the grape arbor and look at each vine separately. Perhaps they have blossomed already . . . maybe the pomegranates are in bloom too—"

"Yeva, darling," he says, "you know that inside my heart the buds have burst already. . . . The whole vineyard is in bloom."

She twines her arms around him and whispers: "My love . . . to you and you alone I'll give all my love. . . . Only to you, Daniel."

The soldier's eyes fluttered open. The first rays of the sun, warm and many-hued, stole between his lids. The wine had gone to his head and spread a warmth through his whole body. He looked up and saw—virtually on top of him, large as a wagon wheel and surely within reach—the blazing sun. . . .

Dazzled by its magnificence, intoxicated by the wine, he glanced up at the hovering faces and smiled. . . . His face was flaming in the glow of blinding sunlight. "Where am I?" he stammered. "Who are you?"

But he was too weak to go on. Trying to sort things out, his mind grew tangled again and his eyes closed.

But for all that, the Doctor managed to glean several words out of him. "The old Inn . . . Avrom . . ."

Alexander Lande removed the cigar from his mouth and turned to—of all people—the coachman. "Did you hear? Did you understand what he said?"

"Why shouldn't I? Don't I know Yiddish, after all?"

24

"But what does it all mean? The old Inn . . . Avrom
. . . What do you make of it?" the Doctor asked.

"Nothing at all," Alexander said with complete indifference, "but I've stopped worrying about him already. Yeva
was right. We'll take him along to my father-in-law's, and
there—"

But suddenly, to everyone's amazement, the woman
shrieked with pleasure and bent to stroke the soldier's face.
"Avromele, is it really you? Avromele?"

The soldier mumbled something, smiled, and went back
to sleep. Yeva did not take her eyes from him.

The others watched her run her finger along his black
brows and the tangled mop that sprouted out from beneath
his cap.

She said nothing to anyone, merely shrugged in rapture.
Was it really he, Avromele, Daniel's skinny twelve-year-old
brother who ten years ago had helped her run away from
home? He, who with Akiva's help had driven her in her
wedding gown through the dark and terrible forest? He, who
had whipped the horse with all the strength of his boyish
body through the pathless, dark woods although even Akiva
had been afraid that their sleigh would be dashed to bits?
The sleigh had, in fact, crashed against the tree trunks but
she hadn't ceased to plead: "Avromele—faster! Faster! My
fate is in your hands!"

No, it hadn't been Avromele's fault that her brothers
had caught up with them and brought her back by force.
. . . She stared fixedly at his bearded face and without looking up remarked to the Doctor: "It becomes more horrible all
the time. . . . How quickly even the bad years go flying
by. . . ."

25

5

UNEXPECTED NEWS ROCKED THE HOUSEHOLD. Yeva had come with her husband. They were at the Inn. Somehow, they had picked up Itzhok's younger son, the soldier, along the way and brought him home. She, Yeva, was there now talking with Daniel under the pear tree. . . .

Chaos followed. The house was in a mess. The Sabbath loaf was still in the oven. Since it was the eve of the Sabbath there was the usual amount of coming and going—and now guests had come besides. And what guests! After ten years of estrangement she had returned in all her splendor, the wealthy, pampered big-city lady. It wasn't as if Aunt Liba had come on foot, for whom an insincere "See here, a guest," would suffice.

The women, screaming as if a fire had broken out, called in their young ones, locked the doors behind them, and commenced to scour their grimy faces with the corners of their aprons. The youngsters squirmed and struggled in their mothers' arms like frightened hens. When it came to selecting new costumes for the children the mothers vented all their frustrations upon their offspring.

"Just a short while ago I made a new pair of trousers for Passover and already too small!" Grow they did, to spite one's enemies, like nettles round a fence. . . .

Having finished with the children they turned their attention to themselves. Aunt Liba assisted tall and skinny Beila who once more wore the felt wrapped round her left foot—heavy with child although six months had not passed since her last pregnancy. Beila struggled to get into her high-button shoes, gnawed on a sour pickle, and grunted isolated words: "They . . done . . . her . . . dirty, they . . . did . . ."

Everyone knew to whom she was referring.

"What did she know those days? She was a balky calf and a calf must be led on a rope."

"She was a wild one, all right."

"What of it? She was madly in love anyhow."

"With Daniel she would have starved."

"She'd be like Malka now, sewing from morning to night. . . ."

"—while he went on coloring those little boards. . . ."

At this, the master of the house, the father-in-law, Gavril Boyar, came barging in. "Women, not another word about that! Not even a single reminder, you magpies and chatterboxes!" And to his sister: "Liba, explain to them that the soul of another is like a dark forest."

And standing in the doorway, without even bothering to turn around, he ordered: "Put on all your finery and tell Velvel, Naftali, Zeinvel, and Simcha in my name to take off their shirts and get into their gaberdines and Sabbath caps!"

And he was gone. The commotion grew even greater and everyone forgot about the invalid, Neha, alone in her small white room with the little buck nestled in her arms.

Far from the house, near the birch forest, Yeva saw her family coming through the meadow to greet her. Her father led the way walking quickly, his face flushed, the skirts of his unbuttoned gaberdine flapping in the wind. Behind him marched her brothers, four abreast, their silk caps tilted to the side, taking long strides in their dung-spattered boots. The women, the cold notwithstanding, were in flowery jackets, deeply pleated and flounced dresses, and high button shoes, and afloat in a sea of children of assorted sizes.

Her mother was not among them. Apparently she no longer left her bed. But from the way they were dressed Yeva gathered that she was still alive. *How hard it will be for me to face her,* she thought. *I can't simply throw myself into her arms and kiss her. . . . I can't! I can't forgive what she did to me.*

Far in the rear, removed from the others, walked Aunt Liba. She had undoubtedly been sent again by Uncle Shmarya to dun her brother for the balance of her dowry. Or maybe she had come to get regards from her daughter? Shifra may have written her that Yeva was coming. Outside of her father and aunt they all seemed like strangers to Yeva, or—if possible—even more alien than strangers.

To her, they were all enemies, particularly her brothers. With silk caps just so rakishly askew, with the same fine smiles and pleasant expressions they had driven her out of the house, more dead than alive, ten years ago after the so-called wedding.

And they had not changed at all since then; only their beards seemed redder now. How much they resembled each other. . . . But he, her father, had changed considerably. She had left him with hair black as a gypsy's. Now it was white as was his beard, and the mustache, stained yellow from tobacco.

And she recalled his visit a year and a half after the wedding when he had come ostensibly to discuss something with her. But she had refused to see him.

She felt as if she were traversing the graveyard of her youth, having just come from the graveyard of her love—at Daniel's—and a feeling of something even beyond grief came over her.

But still her eyes yearned to take in everything, as it always happens when one returns after a long absence to the place of one's childhood.

Hardly anything had changed—a new wing had been added and the house now encroached upon the orchard.

There, round the well, stood the three gnarled alders,

28

their crowns dipping toward it as if eager to drink. On one such sunny, late fall day long ago Daniel had observed: "What could be more horrible than to spend a lifetime near a well and not be able to drink?"

Another time and in the same spot he had told her: "Yeva, I could not live without you. . . ."

Those had not been idle words, she realized now. With her own eyes she had seen that he was dying, dying. . . .

The flowery jackets seemed to sway and her father's snowy beard fluttered before her eyes.

Seeing his daughter spring from the moving wagon, Gavril grunted under his breath to Skinny Beila: "Did you mark that jump? God bless her!"

"Still the same wild goat," Beila remarked to her husband after her father-in-law had moved away. "I'll bet you she's swimming in gravy back there."

Velvel slowly took in his wife's flecked face and unbuttoned left shoe—and groaned. "And even if they kept you in goose-grease for three years do you think it would improve your looks? Yeva is like a lovely, straight pine."

"Why don't you look at her clothes instead?"

"Even if you had her clothes, what do you have to put them on?"

"Velvel, my dear, mind your tongue!"

Gavril broke into a trot toward his daughter and when they came together he took her face in his thick hands, looked into her eyes and said: "I know everything, daughter, don't think that I don't know. . . . The ocean is full of water, still one dies of thirst. May God be our judge." And not giving her a chance to reply he kissed her with his eyes closed, then went to greet his son-in-law and the stranger with the handsome beard.

Even the great distance from the birch forest to the house was not long enough to exchange kisses with everyone. At first, they seemed stunned, so cowed by the large hat with the peacock feathers, the gleaming black fur coat and the blue silk gloves that they did not know how to behave toward her. One nudged the other: "What are you afraid of—that she'll eat you?"

"Stop fidgeting, Gittel, and go up to her."

"And how about you, Beila, didn't you kiss her yet?"

The brothers wiped their palms on their gaberdines, cleared their throats, and stammered something in confusion. They were very much in awe of their wealthy sister.

Once back in the courtyard, however, fearful no other opportunity would arise, Skinny Beila hurled herself at Yeva, kissed and embraced her and would not be untwined. "Yiveniu, my treasure, you're as perfect as a little pickle, may the evil eye spare you! You remember my Aryeh? And these are my little ones. . . . This, Yeva dearest, is my Zorechl, named after my father, may he rest in peace. And this is Uncle Itzele, may he live long. And this is my grandfather, he should enjoy a glorious paradise. This is Grandma Ettele, she should intercede in heaven for us all . . . and this is Uncle Elie. . . ."

But Yeva, her eyes half shut, saw only one thing before her—the back of the Inn where Daniel sits reclining against the pear tree, wrapped in a warm red blanket with a green patch, in felt boots and bareheaded. His hair is still thick, curly and tangled, but it's white as snow now and she can barely recognize him. But when she tries to sit near him he glances toward a window where behind a curtain a head with a great shock of yellow hair can be seen. It is she, of course, Malka. . . .

"We mustn't. It'll grieve her terribly. Yeva, I knew you would come!"

"I couldn't stay away any longer."

"Who is the one with the beard?"

"A doctor."

"A doctor cannot help, my Yeva. . . . It isn't I who is

30

sick, it is my life. It's my life that needs healing, Yeva, and a doctor cannot help."

And now, each of the sisters-in-law stepped forward to present their children.

"This is my middle one, Frumele. You should hear her sing! And this is my Haiml, named after my Aunt Haya, the saint."

And Yeva reached back through generations to clasp the hands of grandparents, uncles, and aunts whose names were embodied in these plump, full-limbed and snotnosed youngsters.

"Asherl, Hershele, Moishele! This is your Aunt Yeva."

And she kissed them and swallowed her tears.

Suddenly, everyone stopped, looked at each other in fear and asked: "How did it happen and what will we do now?"

Yeva saw, running out of the house, a creature that could have been child or crone. It was barefoot, it wore a nightgown, and its white hair had been crudely shorn in a row of graduated "steps."

She sharpened her gaze. No, it wasn't a child—the face was too deeply lined. An odd kind of face too, like a chunk of yellowed bark where two gaping, unblinking eyes had been as if burned in.

Nothing—neither her keen eyesight, memory, or sense of recognition—could have provided Yeva the slightest hint that this was her mother. And even when her father stepped forward and groaned, "Neha!"—even then she could not let herself believe it. She watched the stubby-haired creature dart toward a little girl and snatch a painted wooden toy out of her hand. The child cried: "Grandma, give it back, Grandma! It's mine!"

But the grandmother, the toy pressed to her bosom, ran away. Gavril blocked her path: "Neha . . . Neha . . ."

She stopped and looked up at him. Then she turned, studied everyone, and her face changed. A gleam suddenly

31

showed in her faded eyes. She stared at Yeva as Gavril came charging up and clasped her hand. He knew the terrible things that followed when her eyes lit up that way.

The family stepped aside to let him carry her into the house. A strange, hot and moist feeling came over Yeva. Was this thing her mother? The mother who had slapped her so viciously ten years ago and compelled her to stand under the wedding canopy with Alexander? And from her throat tore a fierce, heartrending moan and she sank onto Aunt Liba's shoulder.

"Cry, Yeva, cry," her aunt urged as she led her inside. "Cry with all your heart, child. It'll make it easier for you. . . ."

6

THE DAY WAS ENDING. The huge, low-lying sun, whipped red by the wind, hung suspended on the verge of setting, as if it would have grown entangled in the thick branches of the old oak that stood alone and nearly leafless in the barren field. The air at day's end held the tang of frost and snow.

Itzhok Boyar sat sideways on the crate of chaff, his feet dangling over the side of the wagon, his broad shoulders moving under his fur-lined coat, one brow lifted as he chewed anxiously on a tip of his beard.

"—that way one can, God forbid, desecrate the Sabbath . . . to drive in such hurry, to shake the fruit down on the bare ground—" he complained to his young companion who lay sprawled in the straw on his belly, leaning on his elbows and was about to sink his white teeth into a cold, green apple. "It should soon be the time to light the Sabbath candles," he added.

"What do you advise, Reb Itzhok?" the young man said, biting into the apple with relish, "that we stop here, go out in the field and inaugurate the Sabbath right there and then? I, for one, am ready to stand before the cantor's desk—which in this case would be the sun—take out my fiddle and play for you the inaugurating chant like it hasn't been played since the world began—"

"Don't be such a wiseacre, Akiva," the older man interrupted angrily. "I cannot live without the Sabbath. One day a week at least I must feel sanctified. During the week, my soul gets used up within me. . . . You've taken enough from me as it is. Leave me a little Sabbath, at least."

Akiva grew so unnerved by Izthok Boyar's tone and expression that his teeth remained suspended inside the apple. Was the innkeeper about to bring up old feuds again? After all, he hadn't thrown it up to him, Akiva, in recent years. Although the old man had enough sense to know that he had been instrumental in helping his daughter run away from home, even though he had never accused him of it directly. Not that he, Akiva, denied it. But afterwards, she, Herut, had left him too and taken her own path without him. Akiva flung the uneaten apple into the field, sat up, and thrust his hands inside his sleeves. "Go on, say it. *I* made you unhappy. It was on my account—"

"Shut up, Akiva!"

Itzhok Boyar turned away and took out his pipe. "The sun can still be seen so it's permissible to smoke. You can laugh all you like, but to me the Sabbath is precious. The Boyars are actually just plain farmers and country folk."

"Yes, yes," Akiva smiled sadly, "the Boyars . . . But tell me better, Reb Itzhok, where did you get this bird and what do you need him for?"

"I don't need him at all, but it's a living creature in trouble. . . ."

A white stork actually lay there in the wagon, his long red legs extended and his red bill raised toward the sinking sun as he flapped his black-bordered wing as if about to fly off.

"A living creature in trouble . . . Who knows, maybe it's a transmigrated soul, the soul of some sinner? Giddy up!" He tugged at the reins. "She's listening already to what we're saying. Well, anyhow, this year I leased an orchard from a German woman on the sands. I hoped for a good crop."

He sighed. "It was generally a bad summer for me. . . . Giddy up! Behind this orchard, almost in the swamp, stands a hut where this old German woman lives. A Von Jorge or

34

something like that. She settled there about a year ago and no one knows who she is or where she came from. She keeps away from people. She goes to no one and no one comes to her. She won't let a person cross her threshold. She's a damned soul, she is. Anyone who hates people is worse than an animal, I always say. Well, when spring came two storks flew in to build a nest on her roof. Apparently they had been doing this for years. But this year she drove them away."

"Why?"

"She had spread fresh straw over the roof and she probably was afraid the birds would mess it up. Three times the storks tried to build the nest and each time the woman destroyed it. Well, spring doesn't stand still, you know, and the days grew warmer. The trees had begun to bloom already. . . . Giddy up! The two birds used to sit on the roof near their ruined nest. One day I saw that a third bird had joined them. At first they all sat there quietly and peacefully. Later, two of them began to fight, probably the two males. They punished each other 'til the feathers flew. Then the newcomer flew away. A few days later he showed up again, not on the roof this time but in the meadow. He spun around, did a little dance, flapped his wings, threw back his head—everything to attract the female. A few more days passed. Finally, she flew away with the dancer. My stork was left there sitting all alone. Sat for days and nights without moving. Didn't make a sound. It broke your heart to see him. A muffled voice . . . couldn't even cry. By the time summer came he was in such bad shape he couldn't even retain his feathers. I did what I could for him. . . . Giddy up! Did you ever see anything like it? We talk, so she won't pull the wagon and stops to listen. A female's soul, beg the comparison, she has to hear and know everything. . . . Giddy up! Well, anyhow, the summer passed and autumn came. The leaves dried up and began to fall. I started to pick the winter apples. One day I heard birds making a racket in the meadow. I took a look. A whole flock of storks had formed in a circle. Mine was there too, I recognized him right away—he was almost bald. Ah, I thought, they've gathered to organize their migration and mine is going to go along with them. Then I saw one of the storks move apart from the others. Obviously their leader, the *starosta*. He stretched out his neck to my stork and said something to him. The others began to chatter too. King Solomon knew the language of birds and beasts, but today, children don't even understand their own parents. . . . Giddy up! But from the way they were hopping around I understood that they were trying to decide what to do with my stork. Should they take him along? How could he keep up if he could hardly stand? Then I saw the *starosta* peck my stork in the head. After that, the others moved in for the kill."

"And you stood by like Aristotle and just looked on?"

"Who could look at such a thing and not step in? I began to yell and ran toward them. They flew away and left my stork on the ground bleeding. God, how much cruelty there is in this world! Giddy up!"

The innkeeper grew silent and puffed on his pipe moodily.

The dun Polesian fields stretched endlessly from both sides of the road. Here and there, the grayness was relieved by a patch of sparse, greenish winter crop. They were not far from the village now and the wind carried to them the dying odors of cabbage and dried sunflower stems and the dull, measured sound of peasants threshing their meager sheaves in the barns. A savage wind caroused over the fields. The later it became the darker and more oppressive grew the leaden sky—and the smell of coming snow hung in the air.

The stork opened his red bill, stretched his long neck toward the fading sun and kept on beating his black-bordered wing.

Akiva settled in a hunched position, his arms inside the sleeves clasping his knees, the lower lip drawn over the upper, one eye fixed on Itzhok Boyar's broad, slightly stooped back.

"The Boyars," he repeated with a wan smile, "the Boyars . . . a most interesting crew . . . the thirteenth lost tribe."

In every village in the region, in every farmhouse you'd meet them, the Boyars. The first Boyar, family legend had it, had settled in the Polesian forests many generations ago. His name had been Ezra. The Boyars called him Father Ezra.

And at every Passover seder, after the first benediction each Boyar would tell his children, and his children's children, the story of how their ancestor had settled in these parts. And they would tell it like this: "In one of the German states there lived a goldsmith possessed of a blessed pair of hands. He fashioned jewelry and precious things for the richest and most important people in the land. The King himself drank wine from a golden beaker made by Father Ezra. This was no mere beaker, however, but a thing of such wonder that it dazzled the eyes. . . .

At one royal repast attended by monarchs of other lands one of the visiting kings could not resist the temptation and slipped this beaker into his pocket.

"But things being as they are," the Boyars would relate, "each person has even more enemies than friends. . . . And the goldsmith was no exception, particularly in that state where Jews were generally hated. Still, his enemies were reluctant to do anything openly because it would make them look bad before the world and it was liable to end in violence, of which they were also afraid, for besides his ability to fashion the most beautiful and delicate articles Ezra could also break a man in half, being a giant of a man."

"We," the present-day Boyars would at this point complain, "are not built along such lines anymore. But to continue—in addition to his strength, Father Ezra also had access to the highest places. So his enemies arrived at the oldest accusation that could be hurled against the Jew—the ritual murder. And as usual this happened just before Passover.

"Mother Bathsheba, as we Boyars call Father Ezra's wife,

37

rose at her usual time before daybreak to fetch wood for the stove. But she noticed that the wood did not seem to be stacked in its usual way in the woodshed and she grew greatly astonished, since no one else besides herself ever went in there and the family kept no servants. She and her husband were all alone; they had not even been blessed by a child after ten years of marriage—clearly a punishment from God.

"So as she rummaged through the wood Mother Bathsheba already had a premonition of evil and she grew aghast when she discovered a dead child lying beneath the logs.

"The hair stood up on her neck and she nearly swooned. But besides being beautiful, Mother Bathsheba was also very wise and she understood everything at once.

"Only after she had arranged and secured everything, did she wake her husband and tell him the whole story. Ezra promptly became panicky and his first words were: 'We must flee!'

"Whereupon she calmed him and drove the thought from his mind. They did not dare run since it would call down suspicion on them and bring probable destruction to the whole Jewish community. They had to wait until after the first days of Passover.

"And you can imagine," the Boyars would repeat as their near ones sat with hearts beating in anticipation, "for our Father Ezra that Passover was a time of terrible grief and sorrow.

"Coming home from the House of Worship, Ezra put on his white linen robe as usual; the holiday candles were burning just as they did every year—but this time, somehow sadly. A dark cloud seemed to be hovering over the table.

"Suddenly, there was a noise in the courtyard. Although they had been expecting it, the couple turned white as chalk. A troop of soldiers had surrounded their house, and their leader walked into the woodshed without hesitation. He obviously knew just where to look and what to look for.

"They dug up the courtyard, turned the house upside

down, ripped up the floorboards, but had to go away empty-handed."

And at this point the Boyars traditionally interrupted the story and refilled the winecups. Everyone drank up and the tale was continued.

"So Father Ezra and Mother Bathsheba left that terrible land to settle in the Polesian forest. And here, God blessed them with a son. This was a true Boyar—a woodsman. They named him Raphael. And now, all their troubles vanished. But Ezra could no longer remain a goldsmith since there were no materials to make precious things from, nor wealthy patrons for whom to make them. So he became a potter. One pot that he made was preserved in the family and passed on from generation to generation."

Akiva, still sitting in the same position, asked: "Reb Itzhok, unless I'm mistaken, that pot is at your house?"

"The family heirloom? Yes, I have it."

"Did you inherit it along with the Inn?"

"Oh no! Not everyone would agree to this so readily. There were many claimants in the family. Gavril moved heaven and earth to get it. He insisted that he had a prior claim. So the family was divided. One faction sided with Gavril, the other—with me. Gavril gave out barrels of mead and flung money around as if it were water. He might have won everybody over but at that time, our great-grandfather, Zorechl, was still living—may he rest in peace now. He had already passed his second Bar Mitzvah. He sided with me and that settled it."

"Gavril . . ." Akiva looked up. "There's a strange one all right. He's got a burr in his saddle, he has. Does he still go to play at peasant weddings?"

"Not anymore. But you are right. He does have a burr in his saddle. You have to admit, however—"

Akiva interrupted him. "I've heard, Reb Itzhok, that a while ago two strangers came to you offering to buy that pot."

"They came from as far away as Petersburg and waved

a bundle of money under my nose. I told them: one does not sell one's grandfather."

"And?"

"They began to plead with me to lend them the pot for at least a month for some exhibition. Such work, they told me, the world has never seen. As if I didn't know it! We knew this even before Jewish pottery became fashionable in Petersburg. . . . Giddy up! Do you have to know everything, you old jade?" he growled at the mare.

"Did you give them the pot?"

"Do you mean, did I lend it? I told them the pot wasn't mine to lend, I was only its keeper. But if they got the consent of every Boyar they could have it. Those two men have been on the road for two years already. There are as many Boyars, may the evil eye spare them, as there are trees in the forests."

"A very interesting tribe, the Boyars," Akiva observed thoughtfully. "They are enemies of despair, stubborn beyond belief, and mighty optimists."

"—which?"

"Opti—believers in God."

"Ah . . ." Itzhok nodded. "What's true is true. We are believers. We believe with all our hearts and souls. One must know how to believe and one must believe to the end. If, God forbid, this faith grows shaky, one is lost—a living corpse. Then, all of one's suffering and pains are as if for naught—senseless . . . one might as well be a madman. Of course, Daniel claims that the Jewish faith in God is a terrible sickness. . . . Giddy up! Look how she wants to mix in in the conversation."

The innkeeper urged the mare on, fearful of riding right into the Sabbath. He kept stealing anxious glances at the vanishing daylight. The wind that always grows stronger at the end of day seemed to be holding the sun back from setting. It still seemed caught there in the few remaining clumps of stew-brown oak leaves.

40

Itzhok Boyar sighed gently. No matter how involved he grew in other matters he could never forget about his children. The youngest, Avrom, dead somewhere in Manchuria . . . Daniel's life flickering out like a candle in the wind . . . Herut, she was like a wound in his heart. And from Rochel— not even a single line.

Akiva pulled out from the straw a long pear, yellow as an autumn mapleleaf.

"Reb Itzhok, I would say that the Boyars accepted the Torah on Mount Sinai. They didn't shrink from the lightning and thunder and the black clouds that hovered overhead. The great voice of the ram's horn didn't frighten them either. When God appeared in fire and smoke and the mountain began to quake, everyone ran away, but the Boyars stood fast. And one among them became known throughout the world, the mightiest Boyar of all—Moses our Patriarch. He is the one who went up to God on Mount Sinai."

Itzhok smiled. "It's a long time since you've been to see us, a half year already. You hang around with comedians, with clowns. You perform in the theatres. Why do you squander your life away? Giddy up! Daniel speaks of you often. He loves you so."

He grasped his long, narrow beard in his hand. "Daniel wanders through the woods. What is he looking for there— his lost luck? I know. You'll tell me again that I must understand him. It's easy for you to say. But even if I did understand him, what then? It tears me up inside to look at him. The 'Quiet Summer' is completely distraught. What mother can stand to see her child wasting away before her eyes? Malka has taken to drink. . . ."

"How is he?"

"How is he? His hands are already shaking and still he paints. He paints on wood, he paints on canvas. You'll have trouble recognizing him."

"There's a fine doctor coming to see him."

"Where does a doctor come to Daniel?"

41

"Yeva is bringing him."

"Yeva?" The innkeeper's brows rose even higher. "What is she coming for—to open old wounds? Is this some of your work?"

"Yes," Akiva admitted. "She is a victim too."

"From one victim to another . . . there are all kinds of victims. Well, thank God, we are already by the windmill. Now we go down to the pond. Hey, look there, Akiva, isn't that Shmulik running toward us? Look at him go, his feet are higher than his shoulders! Watch him pump those arms! What could have happened? Here, take the reins. You'll make it by yourself already, one way or another."

And tossing the reins to Akiva he as if fell from the wagon. Running along the edge of the pond he moved to intercept his grandson.

From afar Akiva watched the boy talking very excitedly to his grandfather who in his confusion discarded his fur-lined coat along with his gaberdine, wrapped the boy up in the garment, picked him up, and in only his shirtsleeves began to race across the vegetable beds toward the old Inn.

7

Running up breathless, his grandson in his arms, to the old Inn that stood almost on the road in the center of the village, Itzhok Boyar turned to his neighbors who were gathered outside. "Has he come, friends? Has he come?"

"He has come!"

"Alive?"

"Of course, alive. Corpses aren't known to walk."

"—nor to rise from the grave. Your son is here, Itzko. He's lying there in bed, smiling."

They moved aside for him. They knew from his appearance that he would be convinced only if he saw his son for himself.

They had also come to see the soldier and to learn some news of the outside world. Had he heard anything about that proclamation giving the nobles' land to the peasants? There was no sign of this yet in Polesie. . . .

Old Vasil had hobbled up on his wooden leg (he had left his in Bulgaria during the Russo-Turkish war), a brand-new woven sandal on his good foot and the St. George's Cross on his breast, to discuss the war and military matters with his fellow soldier. But what was even more important, to ask if somewhere in his travels he hadn't seen that piece of paper signed by the Little Father himself, the Tsar, assigning to peasants land now occupied by the gentry.

But it was useless to speak to the soldier who lay there only half alive, smiling up at everyone while tears gushed from his feverish eyes. He barely understood what was being said to him but he did manage to inform Natalka: "Your husband is alive."

"Is that true? He's alive?"

"Harasim lay next to me in the hospital."

"Where is he, then? Darling, tell us the truth!"

"I am telling the truth. He'll be home soon."

Natalka stood before the Inn sobbing with joy, but old Horpina waited, her back stooped, her shaky, yellow-veined, talon-like hands grasping a cane, her puckered, shrunken face peering out from under the black kerchief as she entreated everyone and no one: "Where is my Pavlo? No one knows where my grandson is. No sons, no daughters . . . I got nobody already but I go on living. Had one and only grandchild and they took him from me . . . left me with only my cane . . . that is my bitter lot. Todoske's son came back. Hvedor's son came back. The innkeeper's son is here. Harasim is alive. But dear God, where is my one and only grandson? Where is my Pavlo, my dove, my precious boy?"

Down the road came Maria, her sick child pressed to her bosom. Her headkerchief was rumpled and the wind ruffled her golden hair. The young widow lamented loudly: "My Mikola won't ever come back anymore. Sonny, Sonny, we don't have our Daddy. . . . They've killed our Daddy. . . . We are drowning, the earth has been flooded! Oh, Mikola, how will we live without you? Sonny, Sonny, we have no Daddy. . . ."

"And for what?" Old Vasil asked. "Do I need Manchuria? I need three acres of land right here." And he swayed on his peg leg. "As soon as that paper comes we'll go after them 'gentlemen.' I'll take off me wooden leg and I'll beat them over the heads with it—like so! Like so!"

"Shut up, Vasil," someone advised. "Hold your tongue."

"Come, good people, why hang around here?"

"That's the truth. There's a cold wind blowing and it feels like snow."

Old Vasil stomped his peg on the ground, pulled down his cap, straightened his St. George's Cross, and began to sing loudly:

> "On the other side of Siberia the sun
>   had already set—
> Hey boys, don't you tarry. . . ."

The brief autumn day expired in the flaming sunset. The wind grew gustier and made the tree branches clap echoingly against each other—the cold had crept in under their bark.

And he, Daniel, snow-white at thirty, threw off the blanket with the green patch, lingered beneath the naked, trembling pear tree, and refused to be taken inside. He peered tensely toward the birch forest and watched the windows glisten in Gavril's farmhouse.

"Yeva is there," he said aloud. "I must see her at least once more face to face. I'll give her those half-burned letters of mine. No, Yeva, I never knew myself how much I loved you. How did I ever endure those ten years without you? Yeva . . . Yeva . . ."

He suddenly realized that he had been talking to his wife and he flushed and began to feel around with his hand aimlessly. His fingers did not encounter anything, however, and he turned to Malka. "Why do you always hover over me?"

She bit her lip. "Daniel, why are you picking on me? Is this any fault of mine? Who told you to put the ring on my finger? You did it on your own, Daniel. . . . Either you yell at me or you treat me like an invalid."

"Malka," he sighed, "do I really yell at you? Forgive me, Malka, my queen!"

He wanted to say something else but suddenly he saw Akiva behind him and he threw his hand around his friend's shoulder.

"Friend Akiva; Akiva, my chum! So you've come? Go inside, Malka. Friend Akiva, have you seen Avrom yet? Did

45

you see his eyes? They're trying to say something. They have a story to tell."

"Has Yeva been here?" Akiva asked.

"Friend Akiva, stand next to me for a moment and let us be silent together. With you only can I converse in silence. It's so much better to have someone with whom to be silent than someone with whom to talk. How good it used to be to share the silence with Yeva. Our silence was like a song without lyrics. What a haunting melody . . . And when our hearts flowed over and we had to speak, we began to recite the Song of Songs together. Are there more glorious words than those?"

"Let us be silent, Daniel."

"Yes, yes, Friend Akiva, I want to be silent. It's so hard to look at such a sunset alone. Stand beside me, Akiva. You see how the sun is hanging there above the earth? Two times a day one must seek the sun in the earth—at sunset and at sunrise. And each is an unforgettable experience."

He grew silent for a moment, entwined his fingers in his white curls and leaned forward. "I don't feel good, Friend Akiva, please take me inside. . . ."

And Akiva recalled a moment months before, when temporarily lifted from the doldrums of his hopeless existence and standing beneath the same pear tree at sunset, Daniel had used the very same expression: "One must seek the sun in the earth. . . ."

But then, the pear tree had still been in bloom with the fragrance of honey clinging to it. And in the birch forest the flowing sap had burst the thin striped bark on the young trees. And the birds had raised such a happy song that not only he, the perennial optimist, but even Daniel, so dour and sober and tortured by reality, had somehow felt that life was just beginning.

They had spent the whole night in the open. "Friend Akiva," Daniel had said, "a night like this is one of the great joys of my life."

It had truly been a magnificent spring night. The sweeping sky had cast a rich, deep-blue glow while gleaming, silvery threads had spun into the bright green, still gummy young flowers.

Daniel had trod ever so lightly over the dewy, moonlit, densely grown meadow striped by the shadows of tree trunks. He had seemed unwilling even by a rustle to mark his escape from his previous existence and the misfortune that dogged his every step.

But he had suddenly halted, thrust his fingers into his hair as he always did in moments of stress, and while the moon highlighted the silvery sheen of his mop he had whispered almost inaudibly: "Friend Akiva, a night beyond all nights. What magnificence! If only I could paint such a night! Listen, Friend Akiva, do you hear how alive the forest is? Even the birds cannot calm down. I love the spring! It has so much tenderness and strength . . . even people grow more beautiful in springtime."

He had stood there in the clearing, his hands in his hair, and moaned in rapture. Suddenly, he had withdrawn his hands.

"Friend Akiva, we must not dwell in the past."

Akiva had understood. Daniel was about to disclose what had been disturbing him in recent months.

"Friend Akiva, I'm far from Herut's ideas. But she is right about one thing—you cannot live in the past. We are already sated with the past, it pours from our gullets. Over and over the same refrain—the good old days. . . . No! No matter how you try to warm it, the past is always steeped in the cold of the grave. Besides, within ourselves the past can never go anywhere. It remains the same for all the generations. Friend Akiva, what we need is a tomorrow. It's true that the tomorrow is bathed in the mist of uncertainty and is as unpredictable as a dark forest with dangers at every step . . . surely no one knows the face of tomorrow. . . . But I want to sit beside you in the wagon, Friend Akiva, and ride into a better life. We dare no longer dwell in the past. Living in the past is a kind of premature death. The future holds strength, and strength is the substance of life. Come, Friend Akiva, let us go down to the river. The sun will soon be rising and we shall be there to greet it. Once, Yeva would come running at this time. . . ."

"One dares not dwell in the past, Daniel."

"Yes, yes, Friend Akiva, let us be silent. Let us live only for the future."

They had rested on the higher bank of the river, watching the sun come up. They had not been able to see the other bank, for the floodwater had inundated land far beyond the fenced pastures. Even the willows had been half submerged. The river had bubbled and rippled and blown a damp mist into their faces. The fragrance of cherry blossoms had grown stronger at dawn.

"Don't look at me, Friend Akiva," Daniel had said, "but there where the sun is rising. Watch the east, see how reddish it grows! What colors! Look there into the fog that billows like a bright cloud of smoke over the ravine. The first ray of sunlight . . . Do you hear the birds? They've started to sing. One must really be stronger than iron. . . ."

And Daniel had grown silent. He had pulled blades of the dewy grass, rubbed them between his fingers, and thirstily inhaled the aroma. A sliver of sun had appeared. Daniel had thrust his grass-stained hands into his hair and watched the sun rise ever higher and higher. His eyes had been hidden behind a warm veil of tears.

"What's wrong?" Akiva remembered asking.

"Do I know? I don't know myself. I feel somehow intoxicated today. And what's so unusual about a drunk crying?"

And then he had added sadly: "My life, Friend Akiva, is already ruined. But if only I had Yeva with me . . ."

And Daniel had not uttered another word the entire following day they had been together. It had even seemed to

48

Akiva that his friend was avoiding him. Only as he was leaving, Daniel had told him that he was going to Kiev to try his luck for the very last time.

But seeing him now, standing so stooped beneath the pear tree, huddled in his blanket and pleading, "Friend Akiva, take me inside," Akiva realized that on that spring night long ago, the same thing had happened to Daniel that had happened to his, Akiva's, mother shortly before she had died.

Following her long sickness, after it had already become necessary to spoon feed her, she who was at death's door had suddenly sat up unassisted. "Ah, it's good," she had said, "everything is so good. . . ."

She, who hadn't been able to utter a single word in three weeks, had spoken clearly and vigorously. "Been sick long enough already. One has to live!"

Pale pink patches had flecked her wasted, yellow cheeks. "It's springtime, isn't it, Akivele?"

From the roofs across the way, sun-filled drops had been falling into the freshly fallen snow. Sparrows had settled on the cornice outside, sharpened their beaks and twittered. "It's good, Akivele . . . everything is so good. . . ."

She had been silent for a long time, then asked: "Is someone coming, Akivele?"

"No, Mama, no one is coming. That's Father getting the wagon ready. He is greasing the wheels."

"So early getting the wagon ready? Is it spring already?"

"Yes, Mama. Shall I get Father?"

"No, Akivele, not your father. . . . Come over here to me, Akivele, come here, my child. . . ."

He had approached the bed but he had been afraid of her, his own mother. Her hair had been so tangled, her eyes so staring and red.

"Mama," he had pleaded, "don't scare me, Mama!"

"God have pity on you, my child; God pity you, my Akivele."

"Mama, you frighten me!"

She had pulled him close. "My son, are you afraid of your mother?"

"No, no, Mama!"

"You're a big boy already, Akivele. You'll soon be thirteen. My God, is it thirteen already?"

She had stared at him with those red eyes.

"Thirteen . . . do you still hang around with the musicians? Would you like to be a musician too? Then be one, my child. Play at poor people's weddings. Be whatever you want, my son. At my wedding, Akivele, there were no musicians. . . . Are you sure that no one is coming?"

"No, Mama, that's only Father greasing the wagon."

"Father? Whose father?"

"Mine . . . my father. . . ."

"Your father, you say? I love him, I love Lazar the coachman. . . . I love that Ashmedai. . . . He hasn't a mean bone in his body, he's almost a saint—but he isn't your father. . . ."

"Mama?"

She had placed her trembling, bony hand over his mouth and her eyes had grown even redder.

"He is not your father . . . not your father. . . ."

And as he had looked on, the redness had vanished from her eyes, her pupils had receded under the lids, and her cold, slimy hand had slid down from his mouth. She had fallen backwards and her head had cracked against the headboard.

To this day the sound of her head hitting the headboard had stayed with him. Whenever he was alone he could hear it again. He was convinced that his mother had as if slammed the door on this world as she was leaving it.

He felt now that he could not get Daniel inside by himself. His friend was leaning all his weight on him. His mother, he thought, had had an easier death. At eighteen, life had dealt her a stupefying blow and only before her death had she regained her full senses and become aware of the world. The sparrows on the cornice outside had sung for her too. But that had been like a momentary flash of light after a lifetime of darkness. Daniel's tragedy was infinitely greater. All the blows life had dealt him had not dulled his capacity to suffer. On the contrary, life struck against Daniel like stone against stone until fiery sparks flew. Pieces did get chipped away, but what remained was still stone.

"Friend Akiva," Daniel said as if he had read his friend's mind, "I am all busted up inside . . . crumbling . . . I don't feel good, I don't feel good at all. Take me to bed." Suddenly he threw his arms around Akiva. "It's a lie what Dostoyevski says. That you can stand a person on one foot on a rock in the middle of the ocean and that he would remain there in that position for the rest of his life." He spoke rapidly, swallowing his words, and held Akiva close—as if anxious to justify himself and to impress his meaning upon his friend.

"It's a lie, Akiva. A human being cannot stand on one foot like a gander. And incidentally, he never specified how long such a life could last. Or was he trying to say that you can do anything to a person? That is a lie too. Such one-footed heroes are only the products of sick minds. Dostoyevski's ideas are generally sick ones anyhow. Yes, yes, Friend Akiva, let us be silent. Man must have the earth beneath him and he must plant both his feet firmly on it. And he mustn't only stand there but move around as well. And the earth where he dwells must not be a scorched desert but a green garden. It must be a thing of beauty, with orchards abloom. Yes, yes, Friend Akiva—let us be silent. . . ."

And leaning on Akiva's arm Daniel turned for a final look at the birch forest where night already held sway, save for the last souvenir of the sunset—a gleaming gold tip of a branch thrusting high into the sky.

In the courtyard, a fur pelt thrown over her loins, her muzzle inside the wagon, stood the big-bellied mare who always had to hear and know everything. And as she fed, she

51

angrily twitched her torn, split ear and flashed her eyes at the red cow who stood beside her and pulled clover out of the wagon with soft black lips.

Daniel stopped to gaze with a bitter smile at the cow with the broken horn. And suddenly he was transported to that blue room with its high, wide windows facing the great city of mediation offices, credit bureaus, brokers, merchants, industrialists, landowners, aristocrats, and princes . . . of screaming gilt signs and gaudy shop windows . . . of droshkies and phaetons with pneumatic rubber wheels drawn by spirited horses and bearing elegantly dressed and bejeweled ladies and their clean-shaven or bearded escorts whose faces glowed like the polished brass buttons on their white cloaks. And somewhere among them was Yeva. . . .

In the mountains alongside the Dnieper the orchards were already in bloom. The chestnut trees bowed beneath their blue-white chalices of blossoms and the church domes flashed golden in the sun. And high on the outskirts of town the small houses were stacked one against another like empty crates in the dump. The Dnieper shimmered and with a loving murmur carried the pleasure boats and tramp steamers. The great city lay bathed in a cloud of dust, noise, congestion, hypocrisy, licentiousness, and sham.

And in that blue room where he waited a kind of pre-festive stillness prevailed. He felt an odd sense of isolation, intrusion, and obligation. As if he were simply another piece of furniture whose only function was to serve as a showpiece. The entire apartment was a monument to false pride and vanity—no real human holiday could ever penetrate this blue citadel with its gilt, ornamented ceilings and gleaming parquets. But it would always maintain its false air of cordiality and respectability to impress the outside world.

Upon the pink marble tables bronze statues were displayed. A husky nude male figure with an Assyrian beard and wings. Farther on, alongside a coffin entwined with garlands, another nude—this one beardless, with a mournful expression and holding an extinguished torch. On another table, in the place of honor, a naked young woman with a wreath on her head and strumming a harp. . . .

"Wherever I looked," Akiva heard Daniel say, "naked-ness, nakedness, nakedness. . . ."

"What are you talking about, Daniel?"

"And I, like a dunce, took my cow there. . . ."

Akiva felt Daniel tremble in his arms. "What are you laughing at? What cow?"

"Yes, Friend Akiva, I did go after all. I tried once more to lay my destiny in the hands of strangers. I brought my cow there. Aren't you even going to ask me about it?"

"If it's anything worthwhile, you'll tell me of your own accord."

"Akiva, for eight days in a row I besieged that famous patron to grant me an audience. I wrote to him twice. And when he finally condescended to see me the first words out of his mouth were: 'You speak only the jargon?' You hear, Akiva? You and I speak in the language of thieves and criminals—a jargon. 'Just as I thought,' he said. 'I read your letters. You live in some forsaken village and your father sells apples. Before you became an artist you were a *melamed* —a Hebrew teacher. Before that, you were a raftsman. I even read your letter to my friends and acquaintances . . . very, very interesting.' And just then, Akiva, a woman in a white silk dress and a large hat with a veil came in—my heart lurched. . . . Yeva! I've got to get away, I told myself. I've got to run wherever my feet will carry me!"

"What are you making up stories for? How did Yeva come to be there?"

"I thought at the time that it was Yeva. But what did it matter if it was this Yeva or another? Was there any differ-ence between them? 'This won't take long,' he said to her, 'sit down, darling.' I felt my insides turning over and the Boyar temper began to flare up. 'Did you study somewhere?' he asked. I felt my throat go dry. I fingered my cap. Where did I study? Where did I learn? And before my eyes materialized the Yeshiva and you and I, Friend Akiva, praying fervently, drenching ourselves in tears, fasting for days at a time. . . . In the winter we immersed ourselves in the stream, through holes cut in the ice. We stood barefoot on dried chickpeas for days at a time, we observed vows of silence for months on end. Why we didn't emerge from there physical and spiritual cripples is to me still a miracle."

"How did you answer him?"

"How could I answer him, Friend Akiva? That I would soon put my destiny in his hands? He studied me with a false, goodnatured smile and I studied him too, the famous patron of the arts. For eight straight days I had been unable to reach him. Every night my hotel had been raided by the police and I had to spend my nights hiding up in the attic."

"Daniel, let us be silent. Let us be silent, Daniel!"

"Yes, yes, Friend Akiva, let us be silent. . . . The patron stood with his side to me. I forgot to tell you that he didn't shake hands with me when I came in, only nodded. He stood, as I said, with his side to me—a tall, thin man with a great bald head, a pale, round face, a cultivated mustache, and a trimmed little Vandyke."

"You describe him so well I can actually picture you two standing there looking each other over—" Akiva laughed. "What about the beauty?"

" 'Well,' he says to me with that saccharine smile intended to encourage and entertain me, the country yokel, 'well, Maestro, show us your work.' I'm just about to untie the bundle when he looks up horrified. 'Not all! Not all! Just one picture, Maestro . . . well, maybe two. Put it there, where the light is strong. Soon, my dear, soon,' he says to her. I tell you, Akiva, my hands were shaking! Yes, yes, I know, Friend Akiva, let us be silent. . . . Anyhow, I showed him the red cow with the broken horn."

"Did he like it?"

"Did he like it? He pulled out a handkerchief and held

it to his nose as if the painting would have given off the smell of manure. 'Soon, dear, soon,' he said to her again. I saw her reflection in the large mirror. She was sitting on the sofa, yawning, and I caught her studying my pants. Unwillingly, I looked down at them, the pants Malka had cleaned and pressed so devotedly for hours. They were as shiny as peeled onions. And from under the cuffs you could see my boot uppers. Yes, yes, Friend Akiva, I won't say another word. Let us indeed be silent. . . . Then I see she's handed me a red piece of paper—a ten-ruble note. . . . Why do you move away from me, my friend? Take me to bed, to bed, my friend. . . ."

8

COMING INTO THE HOUSE, Daniel forced himself to put on a happy face. He was anxious not to mar his parents' joy over Avrom's return. Avrom had already been given up for dead and the family hadn't had an occasion for such a joyous Sabbath in years.

The homemade, yellow tallow candles crackled and burned brightly in the polished brass holders set out on the white tablecloth. The two Sabbath loaves lay covered under the traditional embroidered cloths.

"A good Sabbath," Daniel said as he stepped over the threshold and smiled at his brother, who, beaming, reclined among a great pile of pillows. Still, Daniel saw something in Avrom's eyes—a kind of fear, some nameless horror, some crushing burden. Why hadn't Dobche been sent for? Avrom seemed to be searching for her with his eyes.

Daniel felt grateful to his brother. By coming home, he had done him, Daniel, an immense favor. Now, he, Avrom, would be his parents' comfort and support in their old age. Avrom had inherited their father's strength and their mother's wisdom. One day, he too would be called the "Quiet Summer." And just as she, he would bear his yoke uncomplainingly. The silence of the forest would not enchant him. True, he might one day grow despondent too, but this would not happen so soon. Avrom was not yet one of those who evaluate life and come to their own conclusions. Thank God he was nothing like Herut, Daniel thought with relief.

"A good Sabbath, a good year to you, Daniel, and to you

too, Akiva! And may things be good forever, my children," the "Quiet Summer" said. "But why do you stand there in the doorway? Come in, come in. I just may give each of you a prayer book so that a word of Hebrew might pass your lips. You laugh, Akiva? Go on, laugh at a foolish old woman if you want to, but when I pray my heart grows lighter. You, on the other hand, read and read all kinds of books, if you'll pardon my saying so, but the more you read the more you complain."

"Do you hear that, Friend Akiva?"

"Your mother claims that if we go to the House of Worship, fast and pray wearing two sets of phylacteries, God will send us the Messiah."

"No, no, Akiva, she doesn't mean that at all. She's referring to the soul. She means that a person must have a God, someone in whom to confide and unburden yourself. Don't dismiss her words too lightly, my friend."

And Daniel gazed fondly at his mother in her wide-sleeved dress and silk head kerchief. The tiny wrinkles around her eyes were shining and her eyes glowed like a clear sky after the rain. She kept plumping up Avrom's pillows and adjusting the covers simply for the excuse to be near him.

The father also stood by the bed and held his son's hand between both of his own as he lovingly and fervently ushered in the Sabbath.

"Friend Akiva, close your eyes a moment and hear how much sorrow and piety there is in that voice."

"You don't have to tell me about your father. Why didn't you ever paint him?"

"It's beyond my powers. He is too dear to me that I should attempt this on nerve alone. No, Akiva, it's quite beyond my powers. It wouldn't mean painting a man but an entire generation."

For a moment, the inspiration seized him and he saw that other Itzhok Boyar—tall, rangy, broadshouldered, with the long and narrow beard. But the vision became quickly

57

obliterated—these were mere externalities—this was not the real Itzhok Boyar. Of course, he could portray his stooped back and acquiescent shoulder, but these were not physical defects. His back was bent, the head tilted toward the up-lifted shoulder, the hairy ear cocked, the eyes narrowed—all in anticipation of the inevitable blow. As if they would all be asking: "Is the misfortune still dogging me?" But the ex-pression on the face maintained stubbornly: *Whatever the trouble, it will not break me!*

Deeply mortified and guilt-ridden because his father had indeed been broken, Daniel placed his arm around Akiva's shoulder as if to express his pleasure over his friend's arrival, then shuffled, with his assistance, into the dark room next door.

"I've painted trees, flowers, and all kinds of trifles, but to create an Itzhok Boyar . . . that, my friend, is beyond me."

He halted again.

"And since I cannot create such a picture, may the day be cursed that I took the brush in hand."

Lying there on the bench-bed with his eyes half-shut and watching the pear tree, which seemed to be drawing upon the wall with its crooked branch, Daniel suddenly saw his son poised in the doorway as if centered inside a shining frame. "Shmulikl, where have you been?"

"Mama washed my hair and changed my clothes."

The boy stood there all dressed up and in, apparently, a state of excitement. The still damp chestnut curls clung to his pale forehead and his dark eyes seemed to be all pupil.

"Why are you standing there? Come in and I'll tell you a story."

"What kind of a story?"

Daniel noticed that his son appeared undecided, as if debating whether or not to listen. And he grew puzzled, for there was nothing Shmulik liked so much as a story. Why

58

then did he hesitate? The child's uneven black brows go up: he was obviously trying to make up his mind.

Daniel sighed deeply. What did life hold in store for his son? Would his future be bright? What would become of him? How would he grow up without a father? The questions began to assail him and demand an answer.

And now came the most basic and torturous question of all—*what will become of me?* Was a man actually nothing more than the little heap of dust that remained after him? Was that all there was to it while the world kept on spinning and the sun kept rising and setting?

Suddenly, Shmulik ran up, knelt by the bench-bed and placed his chin on his father's chest while his eyes blazed angrily. "Why do you yell at Mama? She said that you either yell at her or treat her like an invalid!"

Trembling, Daniel stroked the boy's hair. "Did Mother tell you to say this?"

"No, Pa, no . . . Tell me, who is that aunt you were talking with today? Mama cried so when that lady—"

"Shmulikl!" Akiva, who had been sitting by the window and listening, beckoned to him. "Can you play such a whistle?"

Daniel let out his breath. Akiva had come to his rescue. How could he have given the child an answer that would have satisfied him?

He lay there gripped with fear, his eyes closed. Would Shmulik ever understand him? Most likely not. When he grew up he would avoid discussing his father to keep from saying something derogatory about him. But in his heart he would think of him as a kind of interesting bungler, a failure, a rooster gone astray among eagles. Of course he would never confide these feelings to anybody. On the contrary, he would forever be on the alert for someone with a good word for his father.

And Akiva whistled. He imitated the lark's song on a

summer's morn, when the sun has risen and the lark has climbed high above the earth where he hovers flapping his wings so that his song seems to emanate from the sun itself. And now he was a nightingale soaring over budding orchards and shrubs along the river bank on a warm May's night.

Shmulik ran up to Akiva and reached for the whistle in his mouth, but there was no whistle. "What were you whistling on?" he asked in amazement and led him toward the doorway where the light was better. "What were you using?"

"A gold whistle with silver bands."

"And you swallowed it?"

Akiva laughed. "That's right. I swallowed it."

Shmulik's uneven brows rose in anger again. Was Uncle Akiva a faker too?

Last summer his grandfather took him to the fair for the first time. They had loaded the wagon with apples and driven to the village. When they had reached the smooth road Grandfather had turned the reins and whip over to him and said: "Drive!" He had talked to him as if to a grownup. "Watch out so the Gentile lads don't filch our apples. They'd rob us of our whole livelihood if they could."

"Let them just get close and I'll give them such a taste of the whip—"

But he had been taken in completely by the one called Blackie, a boy with a twisted leg and a cap with a missing visor. He had performed such marvelous tricks that he, Shmulik, had stopped chasing the boys away from the wagon and climbed down among them.

Blackie had come up to him and said: "Want to see a good trick?"

"Show me."

"You see this stone? Here, feel it. It's a real stone, so help me God. I found it down by the river. Isn't it a big one?"

"What about it?" Shmulik had asked. "So what if it's a big one?"

"Take it," Blackie had said, "and put it in my mouth." He had opened his mouth and Shmulik had put the stone inside.

Blackie had closed his mouth, winked, and pushed his potato-like nose down onto his upper lip; then he had uttered some mumbo-jumbo and opened his mouth.

"What kind of trick is that? I can still see it under your tongue," Shmulik had said. "I can do that too."

"But soon it won't be there," Blackie had said. "Now it's there, now it ain't. . . ."

He had squeezed his eyes together, stretched out his hands, spun around on his twisted leg several times, and opened his mouth. Empty! Shmulik had been dumfounded. Suddenly, he had heard his grandfather's voice. "A fine watchman you are! I wish you on my enemies! Where are you looking?"

Shmulik had turned around and seen the holes that had been punched in the straw on the side of the wagon by the boys who were now busy stealing the apples.

"A fine watchman indeed! What are you standing around there for like a milked cow?"

Shmulik had felt so humiliated that he had burst out crying. He had been made such a fool! And he had spent the rest of that day brooding in the wagon. But it had continued to plague him—where had the stone disappeared?

That evening, as the fair was drawing to an end, Blackie had shown up again and Shmulik had sprung down to face him. "I'll give you two apples if you'll tell me how to do that trick."

"Four. I want four," Blackie had insisted. "But they have to be big ones."

Shmulik had forgotten all about the argument he had had with his grandfather and had come running up to him to beg four big apples. His grandfather had handed them over.

"This one has worms," Blackie had complained. "Go get me another. A trick like that is worth even six apples."

Itzhok Boyar, besieged and annoyed by his women customers who talked a blue streak at him, had growled with displeasure—but he had exchanged the apple for his grandson.

"Who are you doing business with there?" he had demanded.

Shmulik had been too busy to answer. He had run to Blackie who had calmly examined the apple from every angle, and finding it unblemished, had wiped his bulbous nose with his palm and slipped the apple inside his shirt with the others.

"Well?" Shmulik had asked impatiently.

"Well what, stupid? I simply swallowed the stone." And he had laughed, wheeled on his twisted leg, stuck out his tongue, and vanished among the wagons.

Scowling, Shmulik now looked out from under his uneven brows at Akiva. "You swallowed it too!" he accused him. "But that's no trick."

He came up to Daniel. "Pa, you, you . . . did you ever fool anybody?"

"No, my child. Why do you ask?"

"Pa . . . I'll never, never fool anybody . . ." he cried and dashed out.

Daniel gasped for air. The child's words had somehow sounded like a vow. He was sure the boy was trying to tell him something. It seemed to him that he had just leveled a terrible accusation against him, his father.

"Friend Akiva, children are very perceptive. They have sharp eyes and ears. At his age, I was already probing into everything. I was desperate to know all that there was to know in the world. I've told you this already—at nine I fell in love with Yeva and this has stayed with me all my life. A few days ago, Shmulik asked me, 'Do you have a sister, Herut?' He stood there with his eyes burning, awaiting my answer. How had he found out about Herut? He wasn't even three when she left home. And you know that her name is never mentioned in the house."

He raised himself heavily to his elbows and the bones in his wrists snapped. "Friend Akiva, will my son ever understand me?"

And without waiting for an answer he went on. "You know that I wanted to give at least one person in this world some pleasure. Friend Akiva, I want you, at least, to know that my intentions were always only the best. I wanted to make Malka happy. I wanted to make all her dreams come true. How life laughs at us and makes a mockery of everything! It rubs our finest intentions and purest feelings in the slime just out of spite. It wasn't God but a devil that created the world."

"What are you talking about, Daniel?"

"About that which it is so difficult to talk—and even more difficult not to talk. But let us be silent, Akiva, let us be silent."

He wiped his sweating brow, peered out into the dark night, and watched the stork come up to the bench-bed and peck gently at his dangling hand. "This stork has become a regular house pet. Look there, only two houses have lights on in the whole village—the Milners and the Zinerts. All the others are sitting in the dark. You can see the pitch fires reflected in the windows. All Russia is sitting by the glow of pine-cone fires. . . ."

"If all the pine cones in Russia were put in one pile you'd have such a bonfire the whole paper tiger along with Tsarism would go up in smoke," Akiva said.

"Friend Akiva, I'm afraid of such a fire. Violence breeds violence."

"Would you want change without labor pains?"

"I know that it cannot happen that way. But I feel God has already emptied the full cup of poison over the earth. The bonfire has been burning for two years already and the throne still remains untouched. . . . Do you hear it, Akiva, or am I only imagining it?"

"No, Daniel, you're not imagining. I've been hearing it for a long time already."

From far, far away they heard the words of an army song.

> "Nightingale, nightingale,
> Little birdie,
> The canary, it sings so dirty.
> Hup, two, three, four! Hup, two, three, four . . ."

"Now do you hear it, Daniel?"

Daniel pushed the stork away. "I hear Arakcheev raging. . . ."

"Things haven't been going so good for him. If Nicolai has to send Cossacks to the Polesian swamps the end can't be far away already."

"Maybe . . . " Daniel said thoughtfully. "But until the sun will rise . . . Life, Friend Akiva, is like a tangled ball of thread. And everyone, whether he believes in God or not, throws himself at this ball with whatever comes to his hand to untangle it. They're all filled with a blind rage and they all expect to untangle this mess in the wink of an eye. Their intentions are good but in no time at all they become deadly enemies. And each one wants to teach the others. Each wants to be the leader, the mentor, the guide. Yesterday's friends become tomorrow's enemies, ready to cut each other's throats. And the ball becomes even more tangled and drenched in the blood of innocents. No, Akiva, this problem can only be solved by men of good will, of great wisdom and deep understanding. Men who can deliberate and exercise extraordinary patience. It isn't necessary to tear this ball of thread I call life, nor to sever it. Herut only wants to destroy it with the bare sword."

"Daniel . . ."

"Yes, Friend Akiva, let us be silent. You will stay with me for a few days, at least?"

He caught his breath and went on. "This ball must be untangled gently and delicately. Life is so terribly, terribly tangled! And until it will be untangled, they've robbed man of his most precious possessions, freedom and light. Without these, his will, his courage, and his faith are extinguished. A diamond can sparkle only in sunlight. Nor can a rose grow in the swamp."

He thrust his fingers into his hair as he always did when he grew perturbed.

"It's frightening when you think of the caliber of men who are the leaders of such a huge country with so many nationalities—Pobedonostsev, Witte, Purishkevich, Ignatiev, Plehve. . . . With their hobnailed boots they've trampled the most basic human rights. What cruelties they've perpetrated in the name of order! It's just horrible, Friend Akiva, horrible. . . . And over everything sits God's anointed on his royal throne—a *golem* with a crown on his head and a bloody axe in hand. . . ."

"Daniel, if you won't be silent I will leave!"

"I am silent, Friend Akiva, I am silent. Sit down near me and let us be silent together. But first, see who has come there. Maybe it's the constable again. He's been here twice this week already. Go see who it is, my friend."

Two boys had come bursting into the house. Both wore brand-new, black sheepskin coats, black lambskin hats pulled rakishly down over the ear, and highly polished boots with creased uppers. They filled the house with the smell of freshly tanned leather.

The smaller one held a stick with which to repel dogs in one hand and a lantern in the other. The other lad carried a large package.

Crossing the threshold and neglecting even to close the door behind them they shrilly burst out together: "A good Sabbath Grandfather and the new Aunt Yeva send their best regards to the honored guest Mother asked that you return the tablecloth she lent you!"

Having delivered their message as directed, they stood there not knowing what to do next. Except for Shmulik no one came up to them nor reached for the package.

And to their amazement, Malka took Shmulik's hand and led him away to the kitchen.

The smaller one closed the door behind him and once more began: "A good Sabbath Grandfather and the new Aunt Ye—eva—"

The older one tugged at his sleeve. "We—we've said it al—ready. . . ."

"So we'll say it again!"

"Numskull! Did the Aunt tell us to say it twice?"

Rivka, the "Quiet Summer," glanced at her husband. The two old Boyars, Itzhok and Gavril, hadn't been speaking for ten years already, since the night of Yeva's wedding. There had been no argument—they simply avoided each other. Daniel, it's true, did go to Gavril's house. He had even tutored his eldest grandson. And Shmulik sometimes played there as well. Since Neha had been "punished by God," she, Rivka, would have gone there too but for Itzhok.

The two small Boyars made another bid for attention. The smaller beat one boot against another, supposedly to warm his feet. The older, imitated his father clearing his throat: *Uh . . . huh . . . hum . . .*

Itzhok glanced at Gavril's grandchildren and at the lantern illegally lit on the Sabbath, and he turned toward the wall.

"I neither want nor need any honors from Gavril."

But just then he sensed rather than saw Daniel's gaze upon him and he realized that the present had not come from Gavril but from Yeva, and that it wasn't intended for the guest at all but for Daniel. Why had Yeva come? Daniel's life was flickering out like a candle in the wind. He stood there now, leaning against the wall, having gotten up from bed. Itzhok did not know what to do—he knew that he should accept the gift because of Daniel, but there were complications.

It could cause Malka no end of grief. And what reason was there to punish her? As it was, she went around as if in a daze. Rivka had told him that she, Malka, had been crying all day.

And now, to everyone's surprise, Malka came out of the kitchen and took the package from the children. She unwrapped it and took out two bottles of red wine, a tart, and a box tied in a white ribbon. "Here is the tablecloth, children, and say a great big thank you to your Aunt . . . Yeva. . . . Father-in-law, where are the glasses? Would Father-in-law make a benediction over the wine? Wasn't that nice of her, Daniel?"

9

DANIEL, LEANING AGAINST THE WALL, looked at Malka with an affectionate smile. Her heart skipped. For such a smile she would go through fire, blizzard, and the treacherous Polesian swamps if only the road led to her beloved Daniel.

God, she whispered to herself, *dear, sweet God, tell me how I have sinned. Have I lived even one day for myself only?*

Daniel was, after all, her whole life. From early dawn until well into the night she sat at her sewing machine making linen shirts and coats from dowlas and other coarse goods. At the end of her working day she could not straighten her back, and lying in bed her limbs would ache so that she could not sleep. And she would repeat after her mother-in-law, the "Quiet Summer": "Dearest God, I am not complaining. But why is all this coming to me?"

And on top of it all, Daniel often simply stopped speaking to her altogether. At such times she wondered why she was alive at all, and everything became too much for her—even her child.

On such dreadful days of angry and prolonged silence, when she cursed the day she was born, her mother for bringing her into the world, and herself; when anguish brought her close to even doubting God—on those very days Daniel would ignore her completely and give himself up to his painting. But he would abruptly stop what he was doing, throw down his brush, and after pacing through the house sit down next to her and kiss her eyes. "Malka, my queen, there's such mute sorrow in your eyes."

She would grow confused. Was this some new complaint against her?

He would place her on his lap. "Malka, my queen, your hair is like a yellow pine that smells of sun and mint."

She did wash her hair in mint leaves and Daniel loved this fragrance, but how could hair smell of sun? But undoubtedly he knew better. Her eyes would become misty and she'd grow rapturous. For such a moment of bliss Daniel deserved everything she could give him. Still, she would ask quietly: "Daniel, what do you have against me?"

"I against you? Oh, Malka, my queen, if only you knew the torment of wanting to paint a picture!"

"What's stopping you, Daniel? The child isn't home. I'm out of the way in the corner. Are you out of canvas?"

"It has nothing to do with those things, my queen. I have a fine piece of canvas and Akiva brought me good colors.

"Then why can't you paint?"

"I cannot, Malka, my queen. It isn't in me to paint such a picture. It's more than I can do. I've lost all feeling for life. I feel completely drained, empty, and indebted to everyone."

"To whom are you indebted, Daniel?"

"Malka, my queen, my jewel, I want to paint a summer so dry that the sun has scorched and withered everything. The pasture has burned and the cattle rub their lips against the hot, cracked earth until they bleed and they bellow up to the skies. The leaves have crumbled to dust and fallen from the trees, the forests are on fire. And in the middle of a clear stream stands a man. The water is up to his chin but he is dying of thirst. . . ."

"God pity you, Daniel. Where did you see such a summer?"

Her words would cause him to close his eyes. She simply did not understand.

"Daniel," she would persist, "the man is standing in water, after all."

"Yes, Malka, my queen, but he cannot reach it, don't you see? The moment he bends to drink the water recedes and he is left standing in a black bog."

This would complete her confusion. But at times like these he would seem even more precious and lovable to her. Although his words made no sense she would be proud that he, Daniel, shared his thoughts and dreams with her. But he would also seem alien and distant, as if someone else were holding her. The Daniel who scolded her and found fault was much more familiar and reassuring. It was normal for a husband to yell at his wife. Her father yelled at her mother, and her father-in-law sometimes shouted at his wife. Even she, Malka, would have occasionally made some cutting remark to Daniel if only she knew how. With that Daniel who spoke of dry summers and people who stood in a river and died of thirst, however—

She would press her face against his chest and through the odors of oil and paint trace the scent of his body—of the real Daniel's. She would embrace him and feel a warmth course through her limbs.

"Daniel, do you love me even a little?"

"Whom else have I but you, my queen, my jewel?"

She would be comforted for it was true—he had no one beside her. God Himself had sent Daniel to her and it did not matter to her what other people said, that once Yeva was married Daniel had ceased to care about anything, and knowing of Malka's deep love for him had married her out of pity.

It was true that he had selected her in a strange fashion. He had come to her house on a wintry Saturday afternoon and found the usual crowd of boys and girls there playing their customary game of Pledge and Penalty. The game had a great advantage in that it never repeated itself, and that everyone could participate. And if it happened that a boy had to kiss the same girl every Saturday, no one minded that either.

Daniel had sat on the side, preoccupied, biting his finger-

70

nails, and barely responding to the others. Actually, people rarely spoke to him at that time. The boys felt guilty, as if it had somehow been their fault that an elderly bachelor, a stranger, had taken a local girl away. They should have helped Daniel knock down the walls of Gavril's house, lock Neha and her brother, Abushl, in the chickencoop, and chase the wealthy old lecher out of the village.

The girls, despite their affected sympathy, had been inwardly glad. All it meant to them was one marriageable maiden less and one eligible bachelor more. And what a bachelor at that! Now, each of them could again scheme and hope and wait. . . .

And Daniel had sat there, almost by the front door, and bitten his nails, debating whether to stay or go. This decision, everyone knew, had been based on the fact that Abushl's voice could be heard from the other room and that Daniel was reluctant to come face-to-face with his worst enemy.

In the meantime, the game had continued. But to mask the tension caused by Daniel's arrival everyone had begun to play with exaggerated enthusiasm. One of the boys who had been told to go outside into the bitter cold had asked: "Guess how I'm standing out here?"

And the answer had come back loud and strong: "Like a big dummy!"

The boy, blushing from embarrassment but not angry, had joined in the laughter. Only Daniel hadn't laughed. His surly silence had irked the others. He was spoiling their fun on the one free day they had to relax from the week's drudgery. They had little enough joy living in the village, particularly after the long Polesian autumn when the endless rains and deep puddles left everyone depressed.

Suddenly, he had gotten up. He would also play. But not with that scuffed coin. He wanted a gold ring. No, that ring would not do, it had a stone. He needed a plain ring.

Malka had run to fetch her mother's wedding ring. "Will this do, Daniel?"

And she had cautioned the others. "Please watch out that it doesn't roll into a crack in the floor, God forbid."

Her warning had been unnecessary since everyone knew that the ring was Malka's only possession, her dowry and inheritance from her late mother.

"I'm not worried about this ring," Daniel had said, "since it will remain on your finger." His voice had shook and he had grown pale. He had held the ring over Malka's head between his thumb and forefinger.

"Bear witness!" he had announced, then taken Malka's hand, put the ring on her finger and repeated: "Behold, thou art consecrated unto me by this ring according to the Law of Moses and Israel."

At first everyone had laughed.

"That's what I call a pledge!"

"If it's played, then it's part of the game!"

"But wait, he's taken her as his wife!"

From the alcove above had come charging Malka's father, Zachariah, and behind him, Neha's brother, Abushl the "Sage." He, Abushl, had begun to giggle loudly: *Mazel tov,* Daniel, and you too, Malka! *Mazel tov* to you, Zachariah! You can thank God you've married off your daughter. . . . Go fetch the cake and whisky!"

Only then, realizing what had occurred, had everyone grown as if numb and rooted to the spot. Only Abushl had raced through the house, wiped his palms on his gaberdine, and nearly choked with laughter.

"Everyone blames poor Abush for everything and I didn't even have a finger in this!"

Malka's father, Zachariah, a small emaciated man with a great beard, had stood there stupidly, licked his lips and stammered: "She is an orphan, Daniel, an orphan. To humiliate her so before the world takes a lot of gall! To heap shame on her that way! What do you have against her, such a young girl? She's the only thing I have now—one child left out of eight. . . . We will get a divorce!"

Daniel had answered Zachariah with a single word: "Father-in-law!"

"Daniel, do you mean it?"

"Give us your blessings, Father-in-law. Malka is my wife."

And he had kissed her on the lips before everybody.

More at a loss than the others, Malka had stood there wringing her hands. Her long face had gone so white that even those freckles that did not fade in the winter could be seen. Her pretty, slightly narrowed eyes had gazed with an odd kind of sorrow at Daniel. Neither his words nor his kiss had convinced her. "Why do you mock me, Daniel?"

"God forbid, Malka—you are my wife. My destined one."

She had turned to the others piteously, guiltily, as if in justification. "I am innocent!"

And she had fled into the alcove. There she had chewed the finger on which Daniel had just placed the ring while her heart had pounded within her. A procession of gold rings had danced before her eyes, which had filled with hot tears, and her legs had buckled beneath her. But she had not fallen. Instead, standing with her ear glued to the door, she had heard her father say: "Let it be with lots of luck and happiness. It was fated. A marriage made in heaven. Come, let us have whisky! Daughter, where are you?"

And she had run even farther away, outside into the blue, sparkling snow. The trees had been covered by a thick rime. Through her tears she had glimpsed the reflection of the brilliant, wintry day. A deep longing for her mother had suddenly come over her. She had never needed her mother as she had needed her then. If not for the snow and her tears, she would have gone straight to her mother's grave.

It had been such a lovely day. For three days before it had snowed, and the drifts had made it impossible to go out. But she would carry this bright and sparkling Sabbath-day in her memory for the rest of her life. Her father had been right—it had been fated. God Himself had sent Daniel to

73

her. But why had Abushl pranced around and rubbed his hands with such glee? After all, he was one who was happy only when others were in trouble.

She had run around behind the back room that faced the great forest. She had stood there in only her jacket and the frost had sprayed her with a silvery powder. Her lips had still been burning from Daniel's kiss but a sharp, burning pain had pierced her heart. He loved Yeva. He had never loved her, Malka. And suddenly, he, Daniel, had become hers. No, it was some kind of dream. But she had repeated her father's words: "It was fated." Fated? If so, why hadn't it happened earlier? Had her luck been asleep until then? But Daniel had actually said it in front of everybody: "Malka is my wife." Was it she, Malka, whom he had actually meant? She, who had adored him since childhood? She, who had loved him in secret and kept her feelings hidden from the world lest she be found out and mocked and have her love profaned? Daniel and Yeva, that was a match people could accept. But Daniel and Yellow Malka? And suddenly, Yeva had married the stranger and Daniel, for whom Malka had not even presumed to hope, had proclaimed her his wife before everyone.

She stood now leaning over the table and gripped the two bottles of wine, unable to tear her gaze away from the soft tart and the box so artfully tied in the white ribbon.

"Come, Malka," said her mother-in-law, "let's get the glasses. What are you thinking about so hard? You won't solve the world's problems, my daughter. We have much to be thankful for since the last Sabbath. Avromeniu is home. What a gift from the Holy One! And you, Akiva, don't stand there twiddling your thumbs. Take the corkscrew and open the wine."

"I will not drink that wine," Daniel said.

"Why not?" Malka said, "wine or no wine you still—"

"Children," the "Quiet Summer" interrupted, "don't desecrate the Sabbath. Itzhok, make the ablution and give

74

the benediction. Shmulik, leave the stork alone. That's all I needed in the house, a stork. Avromeniu, does it hurt you to sit up? Maybe you'd like another pillow to lean on?"

She began to bustle around his bed again. "Does your leg still ache, my son? May I suffer all your pains instead. Why are you so quiet, Avromeniu? Talk, my child, I want to hear your voice. Oh, how I missed the sound of your voice!" She dabbed at her eyes with a corner of her apron. "Left home, a boy, straight as a poplar and handsome as can be. And what do they send me back? A living corpse, a bundle of bones. If not for the skin holding him together he'd fall apart, he would. Didn't even recognize him."

"What did you expect?" demanded Akiva, "that he'd come back from the war with a triple chin and potbelly?"

"Am I complaining then, God forbid?" And she walked quietly into the kitchen to help Malka serve the food.

"They messed you up pretty good there in Manchuria," Akiva said, sitting down on Avrom's bed. "You look like a Turkish Angel of Death. You didn't by any chance live on milk and honey there? Didn't eat from the general's bowl? Don't tell me—I know all about it. They put some good wrinkles in your belly, that they did. You think I didn't serve my time, Avrom? Believe me I did. True, I didn't see combat, but even to serve the Tsar without fighting is to suffer. I didn't serve for long, but as long as I did they made things good and hot for me. I had me a sergeant major, a regular relic he was. The spittin' image of Nicolai. They could have come from the same mother. The same little beard, the same mustache, the same sweet personality. Couldn't stand an unpleasant face, couldn't bear suffering, always ready to do anything for anybody. A person was to him something very precious and sacred. In a word—a prince of a sergeant major. He used to line up the company and ask: 'Who are Russia's internal enemies?' And we had to answer together: 'Socialists, students, Jews.'

"I used to remain silent. One time he caught me and

came up closer. 'Who are Russia's in-ter-nal enemies?' I still kept quiet. He asked again. I kept quiet. He dropped his right fist to the floor—he had arms like an ape—and he smacked me one on the left cheek so that the sky took a turn and the good green earth trembled beneath my feet. He had golden hands, that dear sergeant major of mine. From such a benediction the wine promptly began to flow from my nose. But after the first punch, brothers, things began to go easier. It all went according to ritual. He'd smack and I'd keep quiet. That is to say, I didn't only keep quiet but I kept looking straight into his eyes. Suddenly, he barked: 'Forward, double time, march!' I ran. Is there anything I can't do? After all, I had inherited the calloused behind from Noah's son, Shem, and the long legs from Jacob's son, Naftali. I am seen, thanks to the Holy One, in all the world's prisons and all the great fairs. I can swim better than Noah himself. I swim across the world without even an ark. I can actually walk on water! Since I can do anything, when he told me to run I ran. I ran three paces and I heard: 'To the rear, march!' But just then I saw in the distance a pair of blue breeches with red stripes—a general. Probably had come with his staff to ask the troops if they had any complaints. Well, of course, no one ever had any. Let someone just try complaining to a general! But if he just happened to see a bleeding soldier . . . And my sergeant major had spotted the general too and he shouted: 'Halt!'

"But I had suddenly lost my hearing. I kept running. And where did I run? Straight at the general. Let him see me, I thought, and have a good time. He saw me, all right, and stopped me. Then he called the sergeant major. He explaining: so forth and so on. . . . I saw that the general stood there like a pole with his hand to his visor, and started explaining: so forth and so on . . . I saw that the general seemed very satisfied with the report and that I was in for it unless I managed to save myself from the two of them. 'Your Imperial Majesty,' I said to the general, 'if you will just command me I will also fly like a bird. I'll take you along to the moon and from there, Your Majesty, I will lead you to paradise to Queen Sheba. She has such sensuous legs. . . .'

" 'He's crazy!' the general cried.

" 'You are crazy yourself, Your Imperial Majesty!' I cried even louder. 'I've been to the moon more than once already. I wanted to bring you back a present from there—the heavenly plate. Fly with me, Your Imperial Majesty,' I said grabbing his hand. 'The Queen of Sheba is so beautiful and King Solomon is already tired of her. . . .'

"To make a long story short, they packed me off to the hospital. I hung around there for three weeks, heaping abuse on everyone alike. Finally, they discharged me with the diagnosis: oligomania. That means, I was born a little off, with a screw loose."

And Akiva burst out in a childish laugh and slapped his hands on his knees. "There's a windmill going round and round inside my head!"

His laughter enlivened the whole house. Avrom, lying there among his pillows, still could not believe it. Was he actually home? His sunken black eyes sparkled with joy and contentment. Just like his ancestors before him he stroked his black beard that his mother had washed and combed, and the happy smile did not leave his dry, cracked lips. Now, he no longer wanted for anything, for Dobche was already there too. There she sat next to Daniel, blushing. He was probably the one who had told her that he, Avrom, had come home. She had developed into quite a woman during the time he had been away and no longer dropped her eyes before everyone. She sat there redoing a braid. She knew that he loved her long, blonde hair. Itzhok paced through the house with his thumbs hooked inside his sash and prayed under his breath.

How he, Avrom, had longed for such a Sabbath, for the holiday loaves and the candles. . . . He stared at the way they flickered now, and the joy began to congeal within him. Before his eyes formed a procession of lanterns by the cemetery and he was transported to that dark night when Rochel had been buried. He saw himself hopping along on his crutches between the graves, and a lump formed in his throat. He would have to seek Akiva's advice. He was the only one whom he could tell about what had happened to Rochel.

But Akiva was laughing so heartily that the whole family had joined in. Even Daniel was smiling. "You, Friend Akiva, have been blessed by God. You know how to accept life, and I envy you this," he said.

"Daniel," Akiva said, "come with me on the wagon. I'll take you far away down my own special road. We'll ride and ride. It surely will take us long to get there but I'll tell you wondrous tales of the golden peacocks in the golden land along the way. I know that it's far to that land, Daniel, but one day, we will ride into a happy life together."

"Take me too," Malka begged quietly.

"Children," said the "Quiet Summer," standing with a knife and fork in hand, "why not put wheels under the old Inn, hitch up the mare to it, and we'll all ride ever so slowly to that gold peacock. You should only be well, the things you make up, Akiva! Go to the table already! Itzhok, make the benediction, and you, Shmulik, leave the stork alone. . . . You hear those bells?" she suddenly asked. She sprang toward the window and pushed aside the curtain. "He's here again! Woe is us, that makes the second—no, the third time already!"

A wagon had pulled up before the house with a great clamor of jangling bells and snorting horses. The "Quiet Summer" closed the curtain. "Watch over and protect us, dear God."

"God preserve us." And Itzhok Boyar's back sagged, his head tilted toward the upraised shoulder, and the hairy ear cocked. *Was the trouble still far away?*

No, it was already here. The chief constable threw open the door as if he were the master of the household, jumped over the threshold, stationed himself on the side, put his finger to his temple, and let a tall, thin man precede him inside.

"On the dot, Your Excellency."

The ankle-length greatcoat made the newcomer seem even longer and leaner. Two rows of polished buttons glistened down the front of the coat, and on the shoulders he wore brand-new gold epaulets.

"Aha," issued from the chief constable. Short and fat rather than husky, he snuffled through a nose that was broad, squashed on top, fleshy and snub on bottom, red and streaked with greenish veins. He bristled his yellow, pointed mustache like a tomcat and his round, greasy little eyes began, unconsciously, to blink covetously at the two bottles of wine. "Aha! Making a *Shabeskovski Kiddush Lechaiemka?*" he leered, Russifying the Hebrew phrase for the sanctification of the Sabbath. "In honor of the guest? He, he, he. Well, there he is!" he said, indicating Avrom. "The little bird has finally flown back to its nest. Waited a long time for you. What roads did you take coming home? Side ones? Back ones? Natur-ally!"

One thing fascinated Daniel—the tall gendarme's * face. It was strange. As if carved from dark hardwood by a drunken hand. The eyes did not move at all.

Not eyes, Daniel thought, *but two pits of blue ice.* He was anxious to hear the voice but time passed and the gendarme did not utter a single word. His silence cast such a pall that Malka began to pant with her mouth open and Rivka stopped breathing altogether. Watching the chief constable point to Avrom she stationed herself before the bed and her whole appearance seemed to say: *It could mean my death but I won't let you near my child!*

Daniel could only feel the two pits of blue ice. They gleamed coldly by the light of the burning candle. But their owner still did not speak.

* Translator's note: In Tsarist Russia gendarmes arrested persons guilty of political offenses.

79

What could this mean? Daniel pondered. *Undoubtedly one of his methods and a well-tested one at that.* The longer the silence the more fear and terror it generated. They knew well, this gang did, how much easier it was to deal with frightened people who would do anything they were told. And they, the brutes, saw to it that this fear did not leave the houses. The more fear existed at the lower strata the more secure felt those in the upper.

But this silence was prolonged to a point where even the chief constable began to shift his weight from one foot to the other and the green veins in his bulbous nose stretched and scurried like worms up toward the brows. He flicked his nose and the veins began to disperse again.

"Ivan Fyodorovitch," the chief constable said, unable to contain himself any longer. "Your Excellency, shall we begin?"

A deadly silence fell over the old Inn and the only sound heard was that of the cricket behind the stove. A candle snapped, sent off a shower of sparks, and filled the room with the acrid stench of scorched wick and greasy tallow. Shmulik, lying in Malka's arms, began to hiccup from fear. The stork climbed up on the bench and began to peck at the Sabbath loaf.

"Your Excellency, let us begin!"

And now for the first time Daniel heard from somewhere within the long greatcoat a low hissing that seemed to have originated in the toes. The gendarme had begun to fizz like a glass of carbonated water. It mounted ever higher and higher. Now, it was past the stomach, now in the upper chest, now in the throat, and suddenly it erupted in a dry and reverberating: "S . . . so . . . w . . . w . . . what?"

Shmulik burst out crying and the chief constable turned aside and loudly blew his nose.

10

His Excellency, Ivan Fyodorovitch Koblukov, had but two wishes: to add another star to his epaulets and to take his chief's place. To achieve this he was prepared to do anything—not only that which he was ordered, but even that which he had not yet been ordered. He anticipated everything in a flash; what's more, he even made his own evaluations of what would be useful to the Chief in the future. Of course, he did not do all this for the Chief but for himself. For one, his, Ivan Fyodorovitch's, reputation was growing. They had already heard of him at the Ministry. But this was not the principal reason for his overeagerness. The quicker he helped his chief become a general, the quicker he himself would advance. Then, he, Koblukov, would put on a new uniform and take over his section. It was high time already. His Excellency had convinced himself that the higher the rank, the larger, fuller and deeper the gravy bowl grew. Didn't all the higher-ups help themselves with both hands? As did, for instance, his young friend, Sashko, that clod, that overfed good-for-nothing whose only asset was a beautiful handwriting which made his reports easy to read. And that jackass had been transferred to the capital—a fool's luck—while he, Gospodin Koblukov, was still tied to the same place.

He hooked his thumbs now under the cloth near the top button of his greatcoat while the rest of his long white fingers that ended in shining fingernails drummed on the lapel. A kind of wrinkle formed on his smooth forehead. He was deep in thought. Surely such an opportunity would not come up again so soon. He had finally struck a vein of pure gold ore and all that remained was for him to mine it to his advantage.

The two pits of ice glided from face to frightened face and across the furniture. Over the old-fashioned cupboard, the hunchbacked buffet, the narrow wooden benches, and patched curtains.

The jaw moved and Daniel again heard the fizzing followed by the dry, resounding: "S . . . so . . . w . . . w . . . what?"

Koblukov winked at the chief constable, who put his finger to his temple. *At your service, Your Excellency!* And he ran out to the britzska. Soon he returned with a yellow leather briefcase. As he passed the crowd of spectators gathered outside he barked at the soldier guarding the coach: "Scatter them! A taste of the whip!"

His Excellency flung aside his greatcoat and cap and waved his hand for the table to be cleared, indicating at the same time that he hadn't dropped in just for a moment or two but had come for an extended visit.

The fear in the old Inn intensified and the faces grew more despairing. Malka chased the stork and removed the pecked Sabbath loaves. Shmulik, sitting in his father's lap, hiccupped and asked: "Pa, w . . . what do they want?"

"I don't know myself yet," Daniel said, glancing up at Akiva. Maybe his friend had an inkling of what was happening? But Akiva did not respond with so much as a flicker of the eye. He seemed more confused than preoccupied. But his stubborn refusal to meet his eyes told Daniel that Akiva knew more than he was showing.

The chief constable, watching the two bottles of wine disappearing from the table, twitched his mustache and the green veins began to snake their way upwards again.

"Shut that row!" he growled at Daniel. "And stop that chatter, the whole gang of you."

"Understand?" asked His Excellency and turned to the

"Quiet Summer." "And now, little Mother, fetch everything that belonged to the soldier. I mean everything—the great-coat, the boots, the trousers, the tunic"—he paused for a moment—"the . . . kettle." And at the word "kettle" his eyes drilled into Avrom's.

"Why did you get pale just now?" And he answered his own question: "It's obvious why!"

Avrom shrugged his shoulders as if in a trance. He had just now realized that his presence was somehow connected with the uninvited visitors.

"Why would I get pale?"

"You know very well why! Do you have any weapons?"

"Weapons?" A troubled smile appeared on Avrom's swollen lips. "Is His Excellency joking? What weapons would I have? The rifle was left on the battleground. The sword was stuck in the ground. All I remember is a black stream of blood gushing from the horse's mouth. What happened to me after that I can't recall."

"Go on, tell some more! Tell of all your war experiences. You can fool your family with that twaddle but we know all about how you people fight. When your rifle is empty you faint. Com-bat soldiers indeed! Just see there how he dares look me in the face with those shameless eyes! It's unbelievable!"

Ivan Fyodorovitch Koblukov lit a cigarette, exhaled smoke from a corner of his mouth, and, curling his upper lip, displayed a golden tooth. "You spineless creature! I repeat: Do you have any weapons?"

The blood rushed to Avrom's face. "Weapons? Here are your weapons, take them!" he shouted, pointing to the crutches leaning against the bed. "And here, Your Excellency, are more weapons!" And throwing back the covers he bared the grotesquely swollen leg dotted with black and blue specks. "Here are all your weapons, Your Excellency!" He tried to raise the wounded leg, but such an intense, cutting pain stabbed through it that he was forced to close his eyes.

"Hold your tongue!" the chief constable shouted, charging up to the bed. "Shut your dirty Jew mouth!"

Avrom kept his eyes closed. The white egret with the long, black legs was pecking at his temples again.

Daniel put his child down. Any moment now he would throw something at those "guardians of the law." How dared they invade a happy home with such colossal gall and arrogance? But he quickly came back to his senses. What good would it do to throw things at them? Their power was absolute, their authority unquestioned. They represented law and order and he was without rights at all. They, the murderers, had everything behind them—the right to hang, to imprison, to exile. And what could he do except forfeit his life? The best thing was to wait and see.

He rose, supporting himself on the table and on his father's shoulder, and staggered over to Avrom's bed. He covered the wounded leg again and wiped the sweat from his brother's face with a corner of the sheet.

Itzhok Boyar sat with his back bent, awaiting the most terrible of blows. But his head was no longer tilted to the side as if listening for trouble, for the trouble had already come, trouble so grim and ominous that the walls of the old Inn were literally quaking. He picked up his grandchild and sought to console him: "Never fear, my child. We have the strongest God of all."

"Again?" the chief constable snarled. "Wasn't it clearly enough said? No gabbing! You people have to be told the same thing a thousand times. A curse on you all! When you're told to shut up, then keep your damned mouths shut! Choke to death if you must but don't dare open those yaps!"

"Will those things ever be brought?" His Excellency demanded impatiently.

"I'm going, I'm going," the "Quiet Summer" said, and came back with a bundle of rags. Behind her, half-swooning, came Malka. The women started to untie the bundle, but the

84

chief constable ordered them to sit down and be quiet. He personally unwrapped it and began to tap and examine each item: the yellow, shrunken greatcoat; the boots—one still serviceable, the other, worn and cracked, its sole muddy and full of holes; the tunic, torn in the back and white from salty sweat; and the trousers, old and split at the knees.

"Afanasi Lukich," His Excellency said, "leave that junk and get down to business."

The chief constable turned his attention to the knapsack. Two onions, a bowl, a tin cup, and a wooden spoon with a broken handle.

"That's all?" His Excellency asked Rivka.

The "Quiet Summer" did not answer.

"Speak up!" the chief constable shouted, "when the *Nachalnik* tells you—speak!"

"There's a pair of drawers. . . ." She grimaced. "Threw them into the stall . . . crawling with lice they were."

His Excellency sneered and picked up the bowl.

"Didn't you cook anything on the way?"

He spun toward Avrom.

"Why don't you answer?"

"Speak when the *Nachalnik* tells you!"

His eyes still closed from the pain, Avrom repeated with a controlled rage: "Cook?"

"Don't repeat! And open your eyes, they give you away! Answer! Didn't you cook on the way?"

"Of course I cooked. A person has to eat, after all."

"True, very true. In what, then, did you cook? In what, I repeat, did you cook?"

The two pits of blue ice attached themselves like leeches to Avrom's face.

"I cooked in the bowl," Avrom said out of pure spite.

"And you had no kettle?"

"I traded it in a village for a loaf of bread. . . . I was hungry."

"In what village?"

"Who remembers? Stumbled through so many villages. . . ."

"Did you trade the kettle a few days ago?"

"Oh no, Your Excellency, that was before Khabarovsk yet."

"And after that you no longer had a kettle?"

"No."

And before Avrom's eyes formed a picture of the kettle rolling down the bank into the river and being swept by the current to the white-sanded island where it clung to the lonesome pine swaying over the waters. And he wondered: *Why so much fuss about an ordinary kettle?*

To Daniel it seemed that Avrom's reply caused one of the pits of blue ice to grow larger and bluer and glitter in the light while the other pit—just the opposite—grew smaller, darker and nearly extinguished. The answer obviously had displeased the gendarme. But he, Daniel, still could not grasp the thread of the conversation. Why so much stress on a kettle?

He looked up at Akiva, who stood with arms folded, smiling a thin, barely perceptible smile at Avrom. He was obviously pleased at his retorts. Now Daniel no longer had any doubts. Akiva did know something.

His Excellency paced to and fro. Finally, he sat down at the head of the table and took two sheets of paper out of the briefcase. Something resembling a wrinkle again formed on the smooth brow, and he began to write.

Akiva, standing close by, looked ostensibly away but managed to read what the gendarme had written. "This report is being prepared by the Investigator for Special Affairs—"

"Sit down!" His Excellency ordered Akiva sharply. "You've got to stick your nose into everything, don't you? A racial characteristic! You probably think we don't know you, but we know you, all right. You're a musician with a Jewish troupe. You drag around through the villages with the actors. You play and you meet all kinds of people. We'll be talking with you too, but not here. Hey there, no gabbing among yourselves! The one I ask the questions will do the answering. He'll answer to the point, and not repeat after me. And no explanations either! This is a serious matter, I tell you, a very serious matter! If you lie," he said to Avrom, "it'll go even worse for you. Just think of your old mother and father."

And addressing himself to the chief constable: "Afanasi Lukich, write up a report about the old folks. Take off your coat first."

The chief constable's stiff yellow mustache began to quiver and the rubicund nose turned pale. Write? This was one thing, he, Afanasi Lukich, dreaded. He simply had no knack for it. His right hand was forever clenched in a fist and the only time it opened was when someone was about to put something in it. Otherwise it came hard to him to simply straighten the fingers. He actually crossed himself now from perturbation. "Your Excellency?"

"Never mind." The gendarme understood his concern. "It sometimes happens, Afanasi Lukich, that you have to do such things too."

Turning to Avrom again: "Let's have the documents."

"Mama, what did you do with my papers?" Avrom asked in Yiddish.

"Hold it there!" One pit of ice again became bigger and bluer while the other shrank and dimmed. "Speak a proper language!"

Daniel, sitting at his brother's feet, remarked very calmly: "He's speaking his mother tongue."

The upper lip curled scornfully and the gold tooth flashed again. "Nonsense! Jews have no language. But you are an artist. A man who—"

"To you, I am not 'thou'!"

"You're hot-tempered, you are, and you've got to be taught a lesson. We teach you, we teach you, we teach you—

87

and you still can't get it into your thick skulls. What short memories you have! And what was the reason to feel so insulted? Take your magazines, the *Voskhod,* for instance. Your own people write there that you Jews speak a jargon."

Itzhok Boyar, completely baffled, but afraid of another false accusation, laid his hand on his beard. "Believe an old man when I tell you no 'jargon' has ever been spoken in this house!" And he held up his beard as if swearing witness that he, Itzhok Boyar, would not tell a lie.

Biting his lips until they bled, Daniel watched his father grovel, while a hot mist covered his eyes and red flecks broke out on his cheeks. He thrust his fingers into his silvery curls and the tears welled up in his eyes.

Akiva hurried up to his side. "Daniel, is it worth it?"

"Silence!" the chief constable thundered, thrusting his jaw forward.

Akiva ignored him. "Daniel, Daniel, think it over! Is it worth it? Can it do any good?"

Daniel did not answer. His yellow fingers trembled inside his hair as Akiva repeated: "Is it worth it, Daniel?"

Daniel's body suddenly gave an odd twitch. Akiva seized him by the shoulders. "What is it, Daniel?"

"It's nothing, nothing . . . oh, Friend Akiva!"

Akiva left the room. There wasn't a moment to lose. The stony life had just chipped away another chunk of the stony Daniel. He, Akiva, had to hurry to Gavril's to consult with Yeva and to bring back the Doctor.

He hesitated for an instant. Only God knew how hard it was for him to go to Gavril's house! He had been there only once in his life—that night when he had tried to help Yeva run away from the house. But he hadn't managed to snatch her from her mother's clutches.

He started off. It was imperative that he go there. The gendarme and the chief constable were trumping up some very terrible charge. Did it have anything to do with Herut? Whatever it turned out to be, Itzhok would not be able to cope with it alone. He, Akiva, would have to consult with her husband too, that Alexander Lande, who was, after all, a man of high standing and one of the community leaders in the city. His father, Old Nossan Lande, was the only Jew who came face to face with the *Gubernator*.

In the doorway, Akiva bumped into old Horpina. The old woman, her back bent, came trotting up to the table, taking small steps, and pounded her cane against the floor. "Where is my grandson? Where is my only dove, I ask you? What did you do with my baby?" She brandished her cane. "So you'd leave me to my old age with only this stick? Antichrists that you are, why are you disturbing this household? Haven't you enough tears? Maria's child is dying out there in her arms. You accursed breed, do you think you can scare me? Why should I be afraid of you? My life is a hell anyhow. Oh, when will God's wrath descend upon you?"

The people were still gathered around the front door. Even the piercing, icy wind could not drive them back to their shacks. In the open doorway stood a bareheaded peasant holding a piece of paper in both hands, a petition he wished to present. His Excellency winked at the chief constable, who was still having trouble with the pen. It kept sliding out from between his fingers and he was exhausted from his efforts to write. Sweat had broken out over the green veins. The gendarme's wink instantly restored the chief constable's self-assurance and his fingers began to reshape themselves into a fist.

"Rebelling?" He already held the old woman in a tight grip, under the knot of her head kerchief. "I'll show you 'accursed breed' . . ."

He kicked open the door, scattering the peasants with the petition. "Rebelling?" he repeated, and flung the old woman outside. If not for the soldier who guarded the britzska she would have surely fallen under the horses' hooves.

11

Around the huge, wide family table that had to be covered by two tablecloths, in the room that the Boyars called the Hall—here in his younger days Gavril would ride on horseback when in his cups—sat the red-bearded sons, the black-haired daughters-in-law, and the curly-haired grandchildren of the Gavril Boyar clan. Grandchildren as numerous as pits in a watermelon. Gavril did not even know how many they were and refrained from asking, fearing the evil eye.

The Hall, used only on holidays and festive occasions, was furnished with old-fashioned cupboards storing both clothing and dishes. Several tall, broad-leaved rubber plants were placed throughout the room. In the winter, Gavril watered them every Friday evening after the benediction of the candles. Summers, he put them outside in the orchard.

Facing the entrance stood a grandfather clock that was wound only once every eight days. Its pendulum, weights, and chains were made out of silver. Every quarter of the hour a gilded bird would emerge from behind a little door and play the Turkish national anthem. Gavril had bought the clock from the Old Squire, crazy Count Bogushevski himself. His hands folded behind his back, he, Gavril, liked to stroll among the rubber plants and take pleasure in his clock.

A dark wall mirror hung in a corner of the room. Looking into it, one would not see a clear reflection but the dim outlines of a shadowy figure. Between the clock and the mirror stood a high leather sofa which might have been either black or yellow. Twice a year, on Rosh Hashonoh and on Passover, Gavril had it rubbed with fish oil. Afterwards, it would take three days to dry before an open window.

By the opposite wall stood a black chest with copper hoops buffed to such a high polish that it hurt the eyes to look at them. This was Gavril Boyar's strongbox, which not even his sons knew how to open.

On the eastern wall, behind a green velvet curtain embroidered with two gold lions, hung a family heirloom—a Holy Scroll inside a carved ark. The Scroll was used just once a year, when all the Boyars from surrounding villages and farmhouses gathered for the High Holy Days at Gavril's house. They came there out of sheer spite, rather than go to the synagogue in the city.

But the chief attraction here was the chair at the head of the table. Broad, high, its back almost touching the ceiling, it had been carved from a single piece of oak. This was Gavril's chair or, as Akiva called it, "the throne of King Gavril the Fourteenth."

Aunt Liba, the beautiful, good but impoverished Aunt Liba, waited on the table. She served each dish with a smile or a lively remark and no one could guess that her heart was far, far away in her home village with her children and their irascible father, Uncle Shmarya. She would not have stayed for the Sabbath if not for the fact that Yeva had come. But she had lingered to hear some news of her daughter, Shifra, who in the year that she had been away in the big city had written just one letter, as if in atonement.

But she, Liba, hadn't managed to speak about her daughter to Yeva, who hadn't yet recovered from her initial meetings with Daniel and her mother. Liba had put several questions to Yeva's husband, the stout, sallow, smooth-shaven manufacturer with the fat cigar, who had always answered with the same words: "You would be, that means, Shifra's

91

mother? It's immediately apparent. About her, you don't have to worry. We've arranged for her to take courses. She's got a head on her like a man."

From the mother's standpoint, Liba was thrilled. Still, she would have liked to know who were this "we" who took such concern in her child. And what sort of courses were they that she was taking? Then again, in what kind of great commercial ventures was Shifra engaged that required "a head like a man"? But the manufacturer wouldn't elaborate. As soon as she opened her mouth he would repeat: "You would be, that means, Shifra's mother? It's immediately apparent. About her, you don't have to worry. She's got a head on her like a man."

And he would raise his hand adorned with the gold rings as if to say: *You can have faith in me—Shifra is successfully launched in society.*

And Liba would be forced to withdraw. It wasn't easy to talk to a person that saw you, yet did not see you; that talked to you and yet did not talk to you at all. And his every word was coupled with an expression that seemed to say: *You've been granted a great, great favor, that will benefit not only you, but your children and children's children for always.*

God Almighty, she thought, *how can one man put on such airs? Look how he preens himself and lays his hands on the knees to show off his rings! He must think that there is but one God in heaven and one man on earth—himself. . . .*

But she said nothing and waited her chance to speak with Yeva. She kept on serving the dishes, assisted by Stisia, Simcha's fourth wife and Gavril's newest daughter-in-law. Gavril had made Simcha divorce his three previous wives because they had not borne him children. But he laid the blame on his youngest son. Stisia was a Boyar too, a blacksmith's daughter. She came from a poor family and had been a spinster, but she was healthy and industrious. She had helped her father in the smithy and actually even wielded the big hammer. "The fact that she is a spinster is hardly a drawback," Gavril said at the time. "On the morning after the wedding an old maid becomes a young wife. And we'll do something about her poverty too."

He had provided her with a trousseau, arranged a grand wedding, and now waited for her to repay the debt—to provide him with a grandchild.

Velvel was green with envy. Simcha, that luck stiff! Every Monday and Thursday he got a new wife and still people felt sorry for him! But he, Velvel, would be strapped with his calamity of a wife until he went to his grave. Was she a wife then, or, more likely, a plank of wood? But what chance was there to get rid of her when she dropped children like a fish does eggs? "Why weren't you barren too?" he would assail her.

The inside shutters were closed in the Hall and the chandelier over the table was lit. The short, stout homemade wax candles burned within the massive holders and gave off a sweet scent. Since Neha had become sick, Gavril personally lit them every Friday evening. At the head of the table stood the narrow, glazed pitcher of tart birch wine which was drunk in the house all year round. Gavril would not come to the table unless there was a full pitcher before him. "As long as I drink this wine," he now boasted to his son-in-law, "the Angel of Death will not send an oak crashing down on me."

He rose to make the benediction. He picked up the silver beaker in which a half-pint of whisky was concealed, and bawled out: "And the heaven and the earth were finished, and all the host of them—" The rest he as if ground up between his teeth, then tipped the beaker to his lips.

"Daughter," he said to Yeva, who was conversing behind the rubber plants with the Doctor, "maybe you'll take a drop of whisky too? You know that we don't drink wine here, but had I known such guests were coming—who would have figured on it, after all?—I would have bought a barrel of wine."

"There is wine!" his son-in-law said, getting up. And what wine it is—delicate, aromatic; wait, I'll go get it."

"No, there is no wine," Yeva said. "I sent it to the sick—soldier. Give me a little whisky, Father, I haven't drunk from your cup in a long, long time already."

Her husband raised an eyebrow. "You sent the wine?" He stood there fiddling with his rings. "Pity is such a fine trait. . . ."

He thrust his hands into his pockets and looked down. But even though his head was hanging the folds remained in the back of his fat neck. The black, smoothly brushed hair no longer hid the bald spot, and his complexion was as sallow as if he were a victim of an intestinal disorder. "You might say I was carrying the wine for—" He did not conclude but his face displayed only innocent benevolence. "You did a good thing," he said. "Pity is one of man's most commendable traits."

"Whether it was good or not is my business. But you're dead wrong, Alexander. It wasn't out of pity that I did it." And Yeva took the cup from her father and, without even looking how much whisky it contained, drained it with a hearty: "Good health to you, Father!"

And his eyes met hers that were so full of torment, resentment, and reproach. He blinked and looked away. "And you, Alexander, will you not make the benediction too?"

Alexander pointed to the package he had brought to the table. Inside were a bottle of black coffee and a few stale pieces of Sabbath loaf. "This is my supper, Father-in-law. I don't dare eat anything else."

"What do you mean, don't dare?"

The women burst out laughing. Each of their nursing infants ate more. Gavril turned to his grandson, Aryeh, a lad who never came home before dawn. "How about you, Aryeh? Aren't you permitted to drink either?"

"As a matter of fact, Grandfather, I don't feel so well myself," Aryeh said with a roguish grin. "But they say that for every ailment the best remedy is a drop of—or should I say, a few cupfuls of whisky."

"Do you hear that, Alexander? Words of wisdom! They should be carved over the front door of every decent home." And Gavril seized the bottle of coffee and the bread crusts, opened a window, and threw them outside. "That's all nonsense and self-delusion."

He poured a brimming cup of whisky. "Here, drink up, Alexander! A person who runs a factory shouldn't neglect himself the way you do. Why are you looking at the Doctor? He'll already make a benediction by me too. . . . Well, don't think about it, Alexander. To Yeva's health, to the salvation of the Jews—*L'haim!* That's right—to the very bottom! So! Why are you making such faces? It's bitter, is it? I want you to know, Son-in-law, that all of us here have been suffering like this for years!" Gavril said, his eyes gleaming mischievously beneath the thick, bushy brows. "Now, have a bite of something. Liba, bring him a plate of stewed meat! Yes, and put out a bottle on the sideboard for the coachman. Give him a nice plate of food too. Well, Alexander, ready for another drink?"

Alexander stood up and struck his ring against the cup. His face drawn up and twisted, he barely managed to croak: "Another drink? You think I'm a—?"

"God forbid!" Gavril said. "I know who you are—Reb Nossan Lande's son."

"What did you do to me," Alexander said, attempting a smile, "for my burning gut—whisky? Illya Illitch," he said to the Doctor, "I'll probably—"

Gavril forced him down into his chair. "Leave the Doctor alone. Don't you see he's busy talking? Have some chopped liver. Here is shredded cabbage with sour apples. Try some kidney beans ground in goose fat. Here is a plate of rendered fat, some shmaltz herring in vinegar—"

"Vinegar for my gut?"

"Well then, how about gefülte fish with horse-radish or

a piece of calves' foot with garlic, or fried veal? Ah! Here comes the stew! Listen to me, dip an oatmeal pancake in the stew. Even by Reb Nossan Lande's son it'll go down as easy as a yawn. For ten years afterwards you won't need a doctor. . . . Where were you two?" he asked his grandsons who suddenly came in carrying lanterns.

"The new Aunt Yeva sent us to—"

But Yeva led the boys aside and asked intently: "Who took it from you?"

"No one."

"What did you do with it, then?"

"Put it on the table."

"You put it there yourselves?"

"No. They took it from us."

"Who?"

"Aunt Malka."

"Aunt Malka?" Yeva grew pensive.

"She said to tell you thanks."

"Well, all right. Take off your coats and go to the table."

Gavril's eye and ear had missed none of this. He winked at his sons to make the benediction. Three of them, Velvel, Naftali, and Simcha, imitated their father. They recited the beginning words, garbled the rest between their teeth, then drank half of their cups and gave the rest to their wives to finish.

The only one to recite the benediction from beginning to end was Zeinvel. Gavril listened as his middle son did not curtail, swallow, nor muffle his words but measured them out in the same hoarse chant and with the same gestures that he counted his money at the end of a market day. The words rustled and crackled like crisp ten-ruble notes, bill after bill. Gavril muttered to himself: "Zeinvel wouldn't stand for any errors or dodge his responsibilities. On Zeinvel you can rely."

He filled the cup with whisky and each grandchild, according to age, came up and took a sip. Tears came to their eyes but none grimaced or coughed. No young Boyar would allow himself to look bad before his grandfather. Gavril pinched their downy cheeks and watched Stisia drink from Simcha's cup. *With a wife like that you can fill the house with children,* he mused. Suddenly his eye fell on the mirror and he spied his life's tragedy—Neha with her shorn head, sitting on the sofa.

He turned to Aryeh with a sigh: "What do you say to another round, boy?"

"Did I ever refuse you, Grandfather?"

"A bully of a lad!" Alexander exclaimed. "I like this nephew of mine! I've got a fine bride for him and I'll even put up the dowry. A big, fat one too."

"What's the matter with her, is she some kind of cripple?" Gavril asked.

"Why must you assume there's something wrong with her?"

"Because of your sudden generosity."

"She's a cousin of mine. Aaron the Scribe's daughter."

"Me oh my!" Gavril exclaimed. He picked up the pitcher in both hands and poured himself a full glass of birch wine. "They say that once in a forest appeared an old horse with a multicolored saddlecloth, a gold bridle with silver tassels. The mane, tail, and legs were all braided and decorated with silk and gold. The bear, seeing such a gorgeous creature, asked: 'Who are you and what are you doing in our forest?' The horse whinnied back: 'What? You don't know who I am? Why, the Tsar himself rode me to all the ceremonies and parades for twenty years. Before me knelt everyone from a coachman to a count. Now that I'm old, the Tsar has made me a gift of this forest where I can live out my years in peace. So remember, if anyone around here disturbs me or forgets to bow to me I'll have them skinned alive!' Hearing such words the bear grew so frightened that his stomach cramped up and for the next three days his wife didn't give him a taste of honey but fed him on last year's peas. She was such a loyal mate that she ate the honey herself, the poor thing."

97

Laughter exploded around the table. Skinny Beila broke out in a shrill cackle that grated on the ears, and promptly turned to tears. It made the guests uneasy and embarrassed the family. She tried to stand up but no longer could, and Gavril cocked an eyebrow at her. "I'm not telling this story so people should act like peasants. . . ."

Skinny Beila muffled her mouth, and Aunt Liba quickly said: "Go on, Gavril, tell us more."

"The same thing occurred with the wolf and the lion," Gavril continued, lowering his brow. "But then the horse met the fox. The fox, who is always in a hurry, had no time for long discussions. 'Who are you?' he asked. 'What?' said the horse. 'You don't know who I am? Why, the Tsar himself—' 'I heard all that from the wolf,' said the fox, 'but tell me, who are you yourself?' 'I wear the most costly gear,' the old horse whinnied, 'and on me lies—' 'That's fine,' the fox interrupted, 'your saddlecloth is certainly a very fine one, but who are you yourself?' 'I wear a gold bridle with silver tassels. My mane is entwined with rare silks and—' 'That's all true,' the fox admitted, 'but you tell me, who are you yourself?' 'I myself am a horse,' said the horse. 'Then why not say so?' the fox shouted and ran to tell the wolf. The next day the horse's saddlecloth was found among his chewed-up bones."

Gavril Boyar sighed. "Pedigrees . . . I'm up to here with pedigrees already."

Alexander got the point of the story; but did it pay to get involved in discussions with cattle dealers? Once every ten years it didn't hurt to get down to their level. Still, he could not remain competely silent.

"Would you say that heredity means nothing? Don't you understand that the intellectual strength of a people—"

"I beg you, Alexander, speak like a person around here so you can be understood," Gavril interrupted. "What strength? What *Auntie* did it *lick at all?*"

Alexander exploded, now laughing with all his heart

already. His father-in-law, that cattle dealer, was a most interesting individual. Besides, he was rich and it might prove
a good thing to take him in as a partner. The whisky had
worked its wonders on Alexander, and his dark brown eyes
glistened like freshly peeled chestnuts. He did not eat but
bolted everything in sight, even the peppered fish with horse-
radish that Aunt Liba had prepared. Even Gavril's mouth
watered for Liba's famous peppered fish.

"You are good and starved, you poor fellow. Imagine a
person trying to exist on black chicory and biscuits?" And
Gavril filled a second cup of whisky for him. "Come, let us
drink the health of your daughter, my grandchild. What did
you say her name was again—Tamara?" He shrugged. "Where
do you get such names, I ask you? I'll tell you something.
When I first heard your name I thought it was a nickname
too—Alexander. I've lived sixty years in this world already
and never met a Jew with a name like that. What name do
they use to call you up to the Torah—Reb Alexander? Or
do they say a special prayer for you like they do for the
Tsar? You can tell me the truth, after all. Are you named
after some dead relative or is your name taken from the
Haftorah? *

"After a dead relative," his son-in-law said, laughing until the tears came. "I am named for a great man, one of my
great-grandfathers, the Rabbi—" and Alexander began to
enumerate his distinguished ancestors.

"Well now, do you come once in ten years to boast of
your ancestry?" Gavril grumbled. "I knew even before that
the Landes stem from famous rabbis."

"God forbid!" Alexander cried, pulling the napkin out
from under his collar. "I came to you on a different matter
altogether. My factory is on strike. They want to set up so-
cialism there at my expense, so I left. But that has nothing

---

* Translator's note: An extract from the Prophets that is read on the
Sabbath following the reading of the weekly section of the Law.

to do with you. I want to go into a big venture with you—a leather factory. Polesie needs boots—plain, cheap, rough boots."

"What? Would you soil your heredity with axle grease? Well, more about this, God willing, on Sunday. I don't talk business on the Sabbath. You see your mother-in-law there?" Gavril asked, his eyes straying to the sofa. "She's all twisted up with heredity." His eyes flooded over. "Yes, there is your heredity—a golden chain around one's legs."

"I heard the very same thing from Yeva. But she takes more after your side of the family."

Gavril did not respond and grew silent. His feeling of respect toward his son-in-law outweighed his inner rage. Gavril judged people by their possessions only. His son-in-law was esteemed by the *Gubernator* himself. Of course, not he so much as his father. Still, Alexander was the master of a factory that made cotton kerchiefs for peasant women and coarse cloth for men's suits and coats. His son-in-law had a good head on his shoulders and his cunning eyes were forever on the alert for something lying around loose, ready to be snatched up. One factory was, apparently, not enough for him. Still, he did keep Yeva in luxury. With Daniel, she would have been starving for a crust of bread while he kept on with his daubing. What good were all those pictures to him? Who needed painted peasant shacks, poplars and birches when the real thing was in abundance? All you had to do was step out of the house and there were woods there as far as the eye could see. There on the wall hung Daniel's painting of the old Inn that he had brought just the other day. The Inn looked as real as life, that was true, but why had he bothered to paint his father's cow with the broken horn? He was a fine, decent man, Daniel was. God should not punish him, Gavril, for such thoughts, but she, Yeva, had loved Daniel then and she still did. She was to be pitied. But it was too late. God would judge him and Neha for what they had done. . . .

100

"Well, drink up, Alexander, drink up! Look there, Aryeh is already finishing his second cup just to please me. Why didn't you bring the child along?"

"Ask Yeva."

"You hear me, Daughter? Why didn't you bring her? I'm dying to see her."

"I know, Papa," Yeva said, stepping out from behind the rubber plants. "But the road here is so rough and besides, we didn't come on a pleasure trip."

"Yes, Daughter, I understand," Gavril said sadly and glanced again at the mirror which swayingly reflected the bane of his existence. "You're right of course. But come to the table, my child. Why are you standing there?"

"We'll be there in a moment, Papa."

Following her outcry after her first encounter with her mother, and fortified by the whisky, she was now more pensive than concerned. She sat on the sofa, stroking her mother's withered hand, and talked with the Doctor, who stood dejected, hidden by the branches of another rubber plant.

"No, no, I can't agree with you," she said, "too many accidents in life. One at every step. However it may be, there's no one left for me at whom to vent my rage. This is my mother? The one with the eyes so full of hate and rancor? Her brother, Abushl, has the same eyes. But I've never seen such eyes in anyone else. . . ." And seeing that he was about to contradict her—"I'm neither exaggerating nor imagining things. For a while I spent all my time looking into people's eyes. No matter where I was, at home, in someone's house, in the street or at the theatre—all I did was look into people's eyes. I discovered some very strange ones too. Would you believe it? Friends began avoiding me. They somehow felt that I was trying to steal inside their souls. I think that if the eyes of a generation could be assembled and perpetrated they would constitute the greatest human document of all time."

The Doctor took his handsome beard in one hand while

his other slid into the pocket of his jacket. He began to pace in the narrow space between the rubber plants.

"But eyes like my mother's I saw in no one else. My mother never laughed and could not stand it if anyone else did. Even her own children brought her no joy and she drove them away from her. She couldn't even bear to look at me."

He stood there in amazement, unable to believe such a thing. "Couldn't look at *you?* But why?"

"Maybe it was because my father loved me."

"Didn't she love your father?"

"At one time she did and very much so. She is eight years older than he. But later, her love turned to hate. They lived under one roof like strangers."

"How long has this been going on?"

"Ever since I was born. Twenty-eight years. An awful life. And there she sits now, my mother, who so brutally forced me to marry. And she has become something else again before her time—so shrunken, her hair shorn with scissors . . . holding that white buck in her arms . . . and over her head hangs Daniel's painting. No, there is something fatalistic about all this."

A picture actually did hang over Neha's head. It depicted an old crooked building with a mossy shingle roof. In the garden stood a pear tree in bloom. And a lean red cow with a broken horn thrust her head between a black picket fence and bellowed toward the hill where the new grass was sprouting. But the nearby valleys were still covered by a dark snow and high above lay a birch forest veiled in a warm gray mist.

Yeva got up from the sofa, took a few steps forward, then came back to the picture. "Daniel hung it here for me," she said. "He knew I'd be home some day."

The Doctor blinked impatiently. Without his glasses he could not see the picture, much less even Yeva. He only heard her voice. In the five years that he had known her he had never heard her speak this way.

"It's an awful picture," she said, her voice trailing off in a whisper, "and I'll never part with it. I don't know anything about painting but to me it's simply wonderful. It has no light, it has no air, the colors are so drab, but see how much life it contains!"

"You're still so in love with him?"

"Yes. I am cursed with this love . . . look at the cow with the broken horn. That horn says so much to me. The drawn-out neck between those black slats and particularly her eyes. How human they seem, so full of longing! Do you hear her bellow for those few shoots of grass? And look there— there's still some black snow on the ground but the buds in the trees are about to open. If only a frost will not kill them off. . . ."

She turned toward the Doctor. "Illya Illitch, if it's not too much trouble, please throw the shawl around my shoulders. Thank you. It's so good to have you here. I'm not afraid of loneliness—but of wretchedness, terribly, terribly so."

"Yeva," he blurted, "Yeva!"

She looked up. "I'm deeply, deeply beholden to you, Illya Illitch, for all your kindness and goodness, but you must call me Yeva Gavrilovna. I beg this of you. . . ."

His handsome black beard fell back on his breast. "Excuse me." And he broke off a leaf from the rubber plant. She watched him crush it between his fingers nervously and fling it at the ark. He drew his hands inside his jacket sleeves and stood there with his eyes closed. His face, lost in the shadows of the rubber plants, became unrecognizable.

She sensed and knew that she had just then shattered his life.

"Illya Illitch," she whispered, "I've told you how much time I once spent reading people's eyes. You probably never knew that."

"No, I never did."

"Therefore you must also know how much I also flirted.

103

The so-called cream of society flocked around me—lawyers, businessmen, parvenus, wealthy students. I ran a kind of salon. After my wedding, I looked for someone on whom to take revenge. I actually thirsted for it. One evening, this whole pack of them got together and with those stupid, inflamed faces of theirs they drank champagne from an old slipper of mine. After that, I locked myself in my room and life had to go on without me. If not for the child I'd have taken poison and solved everything that way."

The Doctor tore his hands out of his sleeves without noticing that he had also withdrawn from there his long-last eyeglasses. "Yeva, what drives you to make up all these lies about yourself? Oh, Yeva, Yeva, how much better if I had never met you. . . ."

She grew silent for a moment and listened as the coachman was led inside the Hall and Alexander cried out: "Let him sit right here! A man of the people must have the place of honor!"

"Illya Illitch," she said, "you don't know me at all."

"If only I didn't!"

He sounded so terribly angry that she had to smile at him. "Come, let us go to the table and drink to friendship, even to brotherhood. Then, we will go there—"

"To Daniel?"

She nooded, arranged her hairpin, and started toward the table when suddenly she heard: "And me you're leaving alone?"

"Mama, you?"

"Yes, I, your mother. You didn't come to see me but to see him. And you are the good one, the decent one, the fine one. . . ."

"Mother, you?"

Neha pushed the buck off her lap. "All my life I haven't been needed by anyone—" she said in a tragic tone. "My eyes were so full of hate and rancor, were they? You've never seen such eyes in anyone else, have you?" She put her bare feet on the floor. "Your mother was a witch, was she?"

"Mama!"

Neha stood up. "Yes, it's I, your mother. She doesn't please you? She's shorn like a sheep? Go on, take revenge on me, Daughter."

"Mama!"

With her hands held out in front of her like a blind person, Neha advanced at Yeva. "Yes, it's I, your mother. And you were the good one? I alone ruined your life?"

"Mama, I beg you!"

Neha seized Yeva's hands. "Silence! Who are you to me? One thing at least I want to know before I die—who are you to me?"

"Mama!"

And with a voice not her own, Yeva cried to the Doctor: "Illya Illitch, why do you just stand there?"

"I cannot mix into family affairs. Unless you give me permission—"

He came up to the sick woman, put his arm around her shoulder and to lend his voice more authority said in Russian: "You must rest, rest, rest, and rest some more!"

She did not resist and allowed herself to be guided back to the sofa.

When she was back in place with the buck nestled in her arms again the Doctor said to Yeva, still in Russian: "Calm yourself, Yeva Gavrilovna. I've told you before that your mother is not physically ill. Both her depressive and aggressive reactions stem from many causes. They are also compounded by senility. All this, you understand, is related to psychiatry. But to—"

"And she can have complete awareness?"

"Without a doubt."

"That makes it even more horrible."

105

12

No one at the table, with the exception of Gavril and Aunt Liba, had heard what had transpired behind the rubber plants. Gavril's sons, daughters-in-law, and grandchildren were too busy gaping at Alexander's rings, Yeva's peacock feathers, and the stranger with the handsome beard. Was he actually a doctor? Besides, they spoke in Russian. Once he, the Doctor, had even addressed Yeva in some strange tongue that they had later found out was Hebrew. They had been dumfounded. But like children who at first are overly shy and later grow rambunctious, so did the members of the family gradually begin to lose their restraint under the influence of all the rich food and liquor. After a while, Gavril—Gavril the Fourteenth—stopped raising his brow at them to behave in a more circumspect manner, particularly Skinny Beila, and let them be themselves.

And then, even Alexander Lande, the proud eagle, relaxed and began to joke and tease his nephews and especially his grown nieces. After he had run out of witticisms he reminded himself about the coachman and had him brought in from the kitchen. "Let him sit right here!" he called out, "a man of the people must have the place of honor! There is a shortage of real people these days. Over here, Lazar!"

The coachman was forced to enter the wide doorway sideways. And although he kept his head as if drawn in between his shoulders, it still scraped against the ceiling, causing the pointed hareskin cap to fall. The people around the table laughed.

Alexander Lande, who wherever he found himself always felt the need to brag, to show off, and to belittle some other human being, immediately piped up: "In your whole lives did you ever see anything like it? Isn't he a caution? Did you ever see such a walking calamity?"

They had been aware of the coachman even at their first glimpse of him near the birch forest. Size alone would not have impressed the Boyars since they themselves were huge men with mighty beards and ruddy faces. But the coachman was unusual in other respects too. His black beard ended in many points and seemed never to have been groomed. It grew right up to and almost from out of the eyes. His arms also hung to the knees, and the sleepy blue eyes were particularly intriguing.

"Put him at the head of the table, Father-in-law. After all, there must be respect for a man of the people!"

The coachman took in the huge, richly-set table, gulped, and instead of bending, squatted down on his toes to pick up his cap.

Not too lively but a brute of a man, Gavril thought. *I could use such a fellow. . . .*

He extended two fingers to the coachman. "Peace be with you. What are you called?"

"My name is Lazar. Or if you like, Ashmedai. That's what people call me."

Gavril raised an eyebrow. "How? Ashmedai?"

"Father-in-law," Alexander asked with delight, "what do you think of this human misfortune?"

Engrossed, Gavril pushed a bench toward the coachman. "Ashmedai, you say? Sit down, Reb Lazar, and have a glass of whisky with us. You can drink it from the cup, the glass, or the bottle, however you like. Go ahead, drink up and enjoy yourself."

"And you didn't even want to come here, Lazar," Alexander twitted him.

"Why would a man your size be afraid to leave the city?" Gavril asked the coachman.

"Who was afraid? I had no horses."

"Those horses aren't yours? The dun is a handsome animal. I'd buy him from you."

"The horses belong to the Landes."

"A coachman without horses? What did you do—drown them?"

"No, not that."

"Where are they then?"

"In the city."

"I don't understand," Gavril said, taking the bottle of whisky away from his son-in-law who in trying to fill a glass had spilled it into the horse-radish.

"You think I'm drunk, Father-in-law? I could walk a straight line right now. . . ."

"Sit down! Soon you won't be able to walk at all. Tell us, Reb Lazar, did the city take your horses away?"

Alexander, swaying his thick torso on the thin legs, wiped his eyes. "His nags croaked on him, they did."

"What's so funny about that, Alexander?"

"His nags didn't croak at all. That is, they did, but they weren't *his* nags. Not his nags croaked but the city's. His nags didn't croak, the city's did. Every Monday and Thursday nags croak by him."

"Those are horses? Bedbugs they buy me, not horses."

The Boyars continued to be astonished by the coachman. He had already had a big drink of whisky in the kitchen and now he swallowed glass after glass. They, no mean topers themselves, were intrigued by his method of drinking. With maddening slowness he sipped each drop individually. He seemed to be saving the liquor for later, and was merely taking a taste. But the tasting consumed glass after glass.

"This kind of drinking would kill an ox," Gavril remarked.

The coachman ignored everyone, replaced the glass on

the table, wiped his mouth on his sleeve, and began to sniff at an oatmeal pancake. "Horses?" he repeated. "Bedbugs they buy me, not horses. Once I used to have horses . . . my own, they were."

"What's true is true," Alexander said, almost choking with laughter. "I did hear that you had horses of your own. But that was before your first wife yet, right?"

"Enough now," Ashmedai muttered.

"Once," Alexander began in an affectedly grave tone, "while still a boy, he worked in my mother's store. Even then he could lift two bales to his shoulders. He earned a pretty fair salary, supported his widowed mother, and raised his younger brothers and sisters. Did pretty well by them too. Made cobblers and tailors out of his brothers, one even became a watchmaker, and he married off his sisters."

"That was good of him," Aunt Liba said.

"That's what I'm trying to tell you. Then he was left all alone with his mother. Her name was—Lilith. She once beat up a guard in church on a Sunday. They said his mother could get into any store—while it was locked up for the night—"

"Alexander, show a little respect for a fellow Jew," Gavril warned, his brow furrowed in thought.

"Does he know then what I'm saying? Look at him, his head is on his arms and he's asleep. A man who sleeps his life away. He can even sleep standing up. I doubt if he's ever even seen the sun. Not that he needs it. But on the other hand, what does he have to think about? That these days he is held in esteem—a man of the people? The whole intelligentsia bows to him, kowtows to him, flatters him, and makes him out a God. He can sleep in peace. What can he possibly have to worry about?"

"What do you mean—what?" Aunt Liba objected. "They have problems too—your so-called common people. Wives, children. No matter what, one can do just so much. And who worries about his kind?"

"Who? Everybody worries about his kind, that's who."

"Who is this 'everybody'?"

"You are Shifra's mother? Don't mix in! I tell you everyone worries about Ashmedai! Do his horses die? My father is concerned. Does he sleep all day? His wife comes tearing into the House of Worship during Sabbath services and starts hollering: 'Jews, have mercy! A household full of starving children!' So what happens? They buy him another horse. You should see what goes on when he rides by. From every window people lean out and shout: 'Ashmedai, you filthy brute, go easy on the horses! What is it, Father-in-law?'"

Gavril, who had sat listening the whole time with one brow raised, now grinned: "Yes, yes, it's really quite a funny thing. Community horses . . ."

"A ward of the world's," Alexander said, reeling with laughter. "Got used to the world doing everything for him. When his mother, this Dvira-Lilith, died, he was already in his thirties and no girl would marry him. They were afraid that with his size and weight he would—"

The women shielded their mouths and began to shake with laughter. Stisia blushed and the young unmarried maidens shifted their eyes in embarrassment. The mocking smile even vanished from Aunt Liba's lips and she left the table and went to the sofa behind the rubber plants. For a long while already she had heard a series of sounds coming from there and Gavril had signaled her to see what Neha was up to. He raised his bushy brows now at his son-in-law. "Alexander, no more of this. There are children present."

"No, Father-in-law, there's no harm in me telling this. After all, he's asleep. Well, as I said, the girls would have no part of him and he would have surely remained a bachelor all his life. Who would have such a clumsy bear of a man? But Mother-in-law's brother, Reb Abush, arranged a match. My father also helped by providing the dowry—and it was done. They bought him a house and got him married off. They say he was madly in love with her."

"Did he have any children by her?" Gavril asked without looking up.

"Ah, there lies the tale! He gets wives with ready-made children. The first, they say, was a beauty. Only seventeen but already with child. Ha, ha, ha. A lucky stiff, this Ashmedai, he gets everything readymade!"

The coachman's head was sprawled over his hand, his beard pointed at the ceiling, his mouth was open, his nose snorting—everyone was certain that he was sound asleep. But suddenly, his eyes still closed, he crashed his fist against the table and sent all the dishes clattering. "Bastards! Are you still laughing?" And turning to the manufacturer: "Listen you, one more bad word about her and I'll crush your skull right here and now."

From behind the rubber plants came Yeva's frightened, anxious cry: "Mama?"

"Get away from me! So I was the witch, was I? My eyes were full of hate and rancor, were they? Eyes like you've never seen in anyone else?"

Her voice came closer. "Let me go, Liba. Who are you to me, I ask? Who are you to me?"

The blood drained from Gavril's face. He got up but it was already too late. She came to the table, barefoot and in the long nightgown. He stood before her pleading: "Neha . . . Neha . . ."

Breathing with difficulty, she barely managed to make herself heard. "Don't be so scared, Gavril. I kept quiet for so many years, I'll certainly keep quiet now that I'm close to death. God will pay you back for everything already. To us, to me, and to him," she said, pointing a long finger at Ashmedai, "you've left the shame. . . ."

"Neha . . . Neha . . ."

"I'll keep quiet, Gavril, I'll keep quiet. . . ."

The dogs raised a howl in the courtyard. Gavril did not wait for others but ran to the door himself. He silently blessed the arrival, whoever he turned out to be, for pro-

111

viding him the opportunity to flee from the house at such an opportune moment.

He stood hidden in a corner of the courtyard. The night was very dark and cold but thickly strewn with stars. The pounding at the gate grew louder and the dogs strained against their chains. The horses snorted over their troughs in the stalls that exuded the odors of warm manure, clover, and oil cakes. The smells as if revived Gavril and the cold air cleared his head. He lit a pipe. He no longer was angry, but calm and reflective. He thought about his wife with irritation but suddenly he felt deep pity for her. It wasn't her fault either. How could he possibly blame her?

But is it my fault? he pondered. *What was my sin in all this? Did I plan it this way after all? She took forty years of my life, Neha did, forty of the best years. Who'll give them back to me, who'll replace them? And that: "To me and to him you've left the shame. . . ." Was it I who told Ettel to marry the coachman? Was it I who refused Neha a divorce? Didn't I offer to take the children and leave her all the property? I was willing to go barefoot and without a shirt on my back but they said I was crazy. Tied me hand and foot they did, and took me to the rabbi, and that jackass of an alleged saint, may the earth disgorge him, exorcised the dybbuk from my body. . . .*

Someone was kicking the gate but Gavril still did not make a move toward it. A half-moon suddenly came floating out of nowhere across the birch forest and just as quickly vanished.

Gavril Boyar moaned like the bare orchard in the biting wind that now assailed him too. The ground was black but in the corners near the fences the snowdrifts had begun to blow.

If it snows tonight it will stick to the ground, he reflected. *Had Neha calmed down inside? Had Alexander planned in advance to bring the coachman here? Had it all been a calculated scheme? And from whom could he, Alex-*

ander, have learned all this? Outside of Abushl not a living soul knew about it. Chances were Abushl had let a word slip to Alexander. It was puzzling. Abushl wanted his, Gavril's, blood, that was true. But would he compromise his own sister?

Someone was pounding on the gate now with a stone. Gavril finally chased the dogs away and opened the door. A bareheaded, coatless man stood there. He had obviously run out of the house without bothering to dress for the cold weather. Gavril recognized him. It was Daniel's chum, the musician; that wiseacre who made fun of everything and everybody. Two hours before Yeva's wedding he had tried to help her run away from home. And several years later he had also done the same for Itzhok's youngest daughter, Herut. It was a wonder Itzhok allowed him into his house.

He concealed the pipe he was not permitted to smoke on the Sabbath and asked: "Where do you come from in such a hurry and without a coat in the middle of the night?"

"From Itzhok's. To knock on your gate is like to knock on the gates of heaven," Akiva complained.

He looked closely at Gavril. It was the first time they had actually met face to face.

Gavril felt rather than saw his gaze. "Why are you looking at me that way, and what brings you here?"

"I came because of Itzhok. There's some ugly business brewing there. But why are you making me stay out here in the cold?" He stepped quickly into the house.

"What's happened there?" asked Gavril, walking behind him. "You came to see me, didn't you? So why are you running away?"

"I've got to speak to Yeva first. Who is carrying on like that inside?"

"The coachman got drunk."

Seeing Akiva, Ashmedai hurled himself at him with such force that the few dishes that by a miracle hadn't fallen to the floor before, did so now.

113

"Akiva!" he roared. "What are you doing here, Akiva?" He crawled over the benches to hug him.

"Papa, Papa," Akiva pleaded, "you'll crush me. . . ."

But Ashmedai would not release him. "Enough now! Akivaniu, you go all over but you don't want to come to me, your own father! You've forgotten me. . . ."

Neha looked fixedly at Akiva, then shifted her gaze to Gavril who hung back by the door. "I'm keeping quiet, Gavril, I'm keeping quiet. I've kept quiet for so many years, I'll certainly keep quiet now, now that I'm close to death."

"No!" Gavril shouted. "No, don't keep quiet, Neha! Speak up! Speak up! I want you to speak!"

"No, Gavril. You speak, you tell it all. I will keep quiet."

They stood there drained and exhausted. The anger left her creased, shrunken face and the green fires went out inside her eyes that once more became dry, sunken, and burned-out hollows. Suddenly she turned and shuffled back to the sofa. And as she went she beckoned with a long, gnarled, yellow finger and the white buck came bounding back into her arms.

13

AVROM, HALF-SITTING, HALF-RECLINING on the pillows, his eyes
closing from the pain, answered the gendarme's questions
as if he were an outsider not involved in the matter and certainly indifferent to its consequences. He had inherited his
forbearance from his mother, who, if trouble struck or someone transgressed against her, would flare briefly, then aware
of her helplessness and secure in the knowledge that God
settled all accounts, would accept whatever happened with
cheerful resignation. However, the calmer Avrom's voice
grew the paler he became. The "Quiet Summer," standing
by his bedside, silently entreated God: *Frighten me if you
must, O Lord, but don't punish me. . . .*

And with a corner of her apron she wiped away the large
drops of sweat that kept forming on her son's forehead.

Daniel remained at the foot of his brother's bed, his
fingers still hooked in his hair. From the tension and from
clenching his teeth his jaws quivered. He still hadn't managed
to determine what it was the gendarme wanted.

An unspoken fear hovered over the household. It seemed
to Daniel that the fears that had seeped into the old walls
of the Inn through generations had now come oozing out
into the open. The candles went out, tumbling the wicks
into the tallow. Lying there they gave a dying sputter, flickered, then went out forever. The flame inside the lidless
lamp formed into a long point and issued a stifling smoke
from out of the blackened globe. A slice of moon was sud-

denly framed within a windowpane. This was a night he, Daniel, would remember for as long as he lived; a night he would some day paint. But now his brain whirled with one thought only—what did the gendarme want? What was he after?

And His Excellency, fuming and frustrated, turned his back on everyone, placed his right leg on a bench, leaned an elbow on the knee, and smoked one cigarette after another. To hell with them all! He'd make quick work of that spineless creature.

On his way to the Inn he had been sure that he would conclude the entire business in a half hour. But three hours had gone by and he was no closer to a solution than when he had started. He had already used each of his methods— the prolonged silence, the gruff voice, the flashing gold tooth, and what was usually most effective, the piercing glance . . . but even this look, which all of his colleagues envied, hadn't worked. Realizing that force would be useless, Ivan Fyodorovitch Koblukov decided to employ kindness. He would confuse the soldier. First, he would get him to admit to a few trifles. Once he got him "there," however, he would be made to confess to the rest.

He flipped his cigarette and sat down at the table again, pushing aside the papers. "Let us sort everything out calmly," he suggested.

Daniel noted the two pits of ice melting.

His Excellency turned to Avrom. "Nothing personal about all this, you understand," he cooed with extreme gentleness. "What could I possibly have against you?"

"Would I know?"

"And you, Avrom Itzkovitch, surely have nothing against me?"

"How could I? It's the first time in my life I've seen you."

"Good! Then you see that we have nothing against each other. We are both soldiers, however, Avrom Itzkovitch, and you know that a soldier's duty is to obey orders. An order is like a law. Isn't that right?"

"Yes, that's right."

"Good! Then let us sort this matter out very calmly. Perhaps you've forgotten something? Let's try to remember it together, shall we? It's just possible that you've left something out, isn't it, Avrom Itzkovitch? You were wounded, after all, and so long on the road. Your leg bothered you. No one is trying to minimize your services. We'll take everything into consideration. Right, Afanasi Lukich?"

"Of course! I've known him for a long time already and he was always a quiet lad. . . ."

"Used to be," the gendarme corrected him. "Keep writing!"

The chief constable realized that he had said the wrong thing and the green veins began to crawl up the bulbous red nose again. "Used to be . . . of course!"

"We will take this under consideration too, Afanasi Lukich."

The gendarme began to pace through the room and his long, crooked shadow ran up the wall and across the ceiling. The toes of his polished boots gleamed in the semidarkness. He began to speak haltingly, as if to himself: "Is it any wonder? It was no easy matter to hobble along on crutches with the pack on the back. In such a situation everything becomes too much. And the kettle? It bangs against one's sides. A rough trip, all right. And there is the fall weather, the rain and the mud to contend with. What's the use of talking? It's quite understandable that under such conditions dates are forgotten. But you are right, Avrom Itzkovitch. A soldier lives from day to day. He knows the names of the days and months but he is apt to forget the dates."

He stopped to face Avrom. "But that particular day you remember. . . ."

"Not exactly. It may have been a Friday, or maybe a Saturday."

"Saturday. It was Saturday," the gendarme said with an expression that seemed to say: *What is the difference what day it was?* Still, he repeated: "Yes, it *was* Saturday. Quite right. You were brought to the police station on a Saturday. Are you finding it difficult to speak? Maybe you'd like some water?"

"Thanks, I don't need any water. I wasn't the only one to be taken to the police station. Many soldiers were picked up and brought there. All the wounded ones on crutches. They took our names; where we were coming from and where we were going, then they let us go."

"Right!" His Excellency confirmed. "Exactly how it happened. There, you see—your memory is excellent."

"I never questioned it."

The gendarme let the remark pass. "Then you don't deny this?"

"I don't deny *what?* I don't even know what it is you want of me."

"So far, Avrom Itzkovitch, nothing. So far we've only established that you were at that meeting that Saturday morning."

"What meeting? I saw no meeting. And I didn't come to town on a Saturday morning but on a Saturday night."

"And where did you see your sister?"

This question so unnerved Avrom that he opened his eyes and tried to sit up, but he was too weak and his head fell back in his mother's arms.

"And where did you see your sister?" the gendarme persisted.

"At . . . her . . . house."

"What did you talk about there?"

Avrom looked away and did not answer.

"And whom did you see there at your sister's?"

Daniel watched as the two pits of melted ice froze over again and bored into Avrom.

"You might as well tell me everything. We know it all anyway."

Avrom looked up. "I barely made it to her house . . . I could just about stand on my feet."

"We know all that already. So you found your sister in the house?"

"No, not in the house . . . outside."

He licked his lips and seemed at the same time strangely helpless and as if guiltily afraid of his parents. Daniel noticed his tormented expression. "I found her . . . outside. She was cooking jam and all the children were gathered around the pot."

"What children? What pot?" The long crooked shadow weaved over the wall again. "Don't try to change the subject. What children? What pot? I want to hear about—"

The shadow grew immobile on the wall.

"You tell me—" The gendarme took out a notebook and leafed through it. "I want to hear about—Herut."

Itzhok Boyar's back suddenly straightened and his ribs thrust against the straining gaberdine. The long-awaited blow had finally been delivered.

The "Quiet Summer" stuffed the end of a kerchief into her mouth and her mother's cry burst silently out of her eyes. But it was heard throughout the room nevertheless. Even the gendarme was forced to look away and the chief constable blew his nose loudly.

Daniel's fingers clenched inside his hair until they ached. *So Herut was in their hands again! But what connection had this with Avrom?*

Malka carried the sleeping child to bed. She was anxious to take Daniel out of there too. Suppose, God forbid, he passed out?

"Well? Let's hear about Herut."

"That wasn't the sister I saw," Avrom gasped. "Her, I haven't seen for years!"

119

Itzhok Boyar stood up. "She is no sister of his, nor any daughter of mine. Her name isn't mentioned in this house."

His Excellency sneered. "Just because she converted? For that reason only?"

Itzhok bit the tip of his beard but did not answer.

"Don't be afraid, old man. She hasn't strayed as far from you as you think. Children do not abandon their parents. Her conversion was nothing more than another Jewish trick. We know that you people are capable of anything. Your Herut converted so that she could move freely outside of the Pale and so it would be easier for her to agitate against the government and to foster rebellion. She is as much a Christian as he—" pointing to Avrom, "is a Russian patriot. They were all spies at the front. The whole pack of them. For thirty pieces of silver they were ready to sell out all Holy Russia to the Japanese! Don't be so afraid, old man, your Herut doesn't go to church but to demonstrations. She organizes meetings and prints proclamations. She wants freedom—that's what she wants. But what freedom, I ask you? Don't you people have freedom enough? You're running all Russia already, it seems to me. What do you sheenies lack anyway? Come, take a walk with me through the village. Through ten villages. Through a hundred! Find me another house with wine and chocolate on the table, I dare you! You've got nothing to say, old man? Of course you don't. . . ."

He turned back to Avrom. "And you think you can mix me up, you son-of-a-bitch? You're too young and green to do that! And your stubbornness won't help because we know everything already anyway. We know that you were at that meeting where your sister spoke."

"I was not there!"

"The hell you weren't! Your own sister couldn't deny it. You *were* there and we know it! And you hit a Russian patriot over the head. We've got your kettle as proof. You killed a man!"

"I?"

"Yes, you!"

This seemed to revive Avrom. His limbs felt alive and the blood came rushing back to his face. A heat so intense ran through his body that it dried the sweat on his brow.

"I killed?"

"You!"

Avrom looked at the gendarme as if he were some kind of freak. He seemed to be swaying from wall to wall.

"I killed?" he repeated, his voice no longer afraid but completely baffled. "Why would I do such a thing?"

And as the accusation pierced his consciousness the sheer absurdity of it made him repeat: "I killed?"

And suddenly the fear burst like air out of a balloon and he laughed with relief and pure exultation. "I . . . killed?"

Daniel held on with both hands to Malka who stood beside him.

"Don't be afraid. Help me up. Papa, you give me a hand too," he said.

Itzhok's back was again bowed. "Daniel, don't. Remember that we have an Almighty, my son," he said.

Daniel did not answer. He wasn't pale anymore but completely white now. His eyes were veiled by a burning mist and his fingers trembled on his father's shoulder. He had finally reached the stage of the mature artist to whom individual brush strokes mean nothing and who knows that the whole must be conceived before the details become discernible. He stood there with one arm draped around his father and the other around Malka, concentrating—and suddenly everything became clear to him.

"Come along, Daniel," Malka pleaded, "for my sake."

The "Quiet Summer" begged Avrom. "Stop laughing, my child. . . ."

Daniel turned to his mother. "Don't interfere, Mama. Let him laugh. Everyone laugh. Malka, go see to the child. And you, Papa, give me your other hand. Yes, like that."

121

His deep agitation caused him to stutter. "You h . . . heard the l . . . laughter?" he asked the gendarme. "Does that sound like the laugh of a m . . . murderer?"

"Silence them, Afanasi Lukich!" His Excellency barked.

"It's too late for the chief constable to do anything," Daniel said, his normal voice restored. "No, don't interrupt me! I listened to you for hours and I listened patiently. I ask you again—is that the laugh of a murderer? No, don't stop me, Your Excellency. There are a few things I have to say to you. About the fact that my sister—yes, yes, Herut is my sister—and that she spoke at a meeting, this I believe! I know that she attends these meetings because she is so thrilled with her luxurious existence and because she suffers from an excess of freedom. Actually, she has grown quite fond of Siberia and the chains around her legs and the frosts and blizzards. . . ."

At first, the blunt words left the gendarme agape, but he quickly reconsidered. Maybe this brother, the artist, could serve his purposes even better. He was so full of hate that he seemed no longer capable of holding it in. And the gendarme winked at the chief constable not to interfere, and himself began to write in his official notebook.

Daniel, oblivious to everything, went on: "That my sister was at this meeting, I do believe. That some soldier hit some patriot over the head at the same meeting—this is quite possible too. But you weren't able to catch this soldier. In the meantime, a list came from the police station of all detained soldiers. No, don't interrupt, Your Excellency. After all, you're taking it all down in your notebook. So among the names in this list you stumbled across a familiar one, Boyar, the same last name as my sister's . . . the *Okhrana* * promptly established a brother-sister relationship. No, don't bother to raise your voice, Your Excellency. Your screams no longer frighten me. You heard what the old peasant

---

* Translator's note: Tsarist secret police.

woman said: 'my life is a hell anyhow.' Yes, hear me out to the end. So the *Okhrana* began to feed its imagination. What a prize this would make—a brother and sister both! Then you conceived the false accusation and subsequent trial. After all, you had to justify your evil before the world. It was ideal material for Shmakov, Markov, and Purishkevich. . . ."

He could not go on. He uttered the final words with supreme effort, hungrily gasped for air, his pupils expanded—then he collapsed in his father's arms.

14

WHEN DANIEL CAME TO, HE FOUND HIMSELF LYING on the bench-bed by the window in the alcove. He felt as if he had been brutally beaten. His head ached dully. A stone seemed to be crushing his skull and he went so far as to tap around up there, but it was only the pillow. Why then did its feathers feel so hard and heavy?

Malka was applying cold towels to his face. The moonlight made the frostwork on the windowpanes glisten. The odor of pungent, freshly peeled bark hung in the air. Drops from the wet towel dripped noisily into the basin.

Someone was sitting beside him, obviously the Doctor. Who had brought him here, and why?

The other room was bright. Fresh candles had been lit there.

Aunt Liba was bustling about in the kitchen. She had been the first to come. As soon as Neha and Ashmedai had been placated and once Akiva had related the trouble at the Inn, she had come running. She could not wait for Yeva and her husband to settle their differences. Alexander Lande had announced that not only would he not come but also that he forbade Yeva to do so. If anything was to be done for the innkeeper, it would be done back in the city through his, Alexander's, brother-in-law, the lawyer. It was enough that she, Yeva, had gone to visit Herut in prison without his, Alexander's, permission. It was pure luck that she hadn't been allowed near her.

Aunt Liba had even remembered to bring along a platter

of gefülte fish. Gavril had been close behind her, and Yeva and the Doctor a few moments later. She, Yeva, had come all dressed up.

In the kitchen, Gavril was plying the chief constable with powerful whisky.

"Well, Gavrail, Gospodin Gavrail . . . everything will soon be all right. What a daughter you have! The son-in-law is here too? Had a little too much to drink and couldn't make it? Ha, ha, ha, ha. It happens, it happens. How scared they all were here! Ha, ha, ha. Frightened the soldier, we did. . . ."

He drank up. "A strong *Shabeskovski* . . ."

Aunt Liba slipped him a piece of fish and he began to chew. "Good! I like your fish. You ain't stingy with pepper, that's for sure."

He leaned toward Gavril. "But that painter is too much of a hothead already. Is this kind of talk necessary? One must generally keep one's mouth shut these day. Especially in front of the *Nachalnik!* If you can't keep it in any longer and you've got to spill it already, then say it into a pillow. And even then look around a thousand times first. The gendarmerie has long ears, eh? Ha, ha, ha. Where did you get that stork? Look, look at him swallow that roll dipped in whisky! This bird I'm going to bring my grandson for a present."

He dipped another piece of the Sabbath loaf in the whisky and threw it to the stork, who was already tipsy. It flapped its wings, squatted, threw back its long neck—then began to make a circle, hopping, strutting, bending one leg and puffing itself up as if to say: *All the other storks are already there in the warm climes and here I am forced to drink with a policeman. . . .*

"Well, Gospodin Gavrail, to your good health! This stork has the right idea. He drinks and doesn't give a fig for the law. . . . Ha, ha, ha. Oh, did they all get scared here! Ah, ha, ha, ha. . . ."

His eyes vanished completely. They seemed to have been

washed down along with the fiery liquor. He leaned toward Gavril again. "Everybody walks around scared, Gospodin Gavrail, everybody. . . ."

He crossed himself. "So help me God, everybody! What times! Don't think we aren't scared too. You ride into a village. The churchbells ring like they're supposed to, the priest stands where he always does and the peasants take off their caps. Still—you get a funny feeling. The devil knows what it is, a kind of—shakiness. You know that you represent the authority and they're afraid of you, yet—the ants crawl over your belly. Pfui, what times!"

He bent even closer and as if whispered a secret into Gavril's ear while the green veins scurried over his nose: "It comes from up there, this fear, from above!" he said, pointing upward. "They're even more scared than we are! Do you know what brought His Excellency here, Gospodin Gavrail? Nothing else but fear. They can't sleep, none of them can. The fear is so great up there that they can't keep their teeth from chattering. One is afraid of the other. Pfui on it all!"

His muddled brain warned him that he had said too much already.

"No! No more drinking! Ab-so-lutely not—strictly forbidden! Well, all right, another little drop to cheer a grieving heart. My soul is filled with sin. . . . No, no—no more! Gavrail, you devil, no more for me!"

He pushed aside Gavril's hand holding the whisky, hugged the stork, and began to sing:

> "We are going to die
> For death has come,
> Death has come
> From God Himself.
> But dying is so hard,
> That first I'll make merry. . . ."

When Yeva and the Doctor came, the Inn settled down somewhat. The punishment had been temporarily averted. What would happen afterwards was something else again, but even then God would not abandon His children altogether.

The moment the Doctor came in he told His Excellency: "The wounded soldier cannot be moved until his leg gets better. He has fever too and it's cold and blowing outside." Then he went to the other patient, to Daniel.

Yeva interceded too. Surely the officer couldn't be positive that this was the guilty soldier. At this stage, it was merely suspicion and one could not in good conscience take a sick person out into such weather on such flimsy evidence. She, Yeva Lande, and her husband, Alexander Natanovitch Lande, stood ready to post surety for Avrom Boyar. She was prepared to give His Excellency her signature on it.

Daniel didn't hear what was being said to him. His gaze was fixed there on the lighted room where Yeva stood in a long black dress with the plunging neckline, talking to the gendarme. The two pits of ice had already thawed and the blue water sloshed back and forth inside the narrow slits. The gendarme's dark, sullen face was graciousness itself and he smiled very gently, obviously in complete accord with the lady.

Daniel could not remove his eyes from the back of Yeva's sleek black head. Her hair was braided into a huge chignon that lay upon her white nape and shoulders.

Is that you, Daniel wondered, *my faded childhood, my lost youth and dream? Was it the Yeva to whom in summer dawns by the river I said: "I searched for my beloved all night and could not find her?" The Yeva who would answer "I came to you, beloved, in the field . . . I rose before the sun. . . . To you and to you alone I'll give all my love . . . only to you, Daniel." Yes, that was she, but fuller in the bosom and broader in the hips now.* His gaze strayed across her white neck and shoulders. *You are so beautiful, Yeva, even more beautiful than you were. I'm still ready to give my life for you. But something alien has attached itself to you, something very unfamiliar. . . .*

"And how are we feeling?" Daniel felt someone take his

wrist. The glow of moonlit frostwork on the panes blended in the alcove with the luster of candlelight from the other room. A kind of soft, milky, silvery-red mist had formed around the bench-bed. The Doctor sat down within this luminescence and took his pulse. And from behind his glasses his eyes twinkled innocently. "And how are we feeling?"

He had a pleasant voice that Akiva had described correctly as belonging to someone in love.

Daniel tried to raise himself to his elbows. "You can be a friend, Doctor, a real friend. She desperately needs a friend."

The Doctor slid back along with the bench. He gazed curiously at Daniel. Was he talking sense or raving?

"About what and whom precisely are you speaking?" he asked.

Daniel repeated it, this time even more distinctly: "You can be a friend, Doctor. She, Yeva, desperately needs a friend."

"It seems to me I didn't travel sixty versts merely to discuss Yeva with you."

Daniel assumed that the Doctor had not understood him and he answered his original query: "How am I feeling? Thank you."

"I wasn't asking out of politeness but as a physician. I need—"

"I need too, Doctor," Daniel interrupted, "oh, how I need! I would begin from scratch again but entirely differently, exactly opposite from the way I did . . . until now, after all, I've painted everything all wrong. But it's too late, anyhow. My soul has already burned out. You can't give me another soul, after all, and even if you could it would have to be someone else's soul, a stranger's, a corpse's. Living souls are not readily available and even if they were I wouldn't want one. I must have my own! A soul isn't a candle that you buy in the store for a grosz. A soul must not only burn like a candle but also provide warmth . . . a soul must be fire! But mine has already been blown out by the wind."

128

"You hear the chief constable singing?" the Doctor asked abruptly. "Gavril got him drunk. He is kissing the stork. The stork is drunk too. I've heard that you can get a bird drunk but I've never had the occasion to see such a thing."

Daniel lay there with his eyes closed. *He's trying to divert me,* he thought. *He actually didn't come here on my account. He came to me like a leech. And maybe that's all that he is, a leech. . . .*

"The chief constable is on Gavril's monthly payroll. But what do you think, Doctor, should the other one be slipped a little something too?"

"Yes. And not only a little."

"But where will it come from? Where do we get it?"

"About that you needn't worry. Yeva Gavrilovna will see to it."

Daniel suddenly seized the Doctor's hand. "I beg you to excuse me, but please send Yeva to me. Please excuse me, but I beg this of you."

"What's wrong with you? Everything is going well. Your brother won't be moved, I saw to that. We'll hire a lawyer in the city. Why do you carry on this way?"

"Doctor, there's something I cannot tell you. . . ."

"I don't demand that you do. I only want you to stay calm."

"I am calm. Do me the favor and send Yeva to me."

"All right, relax. I'll get her."

"After the Doctor left, Daniel turned to his wife, who had sat there the whole time as if forgotten, holding the wet towel.

"Malka, go get my watch and your ring."

"The ring too, Daniel?"

"Yes, Malka, the ring too. Does it hurt very much to part with it?"

"No, Daniel, not for such an important reason."

"Yes, Malka, the knife blade is poised at our throats. Ask Mother for her pearls and get even Aunt Liba's earrings.

129

Go quickly, my dear, and gather it all together. Wrap it up and bring it to me."

"I'm going, Daniel. Is there anything else?"

"Nothing more, love."

Crossing the threshold Malka bumped into Yeva.

They had never been friends, not even in their youth. Nor had they felt any affinity because they had both been only daughters. She, Malka, was the daughter of Zachariah, Gavril's overseer, and Yeva was the boss's daughter. True, Yeva had never done anything to make Malka aware of the difference in their status. Even after she had gone away to the big city to school and come back on vacations, she had never put on airs or acted superior. But it was a matter of inherent personality. Malka was the minstrel of sad ballads—Yeva, the gay dancer. Malka had never been able to forget that Yeva was Gavril's daughter and that they both loved Daniel—she, Malka, surreptitiously . . . Yeva, openly and proudly.

When the wagon had first driven up to the Inn and Malka had spied Yeva, she had grown as if petrified from fear. She had followed Yeva's every move from behind the curtain. She had watched her sitting alongside Daniel under the pear tree and had gathered from his expression that he longed to throw himself at Yeva's feet.

She had dreaded a confrontation. And now that it had finally happened she cast down her eyes and stirred to get out of the lady's way. Yeva sensed Malka's feeling of inferiority and, blushing vividly, moved to embrace her. "Aren't you ashamed to act this way, Malka?"

"He is terribly sick," Malka whispered, taking Yeva aside. "God alone knows the truth. I haven't spared my health or my strength—"

Her warm breath exuded a kind of entreaty, a justification, a plea for forgiveness; as if Yeva had left a valuable article with her and she, Malka, had allowed it to be damaged.

"God alone knows the truth," she said. "Only God . . ."

But Yeva's lifted brow bespoke only one thing to Malka: *I don't want to hear any excuses, I left my treasure with you and you've let it go to ruin.*

The lifted brow irked Malka, as did the rapidly fluttering lids and cool, patronizing hand on her shoulder. But most of all, the demoralizing scent of costly perfume. And she blurted out: "No one can say you would have done more for him than I did! I gave my life for him and you can believe me when I tell you how hard such a life is."

"Malka, do call me 'thou' and why are you saying these things to me?"

"Why?" The expanse of white flesh from Yeva's deep neckline seemed to dazzle Malka's eyes. "You think of yourself as someone very tragic. But you live in luxury, you're clever, and your child is happy. What about me?"

The tears began to well up in the corners of her narrowed eyes. They gathered there uninvited, generated straight from the heart.

"What about me?" she went on. "Even now Daniel thinks more about you than me. He's trying to find a good friend for you. But it's my fate to live this way. Unloved, my child needing—" She tore loose from Yeva's arms and tried to go, but Yeva blocked her path.

"All right. If that's the way you want it then you listen to me. You, Malka, are a lucky person and a lucky wife."

"I am lucky?"

"Yes. Very lucky. You say you live a loveless life? It's not true. You love Daniel, don't you? Could you part with him? You see, my words alone made you afraid. Would you give Daniel up to me? I think not. Can you imagine a life without him? To whom would you give your life then? It's your life, after all. A big and beautiful life. And what do I have, Malka? To whom can I give my life? What would you prefer—a life with a Daniel who does not love you to one with an Alexander who does?"

A shudder suddenly racked her body. "We are both

women, Malka, so you understand. First I was humiliated, defiled, trampled upon, and drenched with slime. Only then did they wrap me in silks and satins."

Yeva felt that she had nothing more to say. Let Malka complain. She was obviously one of those women who endured a harsh life with a kind of perverse satisfaction. Their only asset was their capacity to suffer. They enjoyed whining to the world and scratching their wounds in public. . . . She tried but could not restrain herself from continuing: "If you recall everything so well and it's all so clear in your mind then may I point something out to you? You didn't 'give' your life to him at all. The word 'give' doesn't apply here. This isn't a thing one gives. It's like breath, like air. Without it, there is no life at all. And if one only 'gives,' then one goes through life as if with a noose around one's neck. Are you showing me your neck in the noose? Are you boasting of your virtue? You say that all you did was make sacrifices? That you didn't spare yourself at all?"

Malka's temper flared. "Is it a lie then? Who else gave their life for him—who else? Who else would like to have a husband and spend all her time sewing? A sick woman with a child to take care of and having to work from morning to night. For the last three years he hasn't lifted a finger. Sits there and paints trees and bushes."

Yeva seized Malka's both hands. "And you threw this up to him? You had the heart to do such a thing?"

"*I* threw it up to him? May God punish me if I even uttered one word of complaint." She tore her hands free. "But how can you say that I didn't give my life for him? Who did it then—you?"

Yeva bit her lip. "Maybe . . ." she whispered, "maybe it was I. . . ."

The sheer gall and impudence of her answer left Malka speechless. A sharp pain stabbed her as if Yeva had driven her long, red, pointed fingernails straight into her heart.

15

YEVA CROSSED THE THRESHOLD and listened to Malka's wooden slippers clacking rapidly against the floor, then fading. The dark alcove smelled of wash, rotten apples, and oil paints. Near the window lay a hoary head, as if a pile of snow had accumulated there. It was Daniel, supine on the bench-bed. Now, she would finally answer the only letter he had ever sent her, six months after her wedding. She sat down on the floor next to him. She did not care who came in and saw her, not even if it were Malka storming in to drag her out by her hair. She had something to say to Daniel and she would say it. But her tongue seemed to have suddenly stuck to her palate.

She sat there as if turned to stone. Only after he had placed his hand on her head and begun to run his fingers through her hair as he used to do long ago did she open her eyes and as if listened to every touch of his fingers. Soon he would say to her as he always did: "Yeva, you will be the happy song of my life. . . ."

But he said nothing.

Suddenly she realized that he wasn't caressing her but tapping her eyes, brow, and hair like a blind man seeking some familiar, reassuring mark. But after a while, his hand seemed so still and lifeless that she grew terror-stricken as she felt his fingers growing cold one by one. She looked up anxiously.

"Is my hand too heavy?" he asked.

"Not your hand, Daniel, your silence."

He did not answer with even a flick of a finger but kept staring through the open doorway into the lighted room where his father sat at Avrom's side. His back was bent, his head bowed toward the uplifted shoulder, and the hairy ear cocked in anticipation again. His torso was twisted in such a manner that he seemed to be sitting not in a room but somewhere in the middle of the river in a boat without oars. This boat drifted farther and farther toward the center of the river and swerved under the impact of mountainous waves.

Across from his father sat his mother, on the edge of Avrom's bed. Her arms hung loosely, her eyes were closed, and her lips clenched tightly to keep back any incipient outcry. *My mother, the "Quiet Summer,"* Daniel said to himself.

"Daniel!" Yeva cried, squeezing his hand. "Daniel, don't be so silent! You know that I wanted to be the happy song of your life. . . . Please, Daniel, your silence is intolerable! You did send for me, after all."

He sat up suddenly and lowered his feet to the ground. "Yes, Yeva, soon I will tell you. But Malka is right."

She cuddled her head against his knees. "You heard?"

"Yes, and she is right. She sat there working while I went on painting trees and bushes. Am I an artist then? I'm a fraud!"

He shook his head, gasping for air. "It isn't a matter of decency or of gratitude—no, don't interrupt me!"

She stretched her hand out toward him. "You needn't go on, Daniel, I understand."

"No, Yeva, you don't understand. I'm not complaining or decrying my fate. It doesn't matter that my life was damned; there's no justification for what I did. Where is my painting of my father sitting in the midst of a raging river in a boat without oars? Since I couldn't paint such a picture why didn't I take an axe and become a lumberjack or a raftsman and support my wife and child?"

"You can still paint that picture, Daniel."

"Yeva, don't. We both know that I'll never paint anything again. And that which I have already painted is junk. My soul has burned out within me and it gives off no more fire, only bitter fumes. My only hope now is my son. Maybe he'll be luckier than I. Maybe he'll achieve something."

"Daniel," she said, frightened, "someone is watching us!"

"Where? Who?"

"Over there! Two glowing coals, not eyes . . ."

He tried to get up. "Malka? Is it you?"

"Yes, Daniel, it's I."

"Why are you standing there like that?"

"I brought the ring, your mother's pearls, and Aunt Liba's earrings."

"Give them to Yeva."

"Why?" Yeva asked. "I don't understand, Daniel."

"You'll give them to the gendarme. Maybe he'll go away."

"You'd take Aunt Liba's earrings but not from me—"

"No, Yeva, no! We don't need your husband's money here!"

Akiva walked into the room, and Yeva came running up to him. "A wonderful thing happened to me this evening. You knew all the time what it was, Akiva."

"I knew what?" His words and particularly his hesitant expression irked and enraged her. She never for a moment doubted that he knew what had occurred and was as sure that he had known the secret long before. Otherwise, why would he have acted at first confused, then sneering and sarcastic? If he truly hadn't known, wouldn't it have been more natural for him to ask what it was all about? And even now when she had just about spelled it out for him why did he act so bewildered?

She drew away from him. Daniel was again stretched out on the bench-bed, his eyes turned toward the frosted, moonlit window. Malka tried to give her the jewelry, but the sight of Aunt Liba's small earring seemed to stab into Yeva's eyes. Had he actually said to her: "We don't need your husband's money here?" Her heart sank. They considered her Alexander Lande's property. Here she wasn't Yeva but a parcel of her husband's estate. And she became aware of the deep chasm that separated her from her family. This was something she hadn't anticipated, although she had known from the onset that the journey home would mean only grief, a final visit to the graveyard of her youth.

Disregarding all that had occurred in her father's house she had found the strength to put on her finest clothes in order to strengthen Daniel's resolve to recover; to show him that she fully expected him to get well. And even this well-intentioned gesture had been misconstrued. She had caught Malka and even Daniel glaring at the gown with resentment.

Despite the fact that she had been repelled by those whom she loved most and that the tiny flame that had kept her alive for so many years had been smothered, she still was thankful that the sixty versts of rough road had permanently shaken loose the dreamy vagueness that had possessed her for so long.

"Well," she remarked to Akiva, "if that's how you want it, so be it. But the secret is no longer a secret. Yes, I've become a stranger in my own home. Apparently, I am destined to be an outsider wherever I go. So be it then," she said and put her hand out to Malka. "Hand over the jewelry!"

"What do you know about Herut?" Daniel asked abruptly in a quaking voice.

Yeva glanced at him anxiously.

"Don't try to spare me," he said, attempting to sit up. "Tell me everything! Is she in their hands again? Why don't you answer? Friend Akiva, you tell me then—after all, you know. . . ."

"Would I keep anything from you? But for the past four months I've been touring the villages with Regaleski's Troupe."

Daniel finally managed to sit up. "You've been touring the villages?"

Akiva felt that he was trapped. But anxious to divert Daniel he assumed a light, bantering tone. "Yes, I've been knocking around with Regaleski's Troupe. One Saturday night we performed in a firehouse right among all the water barrels. 'Two Women in Pursuit of One Man,' the sketch was called. The firehouse was jammed. And just as Bronia Green was doing a gypsy dance on top of a table and her dress flew way up to here who should walk in but the town rabbi. When he saw the bare legs kicking, the bosom shaking, and heard the cymbals clang he began to scream wildly: 'Jews! We are burning!'

"The fireman who was standing backstage drooling over Bronia heard the word 'burning' and he ran up to the tower to sound the alarm. Can you picture all this, Daniel?"

Daniel leaned both hands on the edge of the sofa. "Indeed I can. How dreary life is, Friend Akiva. How terribly sad it is everywhere." He came up to Akiva and looked into his face with a fierce urgency. "And the very next day there was a pogrom, wasn't there?"

"God forbid! What gave you that idea?" Akiva shouted.

His frightened voice made Daniel sag even lower. He tottered and as if anxious to remain on his feet he thrust his his hands deep into his hair. A moment later he asked, "And you, Yeva, you know nothing of Herut either?"

"Daniel, it's I, Malka."

"You, Malka? Where is Yeva?"

"She took the jewelry, Daniel. . . . Please lie down," she pleaded softly.

"No, I don't want to. Why do you all try to make me lie down? Nothing hurts me. The Doctor was just here to see me. Malka, who else came?"

"My father."

"No, besides him. Who is crying in there?"

"Oh that! Old Horpina came with Maria. They brought Maria's sick child to the Doctor."

"Then why do you stay here? Go, Malka, my jewel, maybe you're needed in there."

She slipped out as quietly as a shadow. Daniel shuffled up to the bed where his son lay sleeping in all his clothes, and stood there for a long time watching.

"My son, my last hope, what does life hold for you?"

He sat on the bed and tremblingly kissed his son's dark-brown curls, his brow, eyes, nose, and lips. The boy twitched in his sleep, mumbled something, and threw his arms around his father's neck. Daniel remained completely still, anxious not to wake his son. Only after he was convinced that the boy was asleep did he slowly release him.

"My son, my last hope . . ." he whispered. He kissed the small bare knee, both hands, and each finger individually.

"Friend Akiva, give me a hand. Lead me to the sofa. No, no, I don't want to lie, I want to sit up. . . . Friend Akiva, one day in the future, tell Shmulik . . ."

"Tell him what, Daniel?"

"That I left all my faith and hope in him. Yes, let us be silent, Friend Akiva . . . I know it all, anyhow. What can you tell me? In your place I wouldn't say anything, either. The human language is too inadequate. What word or words could put out the hell that burns inside me? Yes, let us be silent, Friend Akiva, let us be silent. . . . A stone in the wall is liable to begin shouting, but I can no longer cry out. Can you draw water from the stone that I've become? Yes, let us be silent, Friend Akiva. A woe unto our speech and a woe unto our silence. . . ."

He took short, rasping breaths and kept swallowing down the lump that kept forming in his throat. He caught Akiva's hand. "Let us be silent, I say!"

His hand had grown leaner, drier, and more skeletal. To Akiva, it felt like a bundle of frozen bones.

"Is it snowing, Friend Akiva?"

138

"Yes. Winter is here already."

"A heavy snow or a light?"

Akiva rubbed Daniel's hand, trying to warm the icy fingers. Apparently Daniel's senses had deteriorated as well. Couldn't he hear the wind howling and raging outside?

"I love the first snow, Friend Akiva, but I hardly painted this winter. I love the spring too! How much strength and beauty it contains! And those three sunny days, those three numbered spring days—I won't get them anymore. . . . Yes, yes, let us be silent! I'm already all broken, shattered and doomed. I feel the last bit of life fluttering inside of me. *I* feel it but *you* can see it. But I am resigned. There's just one more thing I'd like before I go. I want to ask Avrom something. Death doesn't frighten me. I give you my word that I'm not afraid. But I wouldn't want to go without paying all my debts. If I died indebted, my life would have been all in vain . . . a wasted life . . . a stupid life. . . . I don't want to die that way. It's not so terrible to die; it's more terrible to leave the world empty-handed."

Akiva no longer tried to interrupt. He saw that there was no stopping or diverting his friend. Daniel was no longer talking to him but as if to himself.

"Friend Akiva, I need three sunny spring days. I'd take a large canvas, go out into the field, and paint a wide, stormy river. The water would be a dark, dark blue—almost a black. Yes, the waves must be black but topped by silvery-white caps. No shoreline could be seen except for the very top of a willow, a green crown poking out from the water. The sky would be very clear and very blue, with a few feathery clouds drifting by. Everything would be bathed in sunlight. The air would be transparent. A white vapor would rise from the earth. And on the stormy black waters a boat would be bobbing. Inside it, my father would sit without oars. His back would be bowed, his head tilted toward the raised shoulder . . . the boat would be about to capsize; it would only stay afloat through a miracle. . . ."

139

He suddenly seemed completely drained and exhausted. His breathing grew choppier and more labored. "Friend Akiva, I've paid that debt already. Who is laughing like that in there?"

"Yeva. I believe she has finished the business in there. The gendarme has been paid off and he's getting ready to leave with the constable."

"Will Avrom have to be taken to headquarters?"

"That's something we'll have to face later on. For the present, everything is all right."

A dense fog gathered before Daniel's eyes. "The eternal 'present' . . . the sword remains constantly suspended overhead. . . ."

"Don't think about it, Daniel. Yeva and the Doctor have assumed all responsibility."

"What happened there at Gavril's, Friend Akiva? What secret was Yeva referring to?"

"I'll tell you some other time."

"You keep everything from me. I'm sure Yeva knows all about Herut too. Well, let it be as you say, my friend. Tell me about it some other time." He swallowed down the lump again. "Funny, I did recognize her, yet I didn't. It is Yeva and it isn't Yeva. No, it's a different Yeva. The one I see before me is the other, the one who would come to meet me at dawn by the river. . . . She'd come and sit quietly next to me without so much as a 'good morning.' Or she'd stand by the well among the alders, rinsing the clothes. She'd try to spray me with water, and her braids would dip in the trough. She'd be excited, her eyes would crinkle and a look of wild abandon would blaze out from under her lids . . . and she would laugh. . . . That's the only Yeva I see . . . the Yeva who filled my heart with joy and with great expectations."

He stood up abruptly and walked unsteadily to the table. He opened a drawer, felt around inside with trembling fingers until they encountered a wrapped and tied package. He hesitated for a moment, then took out the package and quickly handed it to Akiva. "Here, put it away, Friend Akiva. One day soon you'll turn it over to Yeva. There are curses in there —yes, and prayers too. . . . Are they leaving already?"

"It seems so." Akiva slipped the package into his pocket and took both of Daniel's hands. "Listen to me and lie down."

"No, my friend, not just yet. After they have gone we will all take a walk. You, I, Yeva, and Malka. We might even hitch up the sleigh. . . . I love the first snow! I love the first whiteness of winter! But now, I must ask Avrom something."

He went into the other room. The candle seemed to him distant and bathed in a dense fog that kept getting denser. He blinked, but it would not be dissolved. His ears filled with a kind of silence that lets no voices penetrate. He thought that he saw his mother standing by the bed.

"Mother, would you get me a glass of warm tea?"

"This isn't your mother. It's I."

"Is that you, Dobche?"

"Yes. Don't you recognize me?"

"I do, I do indeed." He was very anxious to look into Avrom's eyes. His brother had loved this girl even before he had gone to war. "Avrom," he said smiling, "you cannot help but fall in love with such a girl. One would have to be made of iron to resist her . . . black eyes and such blonde hair. It's a rarity, a gift from God. And if I were she I'd be mad about you too. . . . Isn't that right, Dobche?"

She flushed. She knew what he was trying to do. To bring them to say that word that they both found so difficult to utter. And she was eternally grateful to him. But was this the right time and place for it? Didn't he realize what was happening in the house? That even the uniformed men stood around all dressed for the outside but making no move to go? Was he unaware of the terrible tension that had taken hold of everyone? Didn't he know that there on the kitchen table the Doctor was operating on Maria's child? Couldn't he see his father holding up the candles for the Doctor? Or old Horpina kneeling, crossing herself, and beating her head against the floor? Apparently, he saw none of these things, and she whispered to him, "Wait, I'll get the tea for you."

And after she had gone he leaned over his brother. "Is anyone near us?"

"No. Can't you see, Daniel?"

"I see, Avrom, I see. Tell me, when were you at Rochel's?"

"A week ago."

"And she was cooking jam outside? Who cooks jam this time of the year? Out of what fruit—cherries?"

"How do I know what fruit?"

"And the children were standing around the pot, you say?"

Daniel's moist, shining eyes made Avrom shrink deeper into the pillows. "Tell me, brother, did you come on the very day of the pogrom?"

Avrom did not answer.

"And you found Rochel lying . . . outside?"

"Daniel, leave me alone!"

Daniel could no longer remain upright, and toppled into the bed alongside his brother. His hands roamed over Avrom's face and came away wet. Avrom was crying. Daniel clasped his brother's head in both hands, moaned deeply, then lay still.

No one had noticed the little scene between them. They had forgotten the gendarme, the chief constable, even their own existence. Each second dragged by like an eternity. Each such second could age a human being. Later, none of them would believe what they had experienced. But now all eyes were fixed on the kitchen where only the Doctor's back and occasional side view could be seen as he accepted instruments from Yeva. Itzhok Boyar, his face drained white, stood erect with both candles held high and moved his lips beseeching the Almighty's mercy. And finally the strained silence was broken as the Doctor straightened his back and, pulling the gauze down from his face, began to whistle gaily. "Mother, your child will be all right," he said to Maria sitting next to Aunt Liba, who patted her shoulder.

Only now Maria started to weep, and sprang forward to kiss the Doctor's hand. Old Horpina rose from her knees, faced the Doctor, and from confusion began to make the sign of the cross over him. "May God be with you always. May you be God's person forever!"

The old Inn came alive. Only Akiva sat in the dark alcove, his hand holding the package inside his pocket, and looked on horror-stricken at Daniel, lying with his arms around Avrom, who still did not suspect anything wrong.

The "Quiet Summer" came up to the bed, gazed down at her two sons, and said with pride: "May all your troubles be mine instead. May you live long after me. Daniel, my son, you wanted a glass of tea, didn't you?"

Suddenly she began to shriek: "Woe is me, woe is mine!" And wringing her hands she cried: "Itzhok! Malka! What's happened to my child?"

From outside, the sound of creaking wheels was heard as the gendarme and chief constable departed in their britzska. The cow with the broken horn bellowed by the front door. No one had remembered to take her into the stall. All eyes, fearful and expectant again, turned toward the Doctor, who was holding Daniel's yellow hand. They all stood around as if the snow would not be falling outside but straight into their hearts. Only Avrom, who had freed himself from Daniel's embrace, sprang out of bed in his underwear and began to hop through the room on his crutches.

The "Quiet Summer," her lips pressed together tightly, her clasped hands swaying, the eternal outcry ever-present in her eyes, peered into the Doctor's face, and waited. She had waited just this way on a summer's night thirty years before to learn whether she had given birth to a normal child. Her first three had been stillborn, but when Itzhok had exclaimed, "Rivkele, a live baby! A big, healthy boy!" she had commenced to scream exultantly: "My sun! My light! My moon and stars!"

The Doctor put down Daniel's hand, turned away from Rivka's gaze, took off his glasses, and went to the sick child in the kitchen. From the alcove where Akiva still sat, Daniel's last hope, his nine-year-old son, came running, but Itzhok caught him up in his arms.

The "Quiet Summer" ceased swaying and asked in a still, dry tone: "Oh, and is that all?"

Then she held her arms out beseechingly toward the others. "People! Dear people! Good people! My friends! Why do you just stand there?"

And seeing that no one made a move she flung herself toward Daniel to save her baby, but Aunt Liba held her back. "Cry, Rivka, cry. It will make it easier."

But no sound issued from the "Quiet Summer." Itzhok Boyar, his back bowed, his mouth open, his breath as if stopped by the devastating blow, clung tighter to Shmulik, who strained toward his father. Suddenly, the innkeeper gasped oddly, walked up to the bed, and with Shmulik's small hand inside of his own pushed down Daniel's lids, saying: "Praised be the true Judge."

"Itzhok, yes?" Rivka asked in a voice barely audible. "Is it yes? . . . yes? . . ."

He grasped her by the elbows. "Be brave, Rivka. . . . One may not desecrate the Sabbath. . . ."

She looked on silently as Gavril and Akiva carried Daniel to the sofa in the alcove. But when she saw Malka approaching with the white sheet, the "Quiet Summer" burst out: "The sun has been extinguished, and the light, the moon and the stars!"

144

BOOK TWO

BOOK TWO

1

FOR ALMOST A WEEK NOW, a still and restrained holiday-like mood, the kind preceding some unanticipated celebration, had reigned over Aunt Liba's old-fashioned, desperately poverty-stricken home. And this very stillness was rife with the deep provocation and excitement of a beautiful fantasy.

Neither Aunt Liba nor her husband, Shmarya, who spent his life expecting some miracle that would save him, had gone so far as to display their joy openly; both controlled their emotions, terrified of frightening away the good fortune that had suddenly descended upon them. They would curb their enthusiasm until the good fortune had crossed their threshold. And if it actually came about, there would be plenty of time to celebrate afterwards.

Neither really believed that it would happen, especially Aunt Liba, who took a very sober view of life in general. After all, it was entirely possible that Reb Abushl, who had come bursting in out of the blue with the unexpected news, had left out something essential, or exaggerated and embellished the facts. Yet he had said it clearly enough, then repeated it for emphasis—that Avner had taken a shine to their daughter, Shifra, and that she had also found favor with the other Landes—and that he, Abushl, had come at the special bidding of the Old Man himself, Reb Nossan Lande.

And they, the parents, had not ceased discussing the good news well into the long, winter nights. Shmarya, in particular, was ready to be convinced. He clearly saw the hand of the Divine Presence. Clearly, a miracle had occurred—their

147

daughter would be granted the great honor of marrying a Lande. Still, Liba argued, if it were true why hadn't Shifra written herself?

Finally, weary from thinking, judging, weighing, and deliberating, which Liba insisted only multiplied the doubt and worry, they had arrived at a decision. Since Itzhok had lately been going to the city to visit Avrom, why couldn't he stop by and take one of them to Yeva's? And the one to go, Shmarya concurred, should be Liba, whose sharp eyes and ears would quickly size up the situation.

And Aunt Liba had agreed, although she was apprehensive about the trip. In recent weeks she had been feeling nauseous. But Shmarya could not be relied on—he always saw things through rose-colored glasses, and wishful thinking had already supplanted his reason. What was the solution? She would go herself, and since Itzhok would be with her, he could help her determine whether the story had any substance.

"Shmarya, go to sleep!" she admonished her husband. "The last cock hasn't crowed yet."

"Ah, Liba, if only I could . . ."

"Go to sleep!" she insisted. "To sleep!"

But she herself got up. She had to prepare for the trip and to stock her pantry, and she knew the less there was from which to stock and to prepare the longer it would take her, and therefore she had to get an early start. She put on her husband's boots and stole quietly out of the house to avoid waking her children. The lights had already gone on in some of the village houses. She would go to the neighbors and borrow a few things—something here, something there. She did this very rarely—only in times of great urgency such as this.

After borrowing all that she could, she sat with a neighbor's shawl draped across her knees, waiting for Itzhok to come for her. Her flock of children was gathered around her, one smaller than the next. Every three years she had another child, but they all left home at twelve to earn their piece of bread and to help out their father as best they could.

Now, on the verge of departure, she cautioned them, particularly the eldest—the eleven-year-old girl who was left in charge of the household—to behave, to mind their father, to take care of the little ones, and how to cope with any contingency.

The children were aware of something unusual—Father was almost smiling and Mother was actually getting ready to ride in a sleigh! Until now, she had always gone everywhere on foot. And the only place she ever went was to Uncle Gavril's. She would take a cane in hand, pick up her bundle, and strike out, as she would put it, across fields and forests, sands and the Polesian swamps. . . . The older children knew why she went there—to collect the fifteen rubles still due her on her dowry from that liar, that cheat and pig of a brother. Each year she made the same trip and each year she came back spent, humiliated, and empty-handed. For a long time afterwards, a deadly silence would prevail in the house, and if it happened that a child made a joke or, even worse, laughed, the father's anger would ignite like a torch. "Who laughed? Who finds it so good around here that he can laugh?"

The fear would then grip everyone and the oppressive silence would be restored. And he, Shmarya, did not give more than one warning. One squeak and everybody would catch it without mercy. And she, Liba, dared not protest because this only inflamed him further. The only thing that would mitigate his rage was her complete and enthusiastic approval.

But as he flailed away she would hold her hands and beg through tears: "Shmarya, why take it out on the children? Is it their fault, the poor lambs? Shmarya, is it right to beat starving children?"

He stood at the window now with an amiable expres-

149

sion, waiting for the sleigh to show up—a gaunt, dried-out, angry man. When he screamed, it seemed that his bones would crumble momentarily. But he was wiry, powerful, and sinewy, with thick veins. Swarthy of skin, as if he had just come from the desert, his large, sharp eyes glistened with eternal hope. Gloomy, harried, crushed by the effort of providing for his large family, dragging through heats and frosts from fair to fair with the pack on his back to buy a bundle of hog's bristles, a small hide or a lump of wax, he kept looking down all roads and highways for the miracle that would save him.

A deeply pious man, he trembled before the Lord and each morning and evening cried out to Him lamentfully: "Master of the universe, You the Almighty, You the All-Powerful, Hear my voice, O Lord, and see the tears in my eyes! You are holy, holy, holy! Take pity, if not on me then on my little children. Almighty God, open the gates of Heaven and heed my pleas. Father in Heaven, bring closer the day of my salvation. I, Shmarya, am but a nothing, a worm, a mote of dust, a glob of clay in Thy hand, a broken shard, a mere shadow. . . . Answer me, O Lord, answer me! Answer me, Father in Heaven, answer me! Answer, my Creator, answer me! Answer, merciful God, answer me! Answer, Angel of Angels, answer me! Answer, God of my ancestors, answer me! The water is past my chin already. . . . Speak to me now!"

But He, the Awesome and Almighty, He without Whom a hair does not fall from a head, He the Merciful One, remained silent. And at times Shmarya would fall into a deep despair. "Almighty God, when will You help me—after I'm already lying with my face to the ground? God, God, God! Dearest Father of mine . . ."

Standing now by the window, Shmarya rotated his shoulders as if testing whether his burden had been lightened, and looked out for the sleigh. This too seemed a good omen to him—the fact that Itzhok Boyar happened to be going to the city to bring back Avrom who had spent the winter there curing his leg. What a sweet bit of luck that had been—it meant saving a fare for Liba.

He actually smiled. The still and restrained holiday-like mood that reigned over the house gave off the aromas of stewed carrots and chicory that had been prepared for such an honored and opportune guest as Itzhok Boyar.

And from behind the fleecy white cloudlets high in the sky emerged the great toiler of the world—the sun. At night the frosts still prevailed, but during the day, drops like solar sparks had already begun to drip down from the roofs on the sunny side of the village. The coming spring could even be detected in the lowing of the cattle and the rustle of the poplars. In the other half of the house, also resting on two wooden blocks, the blind landlord was playing his lyre. Suddenly he stopped, and the familiar finger tapped against the wall. "Shmarya, can you hear me?"

"I hear you, Panase."

"Will you be going to the fair today?"

"It seems not."

They often had occasion to go to the fair together on market days. At the end of the day, Panase would sit patiently for a long time in the empty marketplace, waiting for Shmarya. He knew that his tenant was at the synagogue, and that his prayer commenced only after the first star could be seen in the sky. And when he finally came, Panase would cross himself as he went past the church and follow him home.

As was the custom, they all sat down for a moment before beginning the journey. From behind the wall drifted the sound of Panase's sad ballad of a widow being comforted by her orphans:

> "Mother, dear Mother
> Don't fret about us.
> When we are full-grown
> Scatter we must.
> We'll fan out all over,

To lands high and low.
We'll fan out all over
To where the four winds blow. . . ."

And sitting there in a row—from Shmarya down to the smallest three-year-old—the eldest daughter, who had been washing dishes but had stopped at Shmarya's request and sat down still holding a plate, read the prophetic message in Panase's sad song and suddenly dropped the plate.

Everyone grew aghast. For breaking a plate in the house Father could kill. The broken shards of the flower-patterned plate lay scattered over the reddish, freshly smeared clay floor while everyone glanced up at him white-faced. But though his jawbones twitched, he only said: "Well, let it serve as a good omen too. No, don't throw out the shards, lay them there on the shelf. Liba, the sleigh! Itzhok is coming. Well, Liba, go with luck! May your journey start on the right foot! Don't you blurt anything out there, you've simply come to visit Shifra . . . a girl all alone, so far from home. The devil shouldn't, God forbid—"

Despite her poverty and eternal struggle not to waste the slightest thing, despite all her problems and cares, Aunt Liba still looked healthy and pretty. True, she had been feeling nauseous the past few weeks, but so far no one knew nor suspected a thing. She hadn't even told her husband yet. If the good news proved true, there would be plenty of time to tell him about the other development. But maybe it would all pass anyway? Such things did happen.

She rose with the borrowed shawl covering her shoulders, and her wise eyes narrowed. She let Shmarya lecture and instruct her and did not interrupt even when he repeated himself for the third time, but when he finally grew silent she turned to him with her good but sad smile: "Anything else, Shmarya?"

"Keep your eyes open, Liba, and don't hide in a corner there . . . and come flying home on wings. If Itzhok has to stay on, grab a ride with someone else."

152

"Shmarya, so far I'm going to the luck, not the other way around. *It* doesn't know me and I don't know *it*. Maybe Reb Luck won't even invite me to sit down there? Who knows, Shmarya?"

"Liba, if necessary, swallow your pride."

"Shmarya, I'm not going there to, God forbid, fling pepper in people's eyes!"

"Forget the Boyar pride for once, Liba."

"But neither will I tiptoe like a mouse on a cymbal."

"Go, wife of mine! A successful trip to you, and take my advice: the less pride—"

"Oy, Shmarya, Shmarya, what do I have to brag about to the likes of them? With one eye I'll look at their wealth, with the other—at my poverty."

2

After Shmarya had escorted his wife out to the broad, slushy, trampled highway; had ceased jogging around the sleigh, warning, admonishing, and reminding; and had been finally left by the poplars in only his gaberdine but with his head still in the clouds—the sleigh had quickly departed the sprawling village and entered the dark, dense, primeval forest.

It glided between the stout pine trunks whose bark was black, puckered and thickly notched on bottom, but grew thinner, smoother, and light golden the higher it climbed. The branches of the evergreens shook off their snow onto the narrow, yellow-rutted path below. With the coming of spring they rustled and jostled each other, vying for an extra ray, an extra droplet of sunshine. And the sun, that mighty toiler of the world, slaked their thirst indiscriminately with curling mists of warm, life-giving light. The snow was a dazzling, brilliant white.

"Are you settled in there nicely, Liba?"

"Yes, Reb Itzhok. Will we get there by nightfall?"

"If God gives good health and fair weather."

In her husband's boots, her old burnoose, and the neighbor's oft-borrowed, checkered gray shawl across her head, she sat in back on the tightly nailed bale of hay and mused about the trip. Who and what was this Avner who was willing to take her Shifra without any added inducements? After all, he was Reb Nossan Lande's youngest son. With his wealth and position he could have married any one of dozens of girls from the same background. Was he a cripple or a sickly man or, God forbid, an invalid?

She would have liked to consult with Itzhok, about whom the Boyars said: His heart is in the right place, he tells people the truth right to their faces and does not see things the way they should be, but the way they actually are.

Yes, she was eager to seek his advice, yet was reluctant to burden one so recently bereaved with such an insignificant matter as a betrothal. Itzhok seemed more grief-stricken than she had ever seen him. What could she say to comfort him? This required a power of speech that was beyond her. She yearned to say to him: "Enough, Reb Itzhok, enough! I can actually see you growing gray before my eyes."

But she remained silent. The sleigh moved forward, drawn silently by the white, big-bellied mare that cocked her split ear, snorted, and trod over the sunny strips that descended onto the path from in between the green branches. No, there was nothing Aunt Liba could say to Itzhok concerning his loss, nor anything that he could tell her, since all the news was already known in the family. After Daniel's death, Rochel's husband, Hershe Leib, had come with his three motherless children to Itzhok's house. *Those orphans must be a great source of sorrow there,* Aunt Liba thought. *Children can intensify the suffering in a house yet at the same time help lighten the worry. After all, everyone needs a laugh at least once in a while. . . .*

The family knew something else. Hershe Leib was anxious to marry Malka, and the "Quiet Summer" was very much in favor of it. This way, the children would not have a stranger for a stepmother. Malka would not neglect them for her own son. But nothing had been resolved. It was said that Hershe Leib's hints had deeply disturbed Malka, and there the matter rested. The marriage ring and the other jewelry that Yeva had secretly replaced under Daniel's pillow the night he died had been sold by Malka for money for a gravestone.

She, Aunt Liba, certainly wouldn't discuss Herut with Itzhok. Herut was still in prison and Avrom had nearly gotten into serious trouble on her account. The Doctor had hired the biggest lawyers in the city, including one from as far away as Petersburg. If the charge hadn't been negated it would have resulted in a terrible tragedy. Nor was there reason to rejoice at Gavril's house. Only a month before, the youngest daughter-in-law, Stisia, had snatched Neha from the jaws of death. Neha kept dying and dying but still could not die. The Angel of Death seemed to be toying with her but would not make the final move. Daniel had once put it very aptly: "Neha's soul having died a long time ago, it is very hard for a body that has no soul to die. . . ."

And with each passing mile the holiday-like mood that had permeated Liba's house revived the long dormant hopes within her, grew ever more raveled with gloom and anxiety. And there was also the nausea. . . . She sat with the shawl across her head, her hands drawn deeply inside of the sleeves, her lips compressed and her eyes, like all Boyar eyes when preoccupied, half shut.

The sun moved slowly over the forest. The dry chuck of a woodpecker pecking a dead trunk hovered in the frosty air and blended with the song of bluethroats and the creaking of towering trees. The bitter tang of a nut tree preparing to welcome the spring assailed their nostrils.

Itzhok Boyar sat in his customary driving position—his legs in the thick-soled, black felt boots dangling over the side of the sleigh. He wore a short brown fur pelt with green selvage, and on his head his grandfather's worn sable hat shiny with age and reaching down past his ears. He held the rope reins, puffed on his pipe, and seemed to be listening to something.

His back was no longer bent nor his head tilted toward the upraised shoulder. Whatever blow was yet forthcoming, whatever trouble lay in store, they could not make him suffer more. He sat erect, one eye narrowed, and he listened.

. . . Someone called, shouted, demanded: "Itzhok, I want to know! What will become of your last remaining daughter?" If only the "Quiet Summer" would say something! But she spoke only with her eyes. Once, he had even begged her: "Rivka, silence your eyes. . . ."

Ever since, she had kept her eyes cast down. "She has begun to display sudden strength and capability," he abruptly remarked.

Deeply preoccupied, Aunt Liba lurched forward at the sound of his voice as if the sleigh would have made a sudden stop. She stared at him. Even during the short time that they had been on the road his narrow beard seemed to have developed two gray streaks. Her head bowed but still smiling her good and wise smile, she asked: "Who, Rez Itzhok?"

"My 'Quiet Summer.' She carries the tub alone, she does all the heavy work and keeps her eyes always on the ground. And they are even more terrible that way than they would be looking directly at me. I can't hide anywhere from those eyes. Giddy up! Giddy up!" he loudly admonished the mare. "Look at her, already she stands still! She has to hear everything that we're saying. Giddy up! Tell me, Liba, what can a simple man like me say to this? Neither my brain nor my heart can break through such a wall. And who am I to take on such a task? Enough that a fine bough has broken off—must I chop down the trunk now?"

And suddenly she realized about whom he was talking and her eyes opened wide in surprise. That Itzhok would talk about his renegade daughter? Everyone in the family had been strictly warned not to mention her name in his presence.

"Don't let it surprise you so much, Liba," he said, relighting his pipe. "Time changes even a stone. Daniel, may he rest in peace, never renounced his sister. Faith, he told me, was a matter of decency and of conscience. Each person, he said, has the right to believe in his own God. 'I don't believe in any gods,' he said. 'It's enough that I'm oppressed from

157

all sides here on earth. I don't need to be oppressed from up there as well. I'd like the heavens to be clear and free of gods,' he said. 'I bow to the sun, to the moon and the stars.' His words made my blood run cold, Liba. Giddy up! Watch, any minute now she'll sit down altogether."

The mare responded with a swish of her knotted tail and a tug of the sleigh. Aunt Liba was thrown forward again but her furrowed brow did not even out. Itzhok thrust the dead pipe inside a boot, palmed his long, narrow beard, and squinted his eye at the road ahead. The forest air grew ever purer, crisper, and more transparent. The sun seemed to be climbing a mountain as it rose higher and higher. But down among the roots the shadows were already multiplying. The snow seemed to be strewn with bluish pearls. The squeaking of the sleigh's runners grew louder as the frost sharpened.

"But it's one thing to be a heretic and another a convert, Liba. How did the God of our ancestors fail her? By being the shepherd of a lost flock? What she did is unforgivable. To abandon a people at a time of crisis and to go seek a fat bone at the table of strangers . . . No, Liba, this is beyond forgiveness. A convert is not merely a heretic. A convert would sell his heritage for a mess of pottage."

He worked his bones beneath the fur pelt. "Tell me, Liba, have our children really sunk as low as that? I keep thinking of the Martyr, Yontel. A plain tailor lad who barely could say his prayers—yet what pride and dignity he possessed!"

"Tell me, Reb Itzhok," she asked gently, "do you consider prison a fat bone?"

He grew pensive for a moment. "If I was that sure that she had done it for the mess of pottage only, would I still mention her name ten years later? I wouldn't be discussing her with you at all now. But do you know what actually got me so stirred up? That gawk of a gendarme, that enemy of Israel. 'Your daughter didn't stray as far from you as you think,' he told me. Those words cut me to the quick. Where *did* she go? Where is she? Not here, not there. . . . Giddy up! There she goes, stopping again. A true obstinate female, beg the comparison. She has to know everything. We'll either have to shut up or else we'll never get there. Giddy up, you!"

He actually stopped talking to keep the mare from dawdling. From under her shawl, Aunt Liba watched his agitated face grow dim, his lips curl into a sneer, and his hands sink to his knees with the palms up while the fingers kept clenching and unclenching as if beckoning to someone.

She looked at him worriedly and overcome with pity, and as if begged: "Reb Itzhok, at times a person must cry himself out . . . the heart must not be allowed to drown in tears."

He smiled imperceptibly and took out the whip from under his seat. "Giddy up! She crawls along like the Messiah. Haven't covered a quarter of the way yet. Giddy up!"

Aunt Liba realized that she had been very foolish to advise him to cry. But what other advice could she have offered him? She wished God would spare even her worst enemy such anguish.

A ringing stillness lingered over the forest. Aunt Liba's eyes became suddenly blinded by the sun, the snow, even by the green pine boughs. The pungent odor exuding from the overheated mare made her ill. The journey became the terrible hardship she had feared it would. At first she had dismissed the nausea, but when it persisted, even spread through her whole body, she grew very uneasy and tensely listened to what was happening within her. The symptoms were all too evident. That's all she needed now. . . . She started to figure out her time.

"Are you that warm, Liba?" Itzhok asked, watching her throw off her shawl. "It's really a fine day but a good frost is coming. Aren't you feeling well, God forbid?"

"I'm kind of dizzy."

"Maybe you'd like to walk for a while?"

He helped her down from the sleigh. "Did your legs get stiff or something?"

"Apparently," she said, and with the good but worried smile added: "no longer a girl . . ."

He stared into her eyes for a long time, then started walking with her, behind the sleigh. Suddenly he seized her by the elbows. "Daniel lies there without a name. Give me your word, Liba."

She blushed. She wasn't ready yet to share her secret with anyone. But feeling his grip and seeing the narrowed eye so full of hope and anticipation she felt that she must buoy his grieving spirit and she stopped. "It's obviously God's will."

"Liba, will you give me your word?"

"I give you my word, Reb Itzhok." And watching his face light up, she fervently added: "As we stand here in this forest before God's heaven and earth I promise that if it is a boy his name among Jews will be Daniel. . . ."

3

FOLLOWING HER SERIOUS ILLNESS, from which no one had expected her to recover, Yeva grew terribly emaciated and her
eyes, grown larger than ever, shone with that impotent revenge that harms no one but the one so afflicted. She had
spent nearly half the night with her head sunk in her arms,
unable to touch the bundle of letters that Akiva had given
her earlier that day. As he had handed them over he had
said: "For you, Sister. I wouldn't give them to you, but that
was his final wish."

She had heard nothing besides the "Sister." That word,
and the way he had said it, had left her so weak with joy
that even as he had turned angrily away she hadn't been
able to make a move to stop him. She had been virtually
glowing. What a precious gift life had handed her!

The moment Akiva had gone out, the new maid, who
had been hired to spy on Yeva, had run directly to Alexander's sister, Judis, the lawyer's wife, to report that Yeva
had actually laughed. Judis had been skeptical—Yeva hadn't
been known to laugh once in the ten years she had been in
the family. But the maid had sworn on all that was sacred
that it was true. And Judis had run with the news to the
younger sister, Esther, and together they had come to the
same conclusion—that the musician had been calling too often on Yeva lately.

The night grew longer, but there under the green lamp-
shade, the bundle of Daniel's letters still lay untouched. The

memory of Daniel's death and funeral stayed constant, distinct, and fresh in Yeva's mind.

The funeral had been a dreadful experience. The moment their wagon had reached the field, the snowdrifts had begun to blow and the path had become promptly obliterated. She could not clearly ascertain how long the storm had lasted—one hour, two, or seventy-two. But when she had opened her eyes, the wagon carrying the corpse had been decked with snow and halted behind a stack of straw, while the ground as far as the eye could see stretched white and still. The horses had buried their heads in the stack and chewed the oat straw with noisy relish. The "Quiet Summer" had scraped the snow from the corpse with her bare hands. New wagons had come rolling from farmhouses and villages as the Boyars had gathered for the funeral. The Doctor had begged Yeva with tears in his eyes, and her father had scolded her—what was she trying to do—commit suicide? The blizzard could start anew at any moment—didn't she hear the horses snorting? After all, the wagon bearing the corpse couldn't very well be driven fast. She would be wise to take another wagon and meet them at the gravesite.

But Yeva had not given in. She insisted on accompanying Daniel on his last journey. That night, he had been brought to his final resting place. The frost had grown so severe that it had been impossible to dig a proper grave. The earth had not frozen but petrified. And Daniel had been buried in a shallow pit in a nearly sitting position. His arm had frozen and could not be straightened. It had seemed to Yeva that he was resisting burial and that he had finally been put there by force.

And over and over again she also kept seeing the night of his death—that cursed and blessed night to which she kept returning. Coming back to her father's house after the funeral, she had been met almost on the threshold by Alexander, and before she could even take off her coat, he had embraced her coarsely and tried to drag her to bed. For a moment she had stood there in absolute dismay. Then a burning shame had seized her along with an almost inhuman pain. Shame as a human being, pain as the wife of such a beast. But she had quickly torn free and, unexpectedly even to herself, had slapped him so hard that he had staggered. "This is for all the ten years!" she had spat at him.

He had been dumfounded. Later, he had asked: "Have you gone off your senses?"

"No, I've just come to my senses!"

"I won't be able to forget this slap nor will I forgive it. That was the slap of an enemy."

"The worst enemy you ever had!" she had agreed, and in order not to give her brothers and sisters-in-law any further cause to gossip she had wrapped herself in her coat and spent the rest of the night on the sofa. Early the following morning, Alexander had gone back to the city with Ashmedai.

The bundle of letters still lay untouched under the green shade. The room was big and empty. The deeper one went into it, the darker and colder it grew. Outside of the bare, red, polished table, the small white iron bed, and the painting of the cow with the broken horn, it was nearly empty. In back of the heavy oak door and under a sheet hung Yeva's dresses from before her marriage. On the first day, after her return from Daniel's funeral, she had thrown everything else out into the hall.

No one had tried to make peace between her and Alexander. No one knew what had occurred between them. Nor did either of them ever utter one word of complaint or make demands upon the other. A silence prevailed between them, but it was a silence of sullen hostility. Everyone had noted that even during her illness Alexander had never entered her room alone, only when others had been present.

Still, when Yeva had been close to death in the first weeks of her illness, Alexander had urged the Doctor, who had volunteered to spend the nights with the patient, to do everything humanly possible, to summon Professor Efros

163

twice a day if need be, and to call in the specialists in the city as often as necessary. Not that, God forbid, he had lacked faith in Illya Illitch, but only to make absolutely sure—

In those days, the Doctor had still believed Alexander's concern and had tried to comfort him. There was no need for despair. Yeva did not need more doctors and specialists but rest—rest and more rest. Despite the gravity of her condition, he, Illya Illitch, was confident that her robust constitution and, above all, her lust for life, would pull her through.

Afterwards, when Yeva had begun to recover, Alexander practically began to avoid the Doctor, and by then the Doctor had already learned the reason. Of course, if not for Akiva, he, Illya Illitch, in all his innocence and with his abiding faith in humanity, would not have realized it as quickly.

Furthermore, he had come to the conclusion that Alexander had been waiting for Yeva to die. Her death would have freed him from a most disagreeable situation and a host of other worries. To the outside world he would have appeared as the tragic husband who had made such sacrifices, spent so much money, and virtually held the patient in his own hands throughout the entire illness. But despite these herculean efforts, the tragedy had still occurred. And after a suitable period of mourning, Alexander would have remarried.

The Doctor had been very much afraid that after her recovery Yeva would go back to her husband. But one morning she had said to him: "Illya Illitch, the moment I get back on my feet I'm leaving this house forever."

By then, the Doctor had been aware of the situation in the house. The spider's web in which she had been struggling like a fly for a decade had been permanently torn during her journey to Daniel, and no truce, not even a superficial one, could ever again be effected between her and Alexander. Still, this was the first time he had heard her say it so clearly, so calmly and so deliberately, and he had been taken aback. She had watched him remove his glasses, pass them from hand

164

to hand, muss his beard, and smile strangely as she had said again: "Yes, the moment I'm on my feet again I'm leaving this house for good."

A second later she had added: "Naturally, taking the child . . . He'll be able to see her whenever he wants, but I'll keep her and raise her alone."

The Doctor's eyes, bloodshot and weary from lack of sleep, had closed and his heart had skipped a few beats. He had thrown himself at her feet then and burst out in a passionate speech, but she had not even heard what he was saying. A warm feeling for this good, self-sacrificing person had gone through her. She had stretched out her hand to him and laid it on his head, and he had seized it and covered it with kisses.

"My house can be your house . . . your child can be my child as well."

"I know, I know . . ." And just as frightened then as she had been by his pleading tone in her father's house, she had withdrawn her hand and sighed, "I know, I know . . . I thank you so very much for everything!"

His sighs and obvious despair had filled her with pity. "Illya Illitch, you are the dearest person I know," she had told him.

"Dearest person," he had repeated with a bitter smile, "the world is full of 'dear people.' "

From that time on, she had grown even more withdrawn.

But this silence had not made too great a stir in her husband's family. Even before, throughout the ten years that she had lived among them, she had been very sparing with her words. She had even replied to her father-in-law, Reb Nossan Lande, the dedicated Hasid, in a clipped and curt fashion, as if to say: All that needs to be said has already been said. She had always been polite but cold toward them all. At first, her reserve had infuriated Alexander's sisters. Later, however, they had grown accustomed to her ways and had even begun to regard them as commendable. Old Nossan

Lande used to tell his wife, the businesswoman: "Nema, after all, you see only her faults. To keep peace in the family you must overlook many things. Don't be a troublemaker. Don't cause any friction between them. Other people could learn much decency from Yeva."

He had even found justification for her when she had thrown out all her clothes and possessions on the first day back from Daniel's funeral. "Don't forget that a person isn't responsible for her acts at a time like that. It's truly queer and outlandish behavior, but remember that she is a bitter, broken spirit. She has suffered terrible grief. After all, she still is a daughter and Neha is already closer to the True World. And what can be said about him? Nema, don't malign her. It will all pass. We've been through this already more than once. If she didn't leave him then she certainly won't do it now. And there is the child to consider too. She loves the child. Don't interfere, Nema; close your eyes to it all. It'll all pass, I tell you. In a quarrel everyone slings mud. Everyone adds a drop and soon the quarrel has grown. As it's said: 'You begin with a jug and you end with a barrel.' A quarrel is like a fire, and don't start a fire in your own home, Nema."

And when his wife, the businesswoman, had asked: "Why, after throwing out all her clothes and furniture, did she also have to go to visit that convert, Herut, in prison? Good thing she wasn't allowed near her. She, that Herut, nearly brought down a tragedy on a city of Jews. And why did Yeva defend that soldier from the gendarme colonel, Koblukov? Who was she to take this responsibility upon herself?"

Reb Nossan had answered again: "Don't start a fire in your own home, Nema."

And this fire had, until now, been successfully contained within the house and kept from the curious, the malicious, and the envious. This, the Landes feared most of all—that strangers should find out. The two daughters, Esther and

Judis, who thought themselves the greatest beauties and the finest ladies in the city and were haughty not only to others but to each other as well; and the two sons-in-law, Jonah Wander, his mother-in-law's partner in the store, and the lawyer and civic leader, Hanan Isseyevitch Levy, known for his golden tongue and steel-trap mind, none of these four discussed Yeva, particularly in Alexander's presence. They knew how he felt and they were in complete sympathy with him. It was high time to rid the house of her. But the one thing that concerned them all was that this be done in great secret and with discretion.

Great effort had also been expended to contain this fire because of the youngest son, the thirty-year-old bachelor, and former profligate, Avner, who had come home after many years of wandering and searching—a penitent. And having donned the long gaberdine, he now accompanied his elderly father to the Braslawer Synagogue every morning and evening where he would stand with his face to the wall and all that would be seen of him would be his shoulders twitching. But from time to time, a cry would be torn from his body. At home he was completely withdrawn, ate very sparingly, hardly slept, and wandered through the spacious, uncluttered, elegantly furnished rooms and corridors of the four-story building with one hand folded high behind him, the other tugging idly at the curly blond beard. Often he sat over a chessboard, playing against himself. In the year since his return he did not seem able to come to himself.

A deadly silence prevailed throughout the house. The night was freezing. A reddish moon came out with one piece as if broken off—and looked straight into the window at Yeva. She knew that no one would disturb her. Outside of Akiva, she had no visitors. Shifra was lately nowhere about either. *What had she, Yeva, done to offend her?* Nor had the Doctor been to see her in two weeks.

The bundle of letters bathed in the light of the green shade lay wrapped in black as if Daniel would have intended to say: "Expect no joy from me." Yeva listened as the cow with the broken horn lowed at the new grass and the horses gnawed the oat straw from the snowy stack with noisy relish. She saw Daniel with his one arm upraised, fighting not to go into his grave . . . and her mother, barefoot and in a nightgown, her head shorn, running after her grandchild, determined to take the child's toy by force. . . .

She tugged at the end of the thread and the knot came loose. Trembling as if she were coming close to a wound that hurts terribly even before contact is made, trembling as if she were approaching something sacred, she began to unwrap the bundle. The paper was yellowed from age and charred at the edges. Apparently, he had once changed his mind and pulled it back out of the fire. Yes, it was Daniel's handwriting, the slanted long-pointed characters . . . letters meant for her but never delivered. But she wasn't angry or resentful. She herself had tried to write to him once but hadn't been able to find the proper words that would both express the truth and still not demean her. Most of all, she had been afraid of his pity. Pity may have caused him to do something foolish, something rash and grandiose. And she would have tortured herself about it the rest of her life. And she had never sent that letter. It still lay in her desk.

Trembling, she began to read page after page. Many words had faded or become illegible. These letters, she saw, were not an appeal to her. They weren't even letters in the true sense of the word, but a kind of muffled outcry. A scream that cannot be given voice, as in a nightmare. She had just had such a nightmare. A horrid one in which she had tried to scream but had not been able and the scream had run out down her spine. . . .

Each page contained a few lines only. And each began the same way, "I am alone. Was our whole love nothing more than a lark, an illusion? The whim of a wild forest nymph? Did I don the blades of a windmill and hope to fly off on them? I waited for you more than a year. I was sure that you would smash all the windows and mirrors and come back to me. No matter how far the homing pigeon is taken it always flies back to its nest. I hoped that you would be the song of my life but instead you became its dirge. Its cup of pain . . ."

"I am alone, but I keep hoping and believing. I spin inside a whirlwind. The tumbleweed catches my feet and my heart is pining. I cannot stand to see the tragedy of our people reflected in my father's eyes. And in my own, all colors fade and are extinguished as is the flame of desire, of longing and endurance. . . . Over me hovers the terrible night, but I still hope and believe. . . ."

"I am alone. Gone are those dreamed-of highways and byways. My paths are strewn with sharp rocks and my feet are bloodied. But I hope and believe. . . . The gray dust makes my eyes smart and dense mists cloud my eyes and will not let the fire of my soul escape. A white sorrow drifts in from the wintry fields, but still I hope and believe. . . ."

"I am alone. Over me hovers the terrible night. But I curse no one, for the first oath must fall upon my own head. I sought in life a holiday, tables covered in cloths of silk and gold and old wine in a crystal chalice. I wished you to be the song of my life, but instead you became its dirge, its cup of pain. . . . My eyes stray over barren fields. I cast them everywhere but they do not see. My soul, once enchanted, now flutters over barren fields harvested by death. My long autumn day is ending. All buds have withered in my soul but still I hope and believe. . . ."

"I am alone. Gone are the days when my eye bathed in the glory of blossoms while my heart bloomed as I strolled through the Polesian swamps under a spell. I felt that I had entered the very core of life, the still rapture of being. . . . Those days have long gone up in smoke as have the cold bonfires of yellow flaming birches and falling leaves. My days are

169

growing fewer and my nights dark and never-ending. But I hope and believe. . . ."

"I am alone. I searched for you nights in my bed. You filled the depths of my soul. My heart has room for no one else. That tiny flame gave me light through the long and endless nights. Over and over I dreamed a hot and thirsty dream, a dream that can never come true. But I hope and believe. . . ."

"I am alone. Each bird has its nest and song, but I have been left without mine. I hoped you would be the song of my life. Is there anything more horrible than to be left without a song of your own? I wander as if through a graveyard and I cannot speak—"

She could not go on. The charred, yellowed sheet fluttered from her fingers. She sat with hands spread out upon the table as if turned to stone. A stabbing chill raced through her body while waves of heat suffused her face. A knock came on the door and she wanted to cry out: "No! Don't come in!"

But she could not control it.

Tripping in timidly in her white apron and cap came the new maid. Her face had grown round and rosy in the short time she had been at the house. It seemed to proclaim the end of a long siege of starvation and the commencement of a glorious period of gluttony.

"I knocked a few times but you didn't answer. She's been sitting in the kitchen for a long time already. I've heated the samovar. But where shall I put her up for the night? I went to Shifra's but she wasn't home."

"Who is this 'she'?"

"Your aunt has come. Shifra's mother."

"Aunt Liba?"

"Shall I bring her in?"

"No, I'll go to her myself." And Yeva ran to the kitchen where Aunt Liba was sitting.

Yeva threw her arms around her. "Oh, Auntie, dearest, why didn't you come straight to me?"

"When one goes visiting," Aunt Liba said, studying Yeva's drawn features, "it's easier to start in the kitchen. That's where you learn all the news. Secondly, it's better to be taken from the kitchen to the parlor than, God forbid, the other way around."

"Yes, Auntie," Yeva said, closing her eyes just like her father, "you are right, as usual. But I was taken into the parlor by force. Who knows this better than you?" She started to elaborate but seeing the maid standing there with her mouth agape, she took her aunt's arm and led her away. "Come, there's so much I have to tell you that the night won't be long enough."

Aunt Liba had some questions herself. Sitting in the kitchen she had felt herself growing more and more uneasy. The fact that Shifra had moved out of the house and into an apartment of her own had certainly been a wise move on her part. It was much more proper that the bride and groom did not live under one roof before the wedding. But why had she stopped coming to the house altogether? And where could she have gone at this time of night? If she was with her intended, that wouldn't be so bad, but the maid had told Aunt Liba that Avner never left the house. *The deeper one goes into the forest, the darker it gets,* Aunt Liba reflected.

If she hadn't been feeling so bad she would have gone to Shifra's herself. But only God knew the truth—she could barely stay on her feet. She would spend the night here and find out what was what in the morning. Circumstances being what they were, she applied the old axiom: "If trouble awaited, tomorrow would not be too late for it. If it was joy instead—it too never came too late. The following day it would be even greater." In the meantime, she was bound to find out something from Yeva.

But the moment she entered her niece's room she forgot

all her own troubles. The maid hadn't exaggerated. Yeva was actually living between four bare walls.

"Just a minute, Aunt Liba, and I'll make the bed. I'll just put together—"

"What are these charred papers?"

"Letters from Daniel . . . But why do you look at me that way, Aunt Liba?"

"For God's sake! How can you get letters from—?"

"You were about to say: 'From the other world?' No, it's from this world. He wrote them to me but he never mailed them. He tried to burn them once too. Before he died, he gave them to Akiva to give to me. Did Itzhok come for Avrom? I'll go to see him tomorrow and to get regards from home. You haven't been there lately by any chance?"

"No, Yiveniu. No."

"I had a terrible nightmare a few days ago. I saw Mother being taken down from a rope. . . ."

Yeva's words made Aunt Liba shudder, but she smiled her good smile. "Do you believe in silly dreams now, Yeva? That would be more fitting for a simple village woman like me." She got into bed and pulled up the covers. "Ah, how good this is! There's no better feeling in the world than to get into a nice warm bed when you're cold and tired. Why are you sitting there, Yeva? Come to bed too."

"Why does your voice quiver, Aunt Liba?"

"Is that so unusual after a long trip? It got so terribly cold at night that I'm still shaking. During the day, it was better because of the sun. It wasn't even too bad in the forest."

And she began to tell Yeva how she and Itzhok had driven into the city and how Itzhok had gotten lost. At the same time, she thought about the promise that she had made to him in the forest, a promise that she had sworn before heaven and earth. Other than causing people worry, Daniel had never harmed a living soul. He had once been hired to paint the symbols of the months on the wall of the new House of Worship. He had pitched in eagerly and devoted the whole summer to it. People had flocked from all around to see the wonders, but just when he was about finished, a fire had suddenly broken out in the House of Worship and destroyed almost half of the village. From that time on, no one would use him again. A kind of a curse seemed to have attached itself to him. She, Aunt Liba, would not go back on her word, but she would be much happier if the coming child turned out to be a girl.

"We kept moving," she continued her story, "and you couldn't see a living person in the streets. A city of the dead. I had always assumed that the streets of a big city would be full of people. But luckily, he showed up. How do you call him? That Ashme—"

And warmed not so much by the cover as by Yeva's burning body, Aunt Liba fell asleep in the middle of the word.

Her hands folded beneath her head, Yeva watched the moon recede from the window and listened as the penitent paced through the large foyer next door. The floor creaked beneath his boots. He spent every night pacing this way. Later, she heard Alexander come in. He walked quickly to his study, knocking over a bench in the process. *The "individual" walks straight ahead and doesn't look to either side. If anything gets in his way he simply kicks it out of the way. . . .* A thought suddenly raced through her mind and left her aghast. *Why not wait until he is asleep, then steal in quietly and choke him to death? Then simply go along with whatever happened later. . . .* At the trial she would proclaim to the world all the crimes he had committed against her. In his letter, Daniel wanted to know why she hadn't smashed all the windows and mirrors and come to him. He had waited for her a year before he had gone to Zachariah's and put the ring around Malka's finger. Yeva began to shake Aunt Liba. One person in the world, at least, had to know the truth.

"Aunt Liba," she cried, "listen to me! On the first day when he led me into the bedroom I said to him: 'You've

173

squandered your money for nothing. You led me under the wedding canopy by force but I'll never be your wife!' He looked me in the eye and walked out. He came back a few hours later and said: 'A spare room has been set up for you. Go live there alone if you like.' I went in. A bed had been made up for me. 'There's a key in the door,' he said, 'so you can lock yourself in for the night.' Then he left. I calmed down a little. I hadn't expected him to behave so decently. He came back that night and brought me food. 'Live here alone!' he said again. I swept the tray to the floor along with the plates but he didn't say a word and walked out. No one came in again. The broken plates and the tray lay on the floor. I locked the door, left the key in the lock, and went to sleep in all my clothes. . . . Aunt Liba, don't go back to sleep, listen to me! When I awoke, it was morning and he was lying next to me! No, don't sleep! Tell me what I should have done! To this day I don't know how it could have happened. That night I became pregnant. Where could I go? Why are you so silent, Aunt Liba?"

"May God watch over you and keep you," Aunt Liba cried, shaking her head. "This is too outrageous to be believed!"

"Tell me what I should have done, Aunt Liba. There was only one thing left for me—to kill myself. But I didn't have the courage."

Aunt Liba took Yeva's hand and put it against her bosom. She began to stroke her shoulder. "Cry, Yeva, cry it all out. It'll make it easier for you."

"It's not for nothing that they call you the beautiful and wise Aunt Liba," Yeva said, nuzzling up to her.

"May the evil eye strike me if I know why they call me this, Yiveniu. When they say 'Beautiful Liba,' I don't argue. All the Boyar women, God bless them, are good-looking. God gives them beauty and takes back the good fortune. But when they say 'Wise Liba' I ask: 'Of what does my wisdom consist? Where is it kept—in a cracked bowl? In a sieve?'

Am I wise because my children have to leave home at twelve and be scattered throughout the world? One here, the other there. My eldest, Dovidl, somewhere in Lithuania at the Vilno Yeshiva, living off charity. Sleeping on a mat behind the stove in the studyhouse. The younger boy, Pinie—I barely managed to convince Shmarya to apprentice him to a tinsmith. For two years already the poor child is emptying the slop buckets and caring for the little ones while the tinsmith's wife robs him of every piece of bread that he earns. . . . Shifra grew up in other people's kitchens. . . . Tell me, Yiveniu, where does my wisdom lie?"

"In the fact that you never complain."

"To whom could I complain even if I wanted to? Am I any better than others? Am I the only one with troubles and cares? And do things improve when you complain, Yiveniu? What good would it do to expose my boils to others? Everyone has enough boils of his own. Wherever you turn, wherever you go, there is grief and sorrow and trouble, each one worse than the ones before. Could I complain to Itzhok? What are my worries next to the tragedies he has suffered? And your heart too has been punctured too many times, my poor Yiveniu."

"So you're left with just one remedy—tears?"

"Remedy or not, unless a person cries herself out the heart is liable to drown in tears, God forbid."

"And then you resume life just as if nothing had happened?"

"Have we any choice?"

Yeva raised herself to her elbows. "I don't want to live that way. I'll divorce him."

"What can I tell you about that? One's own heart is certainly the best judge. But think it over first—then think twice again. Write to your father. He'll surely be opposed to it. Consider it well, Yeva. You want to save yourself from the smoke—see to it that you don't jump into the fire. . . ."

4

YEVA DID NOT CLOSE HER EYES AGAIN the rest of the night. As soon as it was light she carefully got out of bed to avoid waking her aunt, who might have delayed her with further discussion, and went into her child's room. This day, as she had done every day since her illness, she would fix breakfast for her daughter; then, making an effort to be gay, she'd walk the child to school. A busy day loomed ahead for her and she would require an early start. Besides, Shifra would surely be coming to see her mother, and she did not wish to disturb them. For some reason Shifra had been avoiding her lately and Yeva was puzzled. She sincerely felt that she had gone out of her way to do everything possible for Shifra since she had come to live with them nearly a year ago.

This was the first day since her illness that she would be going out. She would go to Ashmedai's house to pick up Itzhok, then go on with him to see Avrom. She was also eager to hear some news of her mother. Since that Sabbath eve at her parents' home, Yeva saw her mother in a different light. At first, she had been certain that her mother was deranged, but her reactions that night, the coachman's behavior, her father's fear of some terrible revelation, and her mother's glance passing meaningfully from Gavril to Akiva had all left their mark on Yeva. Going back to the sofa with the fires in her eyes extinguished, her mother had as if shaken a warning finger at someone. . . .

That Sabbath eve had opened Yeva's eyes and provided a clue to her mother's bitterness. Still, she could not find it in her heart to forgive her. Not so much on her account as on Daniel's.

She walked through the streets very slowly. The frost, the brilliant sunshine, and the wind bearing the scent of the willows from the river intoxicated her and left her light-headed. Only now did she realize how weak she had become. Her feet did not seem to be touching solid ground but sinking into something yielding and unsteady. She leaned against a tree—the light blinded her. Was she on a street of mirrors? She looked up. By the oddest coincidence she was directly across from her mother-in-law's mercery. She quickly turned down another street. A sleigh, its occupants huddled under a bearskin robe, hurtled through the street. The horse, its legs stretched out horizontally front and rear, seemed to be flying. Long after the sleigh had vanished, the sound of its bells kept echoing in the air. The frost, the sun, and the tinkle of the bells left Yeva strangely exhilarated. She even took great delight in the glass doors of the Credit Association and the old doorman with the white beard parted in the center and the black frock coat with the silver piping.

She kept stopping frequently. Until now, she had never really taken a good look at the inhabitants of the city. In front of her walked a group of uniformed high-school boys and girls, all chattering at the same time, laughing and indulging in horseplay. How long ago was it since she herself had attended the *gymnasium* and felt so carefree and uninhibited? Her new-found joy rapidly evaporated. No, those years were so distant now that even memory could not resurect them. As if through a dense fog she glimpsed fragments of summery days and one moonlit night in particular when she had sat on the riverbank with Daniel. She was convinced that she had already been living for centuries . . . that she had outlived her hundred-year-old great-grandfather, Ezra; outlived her ninety-three-year-old great-grandmother, Tzivia; outlived Daniel. And still she went on living. But why? For what purpose? If someone were to ask her: "Who

177

are you, really?" what could she answer except "I am Yeva." And if they should persist: "And who *is* this Yeva?"

And now, not so much from weakness as from preoccupation, her legs grew tangled and seemed again to be treading on something yielding and unsteady. The huge market place was being readied for the annual pre-Passover fair. Regular streets running the length and width of the square had been marked off with canvas and wood. A blaze of color flashed before Yeva's eyes and her ears filled with a cacophony of voices. And suddenly she felt—not only here but everywhere between heaven and earth—so strange, alien, and superfluous. . . .

"Hey there, watch it!"

Something spewed fire over her head and from all sides people shouted and came charging toward her. She glanced up at a horse's gaping mouth looming directly overhead, its muzzle trailing a pink, ropy, viscid slaver. Someone seized her arm and pulled her up onto the sidewalk. A crowd gathered. "Is that a way to walk? How much did it fail for that horse to trample you?"

"She's drunk!"

"It ain't nice for a woman to drink."

"Seems to be a lady . . ." someone else added.

She made it to Ashmedai's house, but the only ones there were a woman and two children. The house was filled with acrid, suffocating, yellow-gray smoke that made the eyes smart and stopped up the throat. The woman barely glanced at the visitor. She knew them only too well, those women from the city welfare department who came poking around with their notebooks, asked a million questions, offered a ton of advice, wrote everything down, then left without doing a thing. Until one managed to extract three groschen from them one could go blind, deaf, and dumb. Experience had taught her that it did not pay to speak politely, to plead, or to cry. To this, their only response would be: "She's a quiet one, she'll wait without kicking up a fuss." And now to prevent the visitor from offering unsolicited advice she began to whine: "Leave the door open, the smoke is thick enough in here to eat out your eyes. No matter how much I beg him, 'Lazar, you loafer, a curse on your father's father, put another pail on the chimney!' he won't move his lazy arse. Is there a shortage of broken pails in the garbage, then? That's one thing you don't have to beg the city for. As soon as the wind starts up it blows all the smoke back into the house. But go talk to a dummy. Don't worry, I'll see to it that he puts another pail on the chimney."

Taking the initiative so that the other could not get away with doing nothing beyond giving advice, as if one needed help to run one's own house, the woman began to heap curses—not, God forbid, on the visitor—but upon herself.

"I'd be better off dead already! I'd be better off rotting under the ground or burning in hell! There isn't even a stick in the house to beat the brats with! I'd be better off blind! I'd be better off hit by lightning!"

Yeva was astounded. Although the woman's eyes were red and puffy from smoke, they still seemed to be laughing. They seemed to say: *Do you actually think that I mean what I say? God forbid! Better my enemies should go blind, rot in the ground, and go to hell. . . .*

Yeva smiled. The woman's bloodshot eyes and bitter, foul curses, intoned in a drawn-out, practiced whine, had somehow lightened Yeva's spirits and left her in a sunnier mood.

"I've come here to see the man who spent the night at your house," she said.

"So why did you keep quiet so long? Did you come here just to plague me before I've even had a bite of breakfast? I haven't seen him myself yet. That's all I got to worry about —guests! Besides all my other troubles, they had to saddle me with some strange brat too. It tears your heart to look at the poor thing."

"Whose child is it?"

179

"What business is that of yours? Playing with matches again?" she shrieked at a small girl. "God help me with this plague of my existence! You want to start another fire? The man you want left before daybreak. His son is staying at the Doctor's. Akiva slept there too. My fine husband didn't even hitch up the horse today. Do I know where they are? Some nag they bought us—a fire on their heads! It pulls the wagon one day, then rests the next three. I'll go to that synagogue next Sabbath and pluck out all their beards! If you go and buy a poor coachman a horse already, then buy him one that will make a living for him, not be another burden. A plague on their father's father's father. . . . You're leaving already? Then go in peace."

And after Yeva had gone a good distance from the house she bellowed after her: "Give us your name, at least, so I can tell him who's been asking for him."

Yeva did not bother to shout back. The woman's laughing eyes had finally irked and depressed her. That poverty-stricken drudge had actually made peace with her miserable existence and taken to it like a worm to horse-radish.

She took a deep breath and began to climb the steep incline. She would ask the Doctor or Akiva about the child she had seen sitting among the soiled, rumpled bedclothes rubbing its eyes. She was bound to meet Itzhok there as well.

* * *

After Ashmedai had finished pounding on the door and his wife had gotten up to let them in, Itzhok Boyar had stretched out on the floor, taking off only his felt boots; had rolled the fur pelt under his head and put the fur robe under him, and had slept the remainder of the night in comfort. He rose at the break of day, ran the tips of his fingers across the frozen windows, which would serve as the ablution, and having said the preliminary prayers, went out in search of a House of Worship, not so much out of an urge to pray in the company of other Jews as to say the mourner's prayer over his two dead children. True enough, a man had been hired to do this back in the village; but no matter how pious and dependable that man might have been, the prayer still came from a stranger's heart.

Gavril would have surely come to the house with his sons and grandsons—a readymade quorum—and given Itzhok and Shmulik the opportunity to say the mourner's prayer at home, but it was more than Itzhok could bear to watch the "Quiet Summer" join in, without crying, without moaning, but in a voice so disturbing, that on the very first day after the mourning period Itzhok had run to the village and engaged the man to recite the prayer from then on.

Leaving the coachman's house, which squatted close to the ground, its black chimney topped by a broken pail jutting out of its sloping roof, the innkeeper made a strange observation. That great city with its maze of streets and towering buildings, among which he strayed on the previous night as if driven on by some evil spirit, had vanished during the night to be replaced by low, snow-covered shacks, narrow little streets, crooked wooden fences, and cross-eyed windows just like those in the village back home.

He walked along, carrying under his arm the prayer shawl and phylacteries without which he never left home for any length of time. The outskirts of town were still dozing, but within the city proper the snow already squeaked under dozens of sleepy feet. Someone yawned loudly. The chimneys exuded stinking smoke.

Stars glowed in the sky like dying embers and the dawn wind flicked the ashes from them. Within an hour, they would burn out completely without leaving a trace. The moon, chilled from a long night's freezing, had huddled against the crown of a poplar where, by a miracle, some spare green foliage had remained, and waited for the sun to come up. After its rise, it would warm itself briefly, then move on to seek a night that was warmer and more inviting.

Itzhok did not have to go far. At the top of the steeply

181

inclining street he saw the familiar rounded windows of a House of Worship. Inside, he found a sizable crowd, particularly around the stove. There, before tables polished to a high glow and by a light cast by the melting ends of memorial candles, Yeshiva students sat hunched over great leather-bound volumes of the Gemara, and recited in that precise, moralizing chant calculated to tug at the heart strings that the founder of their sect, Reb Israel Salanter himself, had initiated and prescribed.

With fervor and ecstasy they smote each other for the benefit of potential patrons who stood around observing and basking in their benevolence. They vied in displaying their devotion and acceptance of the great task that had been assigned to them. Through their efforts, they would win entrance into the True World not only for themselves but also for those who would feed and support them.

Back home, Itzhok was considered a learned man, even more so than Zachariah, but he himself knew his limitations. He stood now and listened respectfully as two of the Yeshiva students launched an erudite dispute.

One, called the Narodicher, after his place of birth, tugged his fair bachelor's beard and flatly refused to concede. He ridiculed all the proofs and examples that his opponent provided and fought as if he were engaged in a life-and-death struggle. The issue was far too important for him to allow it to be disposed of so quickly. Such disregard for truth and order could shortly lead to, God forbid, the destruction of the world.

"But when were these words said? After all is said and done—when were they said? One must take this factor into consideration after all. Tinochas of the House of Rabon would have understood this. Look here, the *Tosefta* says it in black on white: 'An egg laid on the holiday—' "

And from there near the door, as if issuing from the laver itself, a venomous voice chimed in, in the same chant: "A jackass born in Narodich . . ."

Noting where the remark had originated, no one laughed or took exception, but the mood of easy familiarity was destroyed. From the distance that separated them, Itzhok recognized the speaker. Neha's brother, Abushl. Or as he had been nicknamed, Abushl the Nabob.

Abushl, passing by, glanced at the innkeeper. Itzhok knew that he would not address him. Neha's brother did not speak to any of the Boyars. When he visited his sister he did not even shake Gavril's hand. Itzhok noticed, however, that Abushl's round eyes, the black pupils with the white showing all around, seemed to be twinkling with satisfaction. Abushl leaned forward, rubbed his palms together, and growled: "Beadle, light the candles! Time for morning services. Today we will read the Torah and recite the Psalms of praise."

If someone else had insulted the Narodicher and given orders so imperiously to the beadle, he would have been thrown bodily out of the House of Worship. But no one dared talk back to Abushl. No one knew what power lay behind his arrogance and mockery. The Gemaras slammed shut and the crowd dispersed. No one was willing to stand up to Abushl. They all feared his tongue and even more— his eyes. He had recently become the *Gabbai* of the burial society. When the other members of the Society stopped before the House of Worship and Abushl began to absolve the corpse of "its place and all rights" and forbade it to walk among the living, then shouted, "Ta—ake him away!" everyone became petrified and the feeling would spread that the stretcher bore not a corpse but a being that would presently crawl out from beneath the black sheet and spread havoc through the city.

The beadle lit the candle on the cantor's desk. Abushl whispered something into his ear and the other nodded. The services began. Itzhok put on the prayer shawl and phylacteries, feeling the whole time Abushl's eyes fixed upon him. The crowd rustled with curiosity. What had Abushl whispered to the beadle? Each man asked his neighbor, but no one knew. The beadle indicated with his eyes that he would reveal the secret later. He approached the stranger whose gait and appearance labeled him a man from the country and the congregation heard the newcomer say: "I am called Itzhok, son of Menashe, may he rest in peace. No, I'm no Kohen nor even a Levite. I'm a plain Jew, an Israelite."

His modesty impressed the congregation. A man stepped out from behind the stove to welcome Itzhok, asked where he was from and the reason he had come to the city. The innkeeper told him that he had come to take his son home from the hospital and had stopped in the House of Worship to say the mourner's prayer over his children.

The man who had addressed himself to Itzhok was a visionary with dreamy, ethereal eyes, a follower of the Braslaw Hasidic Court, who came to the city twice a year with other members of his sect to pay homage at the grave of their deceased leader, Rabbi Nachman Braslawer. Nevertheless, he had spent many years now seeking a living rabbi to follow. He had already visited all the Hasidic courts and spoken to every great rabbi, but none of the current crop met his standards. Learning that Itzhok lived in a distant forest, he now watched his every move and gesture with his dreamy, ethereal eyes, seeking some hidden omen in the white streaks in Itzhok's long, narrow beard; in the high forehead beneath the worn sable hat, but most of all, in the green selvage of his brown fur pelt. In his heart he was prepared to accept the innkeeper as a hidden saint, a new Baal Shem Tov.

Itzhok prayed facing the wall, turning only to recite the mourner's prayer. Time dragged for him unendurably. Abushl, standing at the cantor's desk, took long pauses and led the services with great pomp, trilling as if he were the cantor himself. Each second was precious to the innkeeper. Avrom was waiting for him at the Doctor's house. How long could he stay at a stranger's house, after all? How much longer could be continue to take advantage of the Doctor's generosity? It was also necessary to inform Liba to get ready. They would be starting for home within a few hours. The "Quiet Summer" could not be left alone for too long either. Of all her children there was only one left now. . . . Itzhok felt someone tugging at his sleeve and he turned quickly.

The man with the dreamy eyes said: "You've been called up to the Torah."

Itzhok strode rapidly toward the platform. He was disconcerted by the unexpected honor, and distressed by the fact that he had not heard his name being announced. The congregation waited. He had already mounted the third step when a loud crash exploded against the bookholder and a dry voice exclaimed: "Don't let him near the Holy Scroll!"

Shouts followed from all sides.

"It's a sacrilege! He raised a depraved daughter!"

"A convert!"

"A rebel against the government!"

"She brought misfortune down upon us!"

"He should be excommunicated! Remember: 'Thou shalt root out the evil from among ye.'"

Itzhok's back bowed under the unexpected blow. The enormity of it staggered him. The tumult and commotion shook the House of Worship. Factions quickly formed. "You mustn't shame a fellow Jew like this!"

"How is the poor father responsible?"

"Who then is responsible?"

"If a child grows up to be outcast the fault lies with the parents."

And Abushl's rasping voice kept interjecting: "'Thou shalt root out the evil from among ye!'"

"A daughter a convert."

"A rebel against the government."

"The misfortune still hovers over the city."

"A rotten tree produces rotten fruit."

And the rasping voice again interjected: "'Thou shalt root out the evil from among ye!'"

185

For a moment Itzhok's temper flared and he was ready to strike out to all sides. But instead, he retired to his place against the wall, took off his prayer shawl and phylacteries, swept away a vagrant tear, and, with his back still bowed, slunk out of the House of Worship.

With the prayer shawl and phylacteries tucked under his arm and the tear still clinging to his palm, he walked through the rimy but now sun-drenched and noisy streets. The odors of herring, oil, kerosene, and axle grease came drifting from the open stores. Sleighs carrying meat unloaded in front of butcher shops. A housewife asked a butcher for a half pound of meat without any bones in it. "Tomorrow, we're going to slaughter a special ox that hasn't a single bone in his body. Even his horns are made out of fat," the butcher told her. In a smithy with its doors thrown wide open, two hammers pounded a pliant, glowing hunk of iron. The iron did not cry out, but fiery sparks flew from it in all directions. From a narrow window, level with the ground, came the clacking sound of a sewing machine while its operator sang:

> "The tailor he sews,
> The needle she goes.
> If this is life,
> What is death, you suppose?"

Itzhok Boyar, his back bowed, his head tilted toward the upraised shoulder, plodded forward in a daze. But his step, firm and solid as ever, left deep prints in the hardened snow. The coachman's house wasn't far from here, and the steeply inclined street should have brought him there a long time ago. But he kept walking and walking until he found himself at the edge of the city. Fields of white stretched far into the distance where they blended with the birch forests.

"And here I've been out looking for you. Go be a stargazer and guess that Itzhok Boyar will be standing by the river enjoying God's sunshine and praising His name for the favor He has granted him."

The innkeeper was overjoyed. "Akiva dear, is it you?"

"Let us both be as healthy as it is sure that I'm me and no one else."

"Friend Akiva . . ."

Akiva trembled. That was what Daniel used to call him. "What, Reb Itzhok?"

The innkeeper told him what had just occurred at the House of Worship. "Why did I have to be humiliated that way? Was it I who led her astray? Is it my fault? No, no, Akiva, I'm not blaming you either. She ruined your life as well. You didn't intend for it to come out this way. Besides, she would have run away from the house without your help. Fire always finds a way. . . ." And he began to weep like a child. "My soul is in flames and all my bones pain me."

"Come along with me, Reb Itzhok. I'll take you in my wagon and together we'll ride and ride until we ride into—"

"Into what?" Itzhok interrupted.

"The land of milk and honey."

"Too many leaders," Itzhok said in a rage, "too many prophets have appeared on the scene. Each one is the Messiah, each one blows his trumpet! Followers of Sabbatai Zevi, all! Would you happen to be going to the Doctor's house?" he asked in a milder tone. "If so, I'll go with you and take Avrom home."

"That's just why I came—to take you to the Doctor's."

"I thank you kindly. I also see that you're anxious to tell me something else."

"Come, Reb Itzhok. We'll talk as we walk."

Entering the corridor of the Doctor's house, Itzhok looked through an open door into a large room where a number of people were present. Everyone kept moving about and talking at the same time. They were mostly young people with pale faces but with eyes that were burning. One stood out especially. He paced through the room, taking long strides, his hands thrust into his pockets, his wild mop of hair bobbing in the air. He wore a thick black mustache and

187

a Vandyke, and his wide, full red lips spewed a cascade of words. But each word was pronounced clearly, distinctly, and in a tone that rendered everyone else's comments worthless unless they happened to coincide with what he had said originally. His had to be the final word, the only one that would bring the world universal justice and salvation. The innkeeper tried to gather something, some meaning from these words, but they were so odd that one could crack one's teeth repeating them: "territorialism, culture-autonomy, Ahad Ha'amism . . ."

"Prophets?" he asked Akiva.

"Prophets." Akiva smiled.

"And my Avrom sits there among them? Call him out here for me this minute! Don't muddle his head with Burian. One is enough, as far as I'm concerned, enough. . . ."

"Oh, there you are," the Doctor said, standing in the doorway. "Welcome, Reb Itzhok and do come in." He stuck out his hand.

"Thank you very much," Itzhok said, taking the Doctor's hand in both of his. "You've done so much for my son and me that I will pray to God in your behalf for the rest of my life. You have a heart of gold, that you do, but I beg you, I fall before you on my knees, I kiss your feet—don't spoil him, for he is pure and innocent!"

The Doctor withdrew his hand. "What are you talking about?"

"One child has been left me, don't spoil him. Don't drag him into your circles. Don't light your fires in his head. One of mine has already been burned by these fires. And one—"

"That's just what I want to discuss with you. You needn't worry about Avrom. He's far removed from such things and no one here wants to drag him into any circle."

"About *her,* there is nothing to be said. I gave her up for dead a long time ago already."

"Please hear me out, Reb Itzhok. Come inside here with me."

188

And out of respect and gratitude for the Doctor, Itzhok let himself be led into a side room. Avrom showed up a short while later. Itzhok was delighted to see him and they kissed. Avrom no longer carried crutches, just a cane, and he limped but slightly.

"Father," Avrom suddenly blurted out. "I beg you, let's take her home."

"Take who home?" Itzhok shouted. "Take who home?"

"Don't raise your voice, Reb Itzhok, but hear me out," the Doctor said. "Hear me out. The Torah says: 'A father must have pity on his sons.' A golden opportunity exists now to have Herut paroled. But only the father can arrange this."

Itzhok Boyar sat down by a window through which the bright late-winter sun was shining. His back was bowed as if in anticipation of new blows to come. At the same time, however, he seemed detached, a stranger for whom the Doctor's words had little bearing. He did not respond with even a word and the Doctor began to grow irked. To him the innkeeper's silence represented sheer impudence. He knew his village people. Whenever it suited their purpose they played dumb. If it had concerned a simple, unimportant matter, the Doctor would have put a quick end to the conversation. But in this instance he swallowed his pride. His voice turned sharp, however. "Forget for the moment that Herut is your daughter, Reb Itzhok. Simply keep it in mind that a human life is at stake!"

Itzhok Boyar turned his gaze away from the glowing windows, shifted his shoulders rapidly, and from his breast issued a deep moan, an indication that he would not endure much more of this torment. "What do you want of me? Why did you bring me here?"

"Don't think badly of me, Reb Itzhok," the Doctor said, his voice faltering. He seemed almost to be pleading. "You're the only one who can do it. Only you. If you refuse, she'll be sent to Siberia. And the transport is leaving this very day. She'll go there in shackles. It's in your hands. . . ."

He said what he had to say, then looked anxiously into Itzhok's face. The innkeeper was gripping the bench with both hands. Avrom, as if a partner to the event, and already deeply regretful that it had gone this far, sat with his hands leaning on the cane, his chin cupped on the hands, his mouth gaping, pale, full of pity for his father, and guiltily afraid. Akiva made a conscious effort to keep out of the conversation. First, he leafed through a book, then he replaced it in the bookcase and picked up a bleached, polished human skull from the Doctor's worktable. He held the skull in both hands and contemplated it at length with a raised eyebrow, a deeply creased forehead and a thin smile on his tightly clenched lips.

And the sun flooded the room with radiant, scintillating light through the high windows draped in richly embroidered floor-length curtains. The Doctor stood with his arms hanging and his pince-nez dangling from the silk cord. He blinked into the glare and waited for even a single word from the innkeeper.

Itzhok slowly lowered his shoulders and straightened his back, but he remained silent. It wasn't that he felt no gratitude to the Doctor, who had done so much for him and for his. He had been the first to defend Avrom against the false accusation and had maintained him for such a long time until he had been cured, and Itzhok would certainly remain forever in his debt. If not for him, he would have been forced to go to Gavril with hat in hand to beg assistance. But it was not only out of gratitude that he stayed and let the Doctor subject him to such nagging and harassment. If not for his great reverence and deep esteem toward him, he would have seized Avrom by the hand and fled the house.

As long ago as the night of Daniel's death he had seen what a kind soul and a humanitarian the Doctor with the handsome beard was, always ready to sacrifice himself. Itzhok Boyar knew that he would never forget that night, not even on his deathbed. And it would not be the vision of Daniel lying there already cold with his arms around his brother that he would see but that of the Doctor spreading the white sheet over the kitchen table, tucking up his beard under a towel, rolling up his sleeves and telling him, Itzhok, to hold the two candles higher over the table. "Give me light, Reb Itzhok!" he had said, "it's the greatest good deed imaginable to perform on the Sabbath!" Then placing the infant on the table, he had made an incision in its tiny belly. It had been a tremendously bold thing to do. Even the tall gendarme had been amazed at its audacity and the chief constable had grown instantly sober. Had the child died, God forbid, dreadful consequences might have resulted. For two weeks afterwards, the chief constable had visited Maria to see how the infant was progressing. Only a heart so feeling, yet at the same time so impetuous as the Doctor's, could have assumed such a crushing burden. If something had gone wrong, the entire Jewish community would have been exposed to terrible danger. Itzhok remembered how frightened he had been, and to this day he wondered how he had been able to remain on his feet and hold on to the candles.

The Doctor paced nervously over the vividly colored rug with its odd pattern of light-red, many-pointed leaves and thick, black-and-white stems extending the whole length of the room. His steps were muffled, as if he were walking through a moss-covered forest.

Perhaps it was on account of this soundless, ghostlike tread, or the silence next door, as if the rest of the company would be awaiting his answer too; whatever the reason, however, Itzhok's heart suddenly cried to him: *One and only daughter remaining—take her home!*

He jumped to his feet abruptly and said: "Don't waste any more effort trying to sway me. Me, you will not break!"

"But that's absolutely inhuman," the Doctor said, coming to a stop, "and what's more, it's incomprehensible. You, who have gone through so much lately . . . one would think

191

that time and troubles would have had an effect on you. Even a stone is affected by wind and rain. Life doesn't stand still, after all."

"Elikl, how much longer will it be? The samovar is growing cold already and your friends are waiting."

"Soon, Mama, soon."

In the doorway, her faded silver hair covered by a black shawl, her eyes shining with pride, on her face an expression that seemed to say: "Nothing shall mar my happiness," stood the Doctor's mother, looking somewhat embarrassed. Looking at her, her son gathered that something else besides the cooling samovar had brought her into the room, and he guessed what it must have been—a patient.

"I can't see anybody now, Mama, even if it's the world's worst pauper."

"Good, my son, good. I'll tell her exactly what you said."

Her voice echoed a subtle, restrained satisfaction, as if the prospect of turning away the visitor would provide her great pleasure, and the Doctor was puzzled. Usually she would object vehemently and urge him: "Don't turn anyone away, my son. A sick person has traveled far to see you. You may be his last hope. Never forget, my child, that if your father had had a doctor in time you wouldn't be bearing his name now." *

Puzzled, he asked: "Has this patient ever been here before?"

"No, never."

"Do you know her?"

"Why shouldn't I know Reb Nossan Lande's daughter-in-law?"

"Yeva? Yeva is here?"

His mother smoothed back her silvery hair and arranged the black shawl. Her eyes, which had been shining moistly with pride, grew hard and dry. She would never per-

---

* Translator's note: It is a custom among Jews to name children after their nearest dead relative.

mit it to happen in her lifetime. She would rather her son remained a bachelor forever! She would not let her Elik, for whom she had sacrificed her life, marry a divorcée with a child. Even before, he had been a frequent guest at the Landes'; but she had closed her eyes to it. But lately, he had been spending more time there than at home. During Yeva's illness she had often found him spending the night in a chair in front of her, Yeva's, bedroom door. To all her pleas he had given one answer: "After all, she is deathly ill! Today or the next day the crisis will come."

"Whose crisis?"

"What do you mean—'whose'? The patient's, of course."

"Oh, I thought yours."

But suddenly, in the past few weeks he had stopped going there altogether. She did not know the reason for this, but whatever it was, she was overjoyed. He had probably realized that no good could come from the whole affair. And was it actually worth it? What if she were beautiful? Was there a shortage of beautiful women in town? Professor Efros's daughter was even more beautiful.

But seeing her son standing there as if lost and twirling his pince-nez while his face changed colors, she said: "What are you waiting for? Go out to her."

And turning to the others she said in a more gracious tone: "Come along, friends, and have a glass of hot tea. Don't make me urge you."

"Is this how you brought me to the land of milk and honey?" Itzhok hissed at Akiva after the Doctor and his mother had gone. "You sit there in your pretty little wagon, you fondle a human skull and you smile with contempt."

"God be with you, Reb Itzhok!"

"With me He certainly is, but is He with you? The skull in your hand isn't only a sacrilege but even more than that, it's self-mockery. On the one side, the new prophets. She, Herut, is one of them too. New Messiahs, New Deborahs. They issue new commandments, they lead people to new

Mount Sinais. Nothing stops them—not lightning, not thunder. They go to Siberia, they go to the gallows. Streets, whole towns run over with blood. And on the table stands a human skull and they flick their cigar ashes into it. . . . Shut up, Akiva, don't make one of your flippant comments. We actually look out through the same window, yet we see two different world. A finger may hurt you, but my whole heart aches. We don't understand each other. I'll put it even better—we don't know each other. Tell me, for instance, who are you?"

And without looking at Akiva, Itzhok tucked his prayer shawl and phylacteries under his arm. "Come, Avrom. I have nothing against you, my son. We'll come back to see the Doctor another time. I brought him a little present, some Antonev apples. Go get Yeva, my son, I have to talk to her. She probably came to get regards from home. Go tell her that her mother was saved at death's door. Go give her the greetings."

But now the Doctor's mother came in again and insisted that she would not let her guests go unless they had a glass of tea first. And Itzhok and his son were taken inside the room where the palefaced young people with burning eyes were gathered. The one with the bushy hair and Vandyke was whispering something to Yeva, and Itzhok heard her reply: "I won't say anything to him. You don't know what this man is like."

And Itzhok snorted into his beard gleefully. *She's one of our kind, after all.* But when she hugged him as if he were her own father, he clasped her elbows as he always did to those whom he held dear, and said: "Thanks be to God that I see you up and about again. I heard how sick you've been. There is nothing new at your parents'. Everyone is well. Beila was blessed with twins—both girls."

And he gave her detailed regards from each of her family separately, leaving out only Neha. Nor did she ask about her mother. She moved closer to the tiled oven, placed both her hands on it, and turned her back to the others. "A warm oven, how nice! I'm a bit frozen."

Outside of the Doctor, his mother, and Akiva, the others paid no attention to her. They were much more interested in the village Jew who sat there in his fur pelt with the green selvage, the worn sable cap tilted to the side, the prayer shawl and phylacteries tucked under his arm, and noisily sipped the hot tea. He sat on the very edge of the bench as if he were being punished. Gulping the tea, he told Yeva that the cow had calved; that Gavril had been going hunting hares lately with Old Squire Bogushevski; that Shmarya, Liba's husband, had encountered a demon on his way home from the fair and that he, Shmarya, had sworn on his ritual garment that the story was true. . . .

But Itzhok Boyar was well aware that these young people, particularly the one with the wild mop of hair, would not let him leave the house without a struggle. They were about to resume their discussion again. Itzhok pushed the unfinished glass of tea from him, tapped on the table at length with his finger, and said: "Gentlemen, you all did a lot for me, which is unnecessary to talk about here. May God be with you in all your endeavors. I also know that that which you want me to do comes from the goodness in your hearts, since actually what is she to you? I also know that you don't want to, God forbid, take advantage of me. Nor did you come here to speak ill of me. Therefore, I'll tell you a story that once happened in my family which will make all further discussion unnecessary. My great-grandfather on my mother's side, Asher, may he rest in peace, had a brother named Todros, may he rest in peace too. The family called him the Miracle Worker. He was, if you'll forgive me, a very common man. He wasn't one of Rabo-son-of-the-son-of-the-son-of-Chone's moguls. He would say grace before going to sleep and the morning prayers after breakfast. On Sabbath eve after the lighting of the candles, he would take his fiddle, go to a party, and stay out all night. He was a tailor all his life, an expert craftsman in whom burned the divine spark of the great Bezalel himself. We have many such talented men in our family. Todros could make royal raiments out of rags—he could weave thread out of sand. He sewed for all the princes and nobles. It didn't matter to him if he was sewing for a man or a woman. He would take the person's measurements with just one glance. Can you see now why he was called the Miracle Worker? Anyway, life went along quietly for him. How does the saying go: Day in, day out, the machine sews on and life goes on. Another dress, another coat. Todros, may he rest in peace, was already well along in years, nearly eighty. A few steps more and the Miracle Worker would go to his glory with the shards covering his lids. But then, something happened." And at this, Itzhok Boyar groaned deeply. "When does life permit one to reach the other world without first seizing one's throat and clawing at it with sharp nails? Pick up the story, Yeva. At one time, you used to tell it very nicely by the first Hannukah candle."

And Itzhok Boyar knocked the slag from his pipe, filled and lit it, and sat back with his eyes closed. Everyone turned toward Yeva. Yes, she would continue the story. She recalled the cold Hannukah nights of her childhood. On the table would stand a heaping plate of hot oatmeal pancakes covered with cloths and a pot of rendered goose-fat scraps. The grandparents would stop spinning the top with the grandchildren and the parents would hide the cards. And she, Yeva, would begin the story. But in those days, Daniel would be sitting beside her. . . . But since it was Itzhok for whom it was difficult to explain himself before strangers, and also because she yearned to bring back those days for a while, she settled herself deeper in the chair, closed her eyes like Itzhok, and commenced:

"One day, the old Count Bogushevski—an ancestor of the current Squire—sent for our Todros, may he rest in peace, and said: 'My daughter needs a new dress and there's no

196

time to send for one from Paris. You'll be given material, but in case you should ruin it, I'll have all the fingers on your right hand cut off. This material has come all the way from Persia.' So the Miracle Worker asked: 'My Lord, by when must this dress be ready?' 'I'm not going to rush you,' the Count said, 'you still have lots of time. We'll set up a machine for you in one of the rooms and you'll be given everything that you need to do the job.'

"And that's how it was. Todros, may he rest in peace, was shown the Count's young daughter; he took her measurements by eye as he always did, and sat down to work. To make a long story short, either the Count had frightened him with his threat or Satan took a hand—whatever the reason, Todros ruined the dress. The Count neither shouted nor became angry, but had the old tailor taken into the courtyard—and his right hand was placed on the block. And as the gleaming sword was raised overhead Todros realized that the game was up and that the Count meant to carry out his threat, and he began to plead: 'My Lord, if I could ruin such an easy job, surely you can wait three more days to chop off my hand. I won't run away. I have a young son and he will fix the dress.' The Squire agreed. The old-time squires still believed in fairness. He ordered the old tailor thrown into the dungeon and had the young man brought to him. And here, the terrible tale first unfolds. . . ."

"Well done, Yeva, well done," Itzhok said, cocking an eyebrow. "You rest a while now and I'll take over." He tapped his pipe against the leg of the bench and picked up the story.

"So the son was brought in, Todros' youngest boy, by his third wife, Yontel by name. He was a handsome and merry lad, full of the devil. Not, God forbid, a drunkard, but he did like a drop now and then. Although this Yontel, blessed be his memory, had a pair of golden hands too, with magic in every finger, he never wanted to sew for the gentry. He preferred to make coarse garments for peasants—coats from

197

dowlas, fur pelts, cotton jackets, things like that, and even with these simple things he performed wondrous things. He worked during the day and at night he stole horses. And he was a remarkable horse thief! Once he led a horse out of a gypsy encampment in broad daylight, so you can well imagine. . . .

"When Yontel came and heard of the trouble his father was in, he called for the ruined dress. He studied it for a long time, took measurements, then whistled and asked that the Count's daughter be brought in. He took her measurements, but not with the eye like his father, and with a song on his lips he sat down to work. He had a voice that was like sweetness itself. Three hours later the dress was fixed. The young man was delighted and the Count ordered that the old tailor be released from the dungeon. He gave the father and son gifts and sent them home in glory. But now we get to the real gist of the story. Up to now it's been, as it is called, the prologue. . . . Anyway, from that day on the Count's daughter started to waste away. She grew so emaciated that she had to take to bed. A great turmoil erupted in the palace. Old Bogushevski called in the biggest doctors but they couldn't do a thing for her. How could they when she couldn't even tell them what was bothering her? Count Bogushevski nearly went out of his mind. What father can watch his only daughter wasting away before his eyes?"

At the last words, Itzhok's voice broke. Another moan was torn from his throat and he turned to Yeva to take over. "Anyhow," she went on, "the girl was flickering out like a candle. She faded like the snow when spring comes. For three days and nights the Count didn't leave her side for a moment. If only she would tell him what it was that she wanted! If she would give him the slightest clue he would move heaven and earth to get it for her. Whereupon the daughter broke down in tears and confessed. She was in love with the young tailor! The Count grew aghast. The most important dignitaries, the greatest leaders, the wealthiest princes and magnates in Europe besieged the palace and vied for a mere glance from his daughter—her beauty was praised throughout the land. And whom did she choose to fall in love with?—some Jewboy tailor and horse thief. The disgrace was unbearable. The old Polish Count with the old-fashioned Polish sense of pride and honor was beside himself. Such a thing could never be! Still, she was dying. . . . From day to day she grew weaker—soon, only an ember would remain. And the old Count gave in and sent a carriage drawn by eight horses for the young tailor. Yontel could not understand why he was being paid such an honor. Apparently the dress had made a big hit at the ball and someone wanted a duplicate. But he was even more astounded when the old Count himself came out to greet him. The Count first stared at him for a long time, then took him on a tour of the palace. Yontel walked through the luxuriantly furnished rooms as if in a dream. The walls were decorated with tapestries, hunting guns, and deerheads with huge horns. Wherever one looked there were gold, silver, costly treasures, silks and satins—everything to dazzle the eye and capture the heart. Finally, the old Squire took Yontel into a magnificent room where a table had been set with all kinds of delicacies. He poured two gold beakers of wine, gave one to Yontel, picked up the other, and said: 'You were born a lucky lad— Drink up!' By now completely bewildered, Yontel did as he was told. He had never tasted such sweet muscatel and it spread a delicious warmth through his limbs. Suddenly, the Count asked: 'Janush, how would you like to own a palace like this?' Yontel smiled at the Squire's little joke. If he chose to call him Janush, what of it? All rich people liked to have a little fun with a pauper, especially a man as important as the Count, and particularly with a Jew. The old Squire had probably been bored and had had him brought there in order to amuse himself a bit. Yontel was very resentful, but what could he do? If one fell into the water one could not complain about the rain. He, therefore, kept quiet and awaited further developments. The Count filled the beakers with a different brand of wine and asked: 'Janush, you've seen my daughter?'

" 'I have,' Yontel said. 'What about her?'

" 'Tell me, Janush, does she please you?'

"Yontel drained the beaker of wine, poured himself another, finished that one as well, and poured still another. As was mentioned before, he could take a bit of strong wine. He was no drunkard, God forbid, but neither would his face flush after a few sociable drinks.

" 'I'm only a tailor,' he said, 'and it's even been said that I'm a horse thief. But I don't like to be mocked. I pray the honorable Lord will permit me to go home.' And he stood up.

"The Count took his hand. 'Your spirit pleases me! Sit down and listen carefully. You were born under a lucky star, my boy. My one and only daughter has fallen in love with you. All that I possess, every bit of my property belongs to you from this day on. But first, you must convert.' The Count repeated it three times more and Yontel realized that it was no joke. The Count was deadly serious, and Yontel began to understand what was required of him. He looked straight into the Count's eye and said: 'No!'

"The Count was dumfounded. Did he know what he was saying? The all-powerful lord was ready to bestow such honors on this Jewboy; to give him his daughter; to make him the master of all his estates and to expose himself to the world's ridicule, and this ragamuffin had the gall to refuse? And his great pride and rage flared up within him. But the more he shouted, threatened, and stormed the more obstinate Yontel grew. Nothing would dissuade him. And the Count made one final desperate move—he took Yontel into his daughter's bedroom and left them alone together. As soon as she saw the youth the color came back to her face.

200

And Yontel? No one should be exposed to such temptation. Before his eyes lay all the beauty that God had created before He rested on the Sabbath. . . ."

And as Yeva paused to catch her breath, applause broke out. One of the listeners, a tall fellow with straight shoulders, long black hair and blue eyes—a young poet with the voice of a pregnant woman—ran toward Yeva, enraptured, and squeezed her hand: "Magnificent! You are an actress with a God-given talent! Your voice strums like a harp. What nuances! What a range! And your face—what expressiveness! What inner fire! And yet, such simplicity, such a feeling for our people, such a quality of innocent humor. Mar–vel-ous! And what eyes! You are a born actress, my dear!"

Itzhok Boyar, the unlit pipe clenched between his teeth, had been leaning back with his eyes closed, listening intently. Had she, God forbid, left out anything? Had she skipped a word? The Boyars guarded their family tales as jealously as if they were the Book of Esther. They passed them from generation to generation without leaving or changing a word. But if someone added an apt, well-turned phrase, it was incorporated into the story and treasured from then on.

When Itzhok heard the applause he opened his eyes in disappointment. He could not understand what was happening. Watching the poet pat Yeva's hand and hearing him call her an actress, he began to glare at her with indignation. Her expression, particularly her eyes, seemed to say: *I don't know why they're applauding, but I've done nothing wrong.*

Cut to the quick, Itzhok jumped to his feet and, by now, shorn of all respect for this crew, slammed his pipe against the table. "We are not play-acting for your benefit nor are we telling you fairy tales. I was taken in here and forced to talk to you people, so the least you can do is have the decency to hear me out to the end." And he stood there and waited until they all grew silent, whereupon he closed his eyes again, and his hand holding the pipe rested on the table.

"But Yontel, like Joseph, withstood the temptation. He ran from the room and the Squire intercepted him: 'Well?' 'No!' Yontel said, blessed be his memory. 'Is it that my daughter displeases you, or is the palace too small for your tastes?'

"Anyhow, nothing would help. The horse thief was given the finest rooms and fed like a prince. Finally, they threw him in a dark, wet dungeon. The Count's daughter stopped eating and drinking altogether. Within eight days she gave up her sinful soul. Don't laugh. To the Gentiles, an unrequited love is like hell on earth."

The Doctor's mother could not bear the suspense. "And the youth?"

"The tailor-horse-thief was buried alive. In the family he is known as Yontel the Martyr."

Itzhok Boyar opened his eyes and began to pluck at the green selvage of his fur pelt.

"In the old days you chopped off a branch, it wouldn't just fall off by itself. People lived very simply then, but they were bigger and stronger inside. Their souls went far deeper. *They* wouldn't dig a well near a river. And the people today? They shake like the willows. First they commit a crime, then they seek an excuse. The most important thing for them is the excuse. They think that finding excuses absolves them of everything, that excuses justify any misconduct. . . ."

"Reb Itzhok, I'll only say two more words to you—"

"*Panie* Doctor." Itzhok stopped him with the pipe held high. "I know what you're going to say. That she didn't do this for riches nor to snatch a fat bone from the table of strangers. Believe me, if she had I wouldn't be here discussing her now. You can take my word on it that my heart goes out to my child even more than yours does." His lids quivered and his eyes filled with tears.

Seizing upon the moment as he saw how distressed the fanatic country Jew had become, the lawyer, Hanan Isseyevitch Levy, he of the famous steel-trap mind and golden tongue, began to castigate Itzhok with passion. He described Herut's sufferings in prison, the tortures to which she had been subjected, and the trouble that he had encountered in quashing the false charges against Avrom.

Itzhok heard him out to the end without interrupting, and when the lawyer—it was he with the wild mop of hair, the thick mustache, and the Vandyke—had grown silent and all eyes had turned toward him again, he said: "I will be beholden to you for the rest of my life. What you did should be carved on a stone for all future generations to see. You've prevented a terrible tragedy. But to take her home and to guarantee her behavior, this I cannot do, this I dare not do. She lays down new commandments for the world to follow. Nothing will stop her. She will not give up her principles— she has shed too much blood for them. No, she will not be stopped. I know what the Boyars are like. Take her home? You might as well hide a torch in a haystack. Come, Avrom. Say goodbye and thank the good Doctor. Thank everybody! What they have done for you can never be forgotten! Your children's children must remember it. Come, my son, come. And I have a request of you too, Yeva. Tell Aunt Liba that I'm ready to go back and tell her not to tarry. If she intends staying on, tell her to let me know at once. Keep well, dear friends, and don't bear me any grudges. A good day to you all and a happy life, always."

AFTER YEVA LEFT, AUNT LIBA STAYED IN BED for a long time.
Although she was a countrywoman accustomed to rising before dawn, she was in no hurry to get up. It was much easier
for her to cope with her problems while lying. She had
heard Yeva get up and leave but had made no effort to delay
her. Yeva was troubled enough. Every house had its own roof
—every individual his own cares. . . . She remained in bed,
therefore, and waited. Shifra would be along shortly. In the
meantime, silence reigned over the house. The sun had
melted the frostwork on the windows—apparently it was already midday. Finally, Aunt Liba got up and went looking
for the maid to find out where her Shifra was staying. She
found the girl in one of the side rooms. Aunt Liba enjoyed
seeing the round, flushed face again with its thick, ash-colored
curl dangling over the sweating brow, the eyes like ripe
cherries, and the smudged nose that kept constantly snuffling.
The girl wore a white apron and dust-cap that resembled a
coronet. She was skating over the floor on a brush **tied** to her
bare right foot and held a chunk of wax in her hand.

"What's your name, girl?"

"Yeva."

"How long have you been called this?"

"Since I've come here."

"What were you called before?"

"Hahve."

"That's more like it. Tell me, Hahvele, what are you
doing now?"

"I'm waxing the floor."

"Isn't sweeping enough? Do you have to do this every day?"

"Yes. It's hard work, but I like it here. I'm my own boss."

"How old are you?"

"Sixteen."

"Do your parents live far away?"

"No, right here in the city. I have a step-mother. . . . Your daughter will be here soon."

"How do you know that, Hahvele?"

"If I say so, I probably know." She gazed sidelong at Aunt Liba. "I was just at her house."

"Who sent you there?"

"This I can't tell you. But I brought her a letter."

Aunt Liba smiled. "All right, Hahvele, I understand. Girls' secrets. How dear and charming they are. . . ." And she thought: *They're writing notes to each other. That's a good deal better than walking the streets together.* A letter forced one's mind to function, to express itself. You could walk for miles, however, and say nothing. Yoel Mattes' daughter, the less said about her the better, spent a whole summer walking with her betrothed. In the end, they broke off their engagement.

Aunt Liba's heart swelled with pride. Her Shifra knew how to do the right thing for herself. Ever since she had been a child things had come hard for her. Finally, God had taken note of her tears and travails and taken pity on her. And just like her husband, Shmarya, Aunt Liba gave in to wishful thinking and reverted to the euphoric mood that had dominated her household for nearly a week before her departure.

Bathed in a surfeit of dazzling sunlight, she walked through the Lande house admiring the costly furniture, the buffets of expensive china, the gold picture frames, and rugs. She shook her head. Why would anyone require so much lux-

205

ury? Later, she grew even more astonished. One did not even have to leave the house to take care of one's needs! All the facilities were actually available inside! This was a virtual paradise. All her children's colds and illnesses could be attributed to having to go out to the privy in all kinds of weather. It was simply amazing how some people lived! Yeva complained about comforts. She had never learned what it was to truly suffer. She had never really had it bad, and, God willing, never would. She had grown up an only daughter whom Gavril had spoiled and pampered to spite Neha and her brother, Abushl. She had spent a great deal of her life in the city, enjoying the best of everything while proclaiming her love for Daniel. True, her heart had been broken. Here, even Gavril had not been able to help. And that which Yeva had told her last night, if it wasn't the ravings of a sick person, was a horrible, unspeakable crime against a person.

"You are the mistress's blood aunt?"

"Yeva's? Yes, a blood aunt. She's my brother's daughter. Why do you ask?"

The girl rolled her cherry-like eyes. "Nothing. Just like that. And Sofia Savelievna is your real daughter?"

"Who is Sofia Savelievna?"

"Shifra."

"My Shifra? Is her name already—"

"Well, Alexander Natanovich calls her nothing else. Are you her real mother?"

"What then, a step-mother, God forbid?"

The girl began to twirl on the brush again. "It's said that Sofia Savelievna was raised by very rich parents."

Aunt Liba detected a faint trace of mockery in the girl's tone. Undoubtedly she assumed that Shifra's name had been changed here and that she was being presented as an heiress. But the girl was no fool. She could see what expensive clothes Shifra's mother had worn for the journey. "God distributes the wealth," Aunt Liba observed. Then added, "Since He has

206

no money of His own, He simply takes from one and gives to another."

The girl pushed back a damp curl and asked with compassion: "Were you rich at one time?"

"Oh, very," Aunt Liba said with her good, sad smile, and went back to Yeva's room. Standing by the window she first realized how high up she was. While climbing the stairs to get here last night she had thought that her heart would explode. She looked out. Beyond the garden that circled the house stretched streets crowded with people. The roofs, partially covered with snow, seemed to press one into the other. Chimneys belched grayish black smoke that the higher it rose the rarer it appeared against the azure sky where it ultimately blended with the fleecy, silvery clouds. The noises of the city barely reached up here but the sound of church bells resounded loud and clear. Through the casement windows drifted odors of newly planed pine boards, of warm, freshly cooked glue, and of tanned leather. Drops fell from rooftops to sills. A tang of something bitter and salty hung in the air, and an undefined essence of spring about to bloom. And off in the distance stretched fields blanketed in glittering blue snow. Set down among those fields, as if somewhere in a wilderness, a village lay. Aunt Liba actually thought that she could hear dogs barking there and cows, having dropped their calves, low in slushy meadows. A forest of mixed trees extended to the left. From among the deep-green firs and pines a few birches thrust their slim white trunks. Three sleighs glided by. What a glorious, God-given day this was! "Were you rich at one time?" "Are you Shifra's real mother?"

On just such a sparkling, sun-drenched day years earlier she had taken Shifra to a strange village to hire out as a maid to a lumber dealer's wife. At that time, Shifra was not yet thirteen. Aunt Liba did not bicker about a salary, merely begged Shifra's new mistress: "Be like a mother to my child. Try to overlook some of her mistakes." The woman promised indignantly. Wasn't she a mother herself? Didn't she know what it was to sacrifice for one's children? And Aunt Liba, somewhat relieved, went into the kitchen to say goodbye to Shifra. When she was already at the front door her daughter clasped her in both arms and began to scream until she turned blue in the face: "Mameniu! Mameniu! Don't leave me here!" They barely managed to pull her off. Shifra's "Mameniu" rang in Aunt Liba's ear for miles afterward. When she came home, she cried for a whole week.

But the real trouble didn't come until a month later. Aunt Liba had become despondent and had not been able to sleep. She was afraid to visit Shifra lest the child cling to her again and beg to be taken home. Only a stone could resist such a plea, certainly not a mother. It was preferable not to see her at all. Shifra would simply have to become accustomed to her lot and to resign herself. But a month later, Shmarya was scheduled to attend a big fair near the village where Shifra was working and Aunt Liba hastily left the children and the house in Blind Panase's care and walked all night with her husband to visit her daughter. When they got there, it was already midday. The sun was blazing and clouds of dust rose from the road. The fair was in full swing. It covered such a wide area that one could not see where it started or ended. Someone had driven a wagon-tongue into a potter's wagon and the whips were already snapping in the air. . . . Aunt Liba was nearly separated from her husband. Noting how far the fair had progressed already, Shmarya's wishful thinking took hold of him as usual and his eyes began to gleam with anticipation. Somewhere within that congestion his salvation was waiting. God forbid that he miss it! Deserting his wife he spun into the vortex of activity like a whirlwind. Aunt Liba somehow found her way to the lumber dealer's house, but just as she was about to step over the threshold the mistress of the house confronted her.

"Barely managed to get here—the sweet, anxious mother! Threw off her child on someone else and was rid of

208

her. You take her straight home! I need a maid, not a wild beast that squats in the corner for days at a time like a wolf ready to spring at people!"

Aunt Liba did not answer. She would not defend either herself or her child. She tied the bundle, took Shifra's hand, and left quietly. They would have to find Shmarya and tell him the truth. He wasn't as likely to lose his temper in public. He worried too much about what people thought. By the time they got home, he would be resigned already to the fact that Shifra was still a child and too young to be on her own. Besides, children did not eat too much nor did they need shoes in the summer. Maybe he would grant Shifra one more summer at home? She would first turn thirteen on Simchas Torah. She could go to work that winter. In the meantime, Aunt Liba was thrilled to have her daughter back. She simply would not let herself think about what would happen later. Things could not get much worse than they already were, anyway.

It was impossible to make any headway through the tangle of wagons, horses, and rushing people. They would never locate Shmarya in this crush. Aunt Liba pushed through the maze holding Shifra's hand and shoulder, fearful of losing her. From wagons lined with green branches a brisk trade was being conducted in white heads of last year's cabbage, in pale-red carrots, potatoes, scallions, garlic, sorrel, fennel, fresh lilacs, and artificial flowers. Bound chickens and geese squawked. A rooster reminded himself that it was day and began to crow. Pigs squealed, cows bellowed. An organ played its lively music, and the ancient parrot, who sat on a perch containing paper pellets predicting fortunes, dozed like a dotard in the sun. The *Starces*, the old beggars, lounged against the glowing gray rocks that lined the road with their legs tucked in beneath their torsos, their sacks draped over their shoulders, tin cups between their knees, and strummed lyres while they bawled their ageless ballads of human misery, injustice, and degradation. A small, bearded peasant—sweating, bareheaded, his tunic torn, barefoot, his white linen trousers belted with a red sash and smeared from tar—lovingly clutched the mane and tail of a runaway colt that trotted beside him obliquely, its head rearing, its ears cocked, its liquid eyes blazing as it whinnied in a thin, frightened voice. The church on the hill cast bright golden rays from its domes as the bells kept tolling and tolling. Scythes rang in the hardware stores. All kinds of clay, glass, and wooden bowls and dishes were displayed on the bare earth—red and white ceramic pots, glazed bowls, wide- and narrow-necked jugs and various shaped basins and trays. Nearby lay yokes, sandals, and soup ladles. The stands featured all kinds of leatherware, cowhide boots, Romanoff fur pelts, ikons in gilt frames, crosses, tin sheaths for *mezuzahs,* Hannukah candelabra, candlesticks, strings of bagels, twisted Sabbath loaves, honey cakes and almonds, and hovering over it all swarmed bevies of green flies. The nostrils were assailed by a plethora of smells, the eyes blinded by a rainbow of colors emanating from coral necklaces, ribbons, rings, brooches, hairpins, earrings, embroidered nightgowns, towels, flowered calicos, silks, and shawls. And a huge sun hung high in the sky and flooded everything in searing, blinding light.

Aunt Liba clutched Shifra's hand and stumbled through the market place. No, they would never find Shmarya this way. Besides, she was anxious to escape the noise and congestion. Her sides were bruised and she had lost all feeling in her legs. Shifra had to be dragged along. She kept stopping and gaping hungrily at everything. The child had to be fed and she herself was starving. Aunt Liba bought a couple of bagels, and a lollipop to cheer up Shifra. She decided to go down to the river bank and to wait by the footbridge among the willows where she and Shmarya had stopped to talk previously. It might even turn out better this way. And suddenly, she spied him standing behind some green branches, shielding himself from the sun. His back was against the wagon-side, his cap pulled halfway down over his eyes, his brows and beard sprinkled with dust, his face a deep yellow-green. The empty sack dangled from his hands while from his pocket extended the green neck of a bottle. He stood there looking depressed, beaten, alien to the huge fair, and mumbled something with his cracked white lips. The symptoms boded no good. And what happened afterward transcended anything that Aunt Liba could have imagined.

When he saw his wife with their daughter and carrying the bundle, he gathered the worst immediately. Shifra had been dismissed. He began to quiver. "But I took five rubles for her! What will I use to prepare for Passover? Woe is me—how will I ever pay it back?"

And before his wife could offer a single word of explanation he thrust one foot between the spokes of a wheel, whipped out a branch from inside the wagon, threw Shifra over his knee, and began to flail away at her exposed bottom.

From sheer desperation to scream out, Aunt Liba lost her voice. The strong urge to do something coupled with her frustration left her as if paralyzed. From under her hands that clutched her forehead she saw the bagel roll somewhere under a wagon and the lollipop stick into the ground. Shifra's dangling pigtails swept the dust and her fingers dug deep furrows in the ground as if she were anxious to bury herself alive.

A deadly silence reigned all around them. Even those denizens of the market place whom nothing could surprise any longer, who had witnessed every variation of human behavior, were dumfounded as the soft, sappy branch descended again and again on the bare young flesh while the sun shone down benevolently and not a single sound escaped either the father or daughter. No one laughed. They just stood there and looked on, holding their breath.

That night, peasants coming from the fair found Aunt Liba lying in the woods. Shame, frenzied shame for herself, for Shmarya and for the child, had caused her to bolt from the scene, her hands still clutching her head. . . .

"Mama!"

"Shifra?"

She saw her daughter poised in the doorway. In the year and a half that she had been away, Shifra had changed almost beyond recognition. She wore a new brown plush cloak with a high collar; the hat and the lapels trimmed with silver-gray fur. She looked tall and strong—a full-grown woman. She brought the smell of sunny frost and of early thaw into the room with her. Yes, it was her Shifra with the familiar beauty mark on the cheek, but the proud, open face was already prematurely tanned by the late-winter sun. A smile hovered over her full lips, and the thin black brows were drawn together as usual. She fanned her long, black eyelashes over her burning eyes so very much like her father's. Seeing her daughter, Aunt Liba forgot that Shifra had neglected her shamefully, and rushed to embrace her. She was consumed not only by a deep longing but also by guilt for that horrible, unforgettable day at the fair, and with each kiss and caress she seemed to be begging: *Forget and forgive, daughter.* . . .

"Mama, let me take off my coat first," Shifra laughed, and laid her hat and coat on a bench. The two black braids, freed from the hairpins, slithered down Shifra's erect back and crept into the folds of the wine-red wool dress.

Pleased yet apprehensive, Aunt Liba took inventory of her daughter's outfit: the sheer black stockings and costly high-heeled shoes; the black silk gloves so carelessly flung upon the table; the muff of matching silver-gray fur draped carelessly over the door. The nails of her daughter's large but shapely hands gleamed with polish. A new ring with a kind of liquid dark-green stone on the finger. Only the old gypsy earrings, which Shifra had cherished and worn for years for some unknown reason, were the same.

How did Shifra earn enough to not only support herself but buy such luxuries as well? She could not possibly have saved up enough in the short time that she had been working here. It was true that she had dressed nicely wherever she had worked, particularly in recent years. But Aunt Liba knew nothing about her daughter's life in the city. In the year and a half that she had been away she had sent no more than a couple of obligatory letters. Nor had she written from the other cities where she had worked previously. Each year she had moved farther and farther away from her home town. And each year at about this same time, just before Passover, she had sent a five-ruble note.

Alexander's sketchy, "About her you don't have to worry. . . ." at Gavril's house had told Aunt Liba nothing. But even as Shifra stood there before her now, so straight, so full of the juices of life and ripe as an apple, and laughed in a pleasant, soft voice completely devoid of rancor—even now Aunt Liba did not feel free to demand an accounting of her life and behavior. Did she have this right? What had she, the mother, ever done for her daughter?

Despite the pride apparent on her mother's face Shifra knew what she was thinking. If it were not for the fact that there was something far more important to discuss with her mother, she would have hugged her and reassured her that all her finery had been purchased with her own money, which she had managed to save up even before coming here. Besides, for nearly a year and a half now she had been working as an assistant pharmacist and earning a fair salary. But having learned to control, even to smother her noblest inclinations if they distracted her from her prime course, Shifra said nothing. Let her mother remain in doubt. Better still—let her think the worst of her. And to top it off, she began to discuss her hideous childhood years. True, she did this without bitterness, without resentment, even smilingly, as one discusses a long forgotten tragedy. But her purpose was clear enough nevertheless—to prevent her mother from acting too righteous.

"No, I never forgot, Mama. And the path that you pointed out to me has stuck in my mind ever since."

213

"What path?"

"Do you remember, Mama, when you called for me during that immemorable fair? I want you to know that my first mistress was a person with soul. When Papa brought me back there after whipping me, she sat up with me the whole night. She held me in her arms as if I were her own child, she cried with me and urged me to forgive my father, who was, after all, only a victim himself. But Papa had become my worst enemy then and I kept praying for his death. I never said it aloud, but oh, how I begged God to make Papa die! I wanted to die myself . . . I saw myself lying on the floor with the candles lit at my head while he cried over me. Remember, I was only a child then."

"But now you understand your father. And you forgive him."

"I understand. But to understand does not mean to forgive. I was so terribly angry at you too, Mama. How could you have left me there to his mercy? I don't hold any resentment against you now, Mama. But at that time— When the mistress complained that I crouched in the corner with eyes like a wolf . . . that was when I got my first period. The pain was so intense I almost bit off my fingers. After all, I didn't know what it was all about and I was so terribly frightened. And I was deeply ashamed too. . . . And then my own father bared my nakedness to thousands of strangers. Did you ever wonder why I still wear these plain gypsy earrings, Mama? I'll tell you. That time when I was clawing at the ground with my bare nails, not so much out of pain as out of shame, something caught in my fingers. I didn't even notice it until after Papa had brought me back and the mistress had washed me and found them inside my clenched fists. I'll never take off these cheap gypsy earrings. I wear them as a symbol, as a reminder. After that fair, I only wanted to get as far away from Papa as possible. Later, this feeling changed so that I wanted to get away not only from him but from all the villages with their stinking streets and their greasy Jews, with their grated radishes, their cold Sabbath lima beans—their tricks and wiles . . . I grew to hate their fairs and their side-locks, their piety and cruelty to children."

Aunt Liba, who had kept silent, only wiping her lips occasionally between her thumb and forefinger while she admired the color of her daughter's handsome face and the almost gay smile with which she was talking, began to understand what had estranged Shifra from the house and compelled her to go ever farther and farther away. Finally, unable to hold it in any longer, she blurted out: "What you're saying, Daughter, is that I pointed out this path to you?"

The thin brows drew closer together. No longer smiling, one leg crossed over another, Shifra pulled the muff toward her as if about to extract something from it, but her left hand remained on the table.

"Don't be so afraid, Mama. No one will say that Shmarya's wife led her daughter down the primrose path. But you didn't steer me on the path of righteousness either. I took it on my own. It's true that I remembered your good advice and always clung to it. You recall what happened some time after that fair when we sat together near the fence of the priest's house? It was in the middle of summer. After we had had a good cry you told me how once when you were walking through the woods in the evening you suddenly got lost and you became very frightened. Night was coming, and with it a terrible frost. But you got hold of yourself and you followed a bright star that led you to a farmhouse. 'Shifreniu,' you told me then, 'never be afraid. You'll always find your way, for all paths lead to life. . . .' That lesson stuck in my mind, Mama. One has to walk straight ahead always and not be distracted to other directions or wait for others to show the way. One has to follow one's own path and look to the stars."

"Where did you go, Daughter, and what star did you follow?"

"In the three years that I stayed with my first mistress—

and I'll never forget her—I learned to read and do figures from her children. And when I had nothing more to learn there, I went to a wealthy home for practically no salary, for my board only. But there were *gymnasium* students there and I learned from them. I worked all day in the kitchen cooking and washing, and at night I did their homework. They would copy it over in the morning and bring home the best grades. Their parents used to buy them presents for it."

"May all your troubles be mine instead," Aunt Liba said, dabbing at her eyes. Her heart filled with pride again, "Give me your pretty brow, Daughter, so that I may kiss it."

"And later," Shifra continued, nestling her head on her mother's breast, "later I went to a house where the daughter took piano lessons. She was a real nincompoop. All she thought about was boys and didn't want to study. Her dowry was already all arranged. So the mistress fixed it that we should take the lessons together. This way, her spoiled brat managed to learn something too. And that's how I walked through the woods, on a winter's evening, Mama, looking straight ahead. For the last two years, before coming here, I was a tutor to rich children."

"What's that, Daughter?"

"Someone who teaches at home." Facing the sun-drenched window, her head still cradled on her mother's breast, Shifra batted her long lashes over her burning eyes. "How I hated the rich homes and those mighty industrialists whose only pleasure was stuffing themselves. They cooked and baked there from morning 'til night. The people staggered around as if in a daze and rubbed their bloated bellies. The rich man crawled away from the table after a greasy, heavy dinner with all his buttons open, sweating, flushed, his tongue hanging out. 'What's wrong, Hillel?' his wife would ask, afraid. 'Nothing, Zelda,' he'd say, 'I just have to give a belch . . . get me a glass of seltzer.' "

216

She stood up suddenly and picked up her things. "Enough of that. What's over is over. We have more important things to talk about. Come, Mama. We'll go to Alexander's study. No one will disturb us there."

6

THAT MORNING, THE SILENCE IN THE LANDE HOUSE was shattered forever. It was a white four-story building with towers and balconies supported by hunchbacked stone gargoyles and monsters with hollow eyesockets and braided beards. It was located in the finest section of town, among the homes of the aristocracy. It differed from the others in that it was more deeply recessed from the street, but like the others it had a garden containing fruit trees and silver poplars and was bordered by a red picket fence. The two sons-in-law occupied the two lower floors; the old couple and the youngest son lived on the third floor; and Alexander and Yeva, on the fourth.

As soon as the new house had been erected, old Reb Nossan Lande had refused to move into it. What was wrong with the old house in the Jewish quarter? On Sabbaths and holidays when candles were lit all around it warmed one's heart to see them in the neighbor's windows—the plain ones, the Hannukah tapers and the fat, twisted wax candle used to usher out the Sabbath. You could hear people saying the benedictions and singing the Sabbath hymns. On Purim, they sang the hymn *Shushan Yakov;* on Simchas Torah there was dancing in the streets. Sweating, excited Jews would besiege the house, help themselves to *kugel,* and share the homemade cherry and grape wine.

Nor could Reb Nossan be a party to such extravagance. It was a far nobler thing to give money to the poor and needy; to widows, orphans, and impoverished brides. No, he would not leave the old quarters. He would not dwell in that heathen palace with its idols and statues, a flagrant violation of the Torah.

And he stuck to his resolution and remained all alone in a small garret of the abandoned house. A small, wispy man with a rounded back, he wore a mohair gaberdine that made him seem taller and broader; white woolen stockings; slippers, and a round, velvet skullcap on his huge head. He spent the daylight hours poring over the ancient, dusty volumes of holy works. He would stand near the window, letting the light fall on the pages, lean one shoulder against a frayed patch of wall, tuck the left hand under his sash, and holding the Zohar * close to his myopic eyes, shake his head with reverence as his sparse white beard swept the dust from the crumbling, tobacco-stained pages. The nights he spent hunched over the plain, unpainted table, where, by the meager light of the seven-candle candelabrum he dipped his goose quill in a horn inkwell and wrote in his manuscript, *The Sanctity of the Godhead.*

Old Nossan Lande was determined to probe the mysteries of the Torah and the deep secrets behind Rabbi Leib Sore's deeds, such as his chastisement of the rich men who refused to contribute toward the redemption of Jewish prisoners. He showed proofs in the writings of rabbis that a saint who had been touched by the Divine Presence did in reality become "one who sees but is himself not seen. . . ." Huddled at night in the woolen shawl that spanned his rounded back, straining in the dim light, clutching the goose quill in his yellowed hand, old Nossan Lande waged war against "the little foxes that spoil the vineyards," against the proponents of Enlightenment; against the slanderers and sycophants the likes of Joseph Pearl who urged the arrest of Jews who blessed the new moon; and against those who

---

* Translator's note: book of cabalistic commentaries on Scripture.

219

had informed against the Zydaczower Rabbi to the police and thus helped delay the redemption.

Through long winter nights, as the moon cast its cold, impersonal light through the frozen windowpanes, the aged mystic chanted the Cabala, equating the seven musical scales with the seven days of Creation and the Spheres.

As blizzards raged outside, the revelation came to him that the Divine Presence permeated all Hasidic table chants and dances, particularly when they achieved such ecstasy that bared the hearts themselves. When those select, dedicated Jews formed their circles, a ring of fire actually trailed behind them. With each dance a fiery angel was born. Finally it came to pass that the souls ascended to heaven. Yes, the root of every benediction was contained in a Hasidic dance. A dance made it possible to worship with intensity, to reach up to God more directly than through a common prayer. A dance made it possible to keep the soul alive. . . .

And Nossan Lande, burdened as he was by the heavy yoke of heredity linking him with such distant ancestors as the Miracle Worker who never accepted a fee for his services, the older he grew the more he clove to the path of seclusion, a path taken by a still more distant ancestor, the recluse who for the last forty days of his life had slept on a stone slab. He, Nossan Lande, had gone so far along this path as to sleep on the bare bed slats and to sustain his body just enough to maintain its soul. Through long winter nights he wrote in his *Sanctity of the Godhead* and waged a life-and-death struggle with the "grandsons" of the true saints, those rabbinical heirs who ruled with all the authority of their holy ancestors, issued remedies and amulets, yet lived in magnificence that far outshone that of the noblest Polish princes and magnates. His weapon the sharpened goose quill, he fought the descendant of Rabbi Avrom Melech who had engaged the greatest artists and architects in the world to build his palace in Ruzhin, and he displayed this ostentatiousness not only on the outside for the benefit of strangers, but inside as well, for his own enjoyment. Everything there was of the best, the finest, the costliest. The floor was tiled in silver rubles, all the door and window handles were of amber. There were magnificent gardens and a stable of blooded horses. The "grandson" liked to take rides, like some monarch, in elaborate carriages drawn by six teams of horses. The court attendants, the various deacons and beadles, had managed to convince the average follower of the court that their rabbi was a saint on a rank with royalty. And even the lesser rabbis, like the Czernobiler, lived in magnificent splendor, each vying to outdo the other in opulence. If the Trisker Rabbi got a pure gold chandelier the size of a man, the Talner Rabbi ordered a silver chair engraved with the name of David, King of the Jews. And the decadence worsened and worsened until it happened that the Kozienice Rabbi's chief attendant, whose only claim to fame was his ability to pave a street standing up, was elevated to the post of a rabbi who reigned over Hasidic banquets and interpreted the Torah.

And the goose quill in the parchment-yellow hand scraped over the foolscap: "Woe unto us all what corruption has befallen us: Prior to Messiah's coming, the shame multiplies. We live in a time that is neither day nor night. . . ." The old man wrote page after page, while from time to time his dark-gray, febrile eyes strayed from the flickering candles to the frost-covered windows. His legs were cold and his spine aching. The candles sputtered out and the charred, blackened wicks toppled into the melted tallow. The candelabrum exuded an acrid, fumy smoke. Reb Nossan sat in the dark and stared at the frost patterns. For whom was he writing? What was he but another voice in the wilderness? *There is no forest. There are no bears. And the strength is waning, O Lord!* His eyes began to close. Somewhere, far off, he heard the roosters crowing. But soon he nodded off by the blue-metallic shine of the frozen moon. The huge head sank onto the table, the goose quill remained gripped in the outstretched hand.

For seven weeks the family left him alone in the deserted house to indulge his obstinacy. The continuous rains had turned the decrepit wooden houses black and washed the green moss on their soggy, shingle roofs clean of the dusts of summer. The bare trees stopped rustling only in the evenings when the east wind subsided. In a corner of the attic window, a sere willow leaf nestled, a faded memory of the sun. The covered wagons moved slowly through the muddy streets below. The draught horses—their heads lowered and knotted tails lifted high—plodded with hairy, sinewy legs through the sucking mire. The smoke from the chimneys drooped sluggishly toward the ground and permeated everything with its noxious stench. Nossan Lande did not once leave his cell with the four bare walls and network of spiderwebs in the corner. By the threshold lay a cracked jar of apple preserves with a thick layer of foamy mold on top. Objects once useful and suffused with the warmth of life lay scattered underfoot. And over everything hung the smell of dank ruin, and the dense, sweet-sour reek of naphthalene. In the kitchen, the white cat took refuge in the black cavity of the stove and licked the pads of her black paws with a pink, narrow, rigid tongue.

The winter that year came all at once, and with it deep snows blanketing the ugliness in loneliness and a niveous silence. The small attic window grew completely covered with frost. Each night at the same time, Ashmedai came from the new house bringing seven candles, a pot of food, a hard-boiled egg, and a chunk of black bread. He deposited his burden on the corner of the kitchen table, fitted the candles into the candelabrum, lit the stove, and left in silent awe and fear.

When Nossan Lande returned from saying the evening prayers at the synagogue he would light the candles, quickly break his fast, and with goose quill in hand and shawl around his shoulders resume writing in his manuscript showing the relation between the seven scales of music and the Spheres and waging the struggle against the slanderers, sycophants, and proponents of Enlightenment. . . . But one morning when he returned from the synagogue he found his little attic room stripped bare. Everything had been removed. The workmen had even torn down the walls.

"My manuscript! My books!"

"Everything is where it belongs, among your children and grandchildren in the new house, my husband," his wife told him. "Enough, Nossan, enough. You've caused us untold shame. . . . The whole city is laughing at us. . . . This house is being torn down for its lumber, which will be distributed among the poor."

And the old man had been forced to give in. No one took notice of his arrival in the new house. They had appraised the situation correctly. Wreck his room, tear down his walls, take away his books—he'd have no choice but to capitulate. The fact that he had held out for seven weeks and given people good cause to laugh and gossip about the Landes—this they would never forgive him. But before strangers, they continued to treat the old man with even more esteem and humility.

* * *

And that morning after Yeva had gone out and while Aunt Liba was talking with Shifra, the turgid silence of respectability in the Lande house was shattered forever. No one could have anticipated it. The mother and her son-in-law partner had long since left for their store. The other son-in-law, Hanan Isseyevitch, a participant in the All-Russia Lawyers' Conference—he who had spoken for a full fifteen minutes with Miliukov himself—had been convinced that with a quote or two from the Midrash he would quickly overwhelm the country Jew and persuade him to take his daughter Herut home. It wasn't that he gave a fig for her. As a Social Democrat he was as violently opposed to Karl Marx as the old fanatic himself. Still, it would have enhanced his reputation as an attorney to pull it off. It also would have demonstrated, now that the election for the Duma was imminent, that only the members of the workers' intelligentsia, those men of "spiritual effort," could effectively oppose the police powers, and rallying all Russia under the green flag of the Party, guide it to freedom and democracy.

Even the two sisters, those fierce and implacable foes and competitors who usually did everything to spite each other, joined forces that morning out of fierce curiosity and sent for the new maid to ask where Yeva had gone, what she and her aunt had talked about, if Shifra had met with Yeva, whether Alexander had slept at home, and what Shifra and her mother were saying. They admonished the girl to remain on the alert and to report all new developments. Then the elder sister made slanderous remarks about Professor Efros' young, second wife who was making eyes at the rising young poet who was just as eager to wed the Professor's eminently marriageable daughter. She whispered something else to her younger sister and went off to dress. She was going to court later to watch her husband defend a peasant who had murdered his brother for plowing a piece of land that belonged to him. She would enjoy parading around the courtroom in her finery while people pointed out the elegant and fashionable Madam Levy. The younger sister, left alone, cried into her embroidered pillow. Eights years of marriage had left her childless. She had taken her Jonah to all the health resorts, even to Carlsbad. He had consulted the finest specialists, but to no avail. On the other hand, each year he increased his holdings in the business, kept taking it over bit by bit so that the mother-in-law would not suspect. He planned one day to open a huge department store of readymade dresses. Meanwhile, he kept acquiring shares and playing the stock market. She, Esther, could not even talk about this with anyone. Her life was intolerable. If only she could launch a salon in her apartment, just like Professor Efros' wife. . . .

Old Nossan Lande had gradually become accustomed to his new quarters too—particularly to his room. No one kept him from sleeping on the bare bed slats; no one stopped him from fasting. The seven candles stood as always in the candelabrum. He was anxious to make donations to charity but he had been strictly warned not to allow beggars and ragamuffins into the house. Nor did Jews come on Simchas Torah to share his food or dance on the tables.

That morning, coming home from the synagogue with his son, the penitent, he crossed the garden with eyes half shut as usual—to avoid seeing the idolatrous statues on the building—and stationed himself in his customary place by the window with the light falling on his pages and his shoulder rubbing against the frayed spot on the wall. He was happy. Only this day he had recognized his son as he once had been, when, betrothed to the Mozirer Rabbi's grand-daughter and scheduled to take over the rabbinical chair, he had suddenly strayed from the path of righteousness and gone off to roam through the world. Then, having come home with the dust of the road still upon his face, he had begged: "Father, take me back under your wing. . . ." And he had kept his word, growing more pious daily. Having watched his son stare at the sky through the synagogue windows with burning eyes, the old mystic had become alarmed. His son seemed to be looking into the other worlds and reflecting God's light in his eyes. But Reb Nossan had quickly grown enraptured. Now he was convinced that Avner would take up the golden chain of Jewishness and piety from him, his father. A penitent could accomplish so very, very much after all. . . .

And on that morning, Avner, having come back from the synagogue with his father, began to pace again through the house, up and down the corridors, and finally wandered out into the garden. But once outside, he grew as if frightened by the sparkling sunshine, the gentle breeze blowing through the silver poplars, the clear skies and the rivulets trickling down into the crusty, yellow-pitted snow, and he dashed inside, not back to his parents' apartment but to the top floor—to Alexander's. He headed for his brother's study, confident that this was the most likely place to find him, but seeing Shifra there with an older woman he stopped, grew even paler, then quickly excused himself. He had not expected to meet anyone else there. Today Shifra looked just as Akiva described her: the Shulammite of the Polesian forests.

"If I possessed even one spark of the immortal Petrarch I would laud you in sonnets as he did his Laura. . . ."

Shifra walked up to him, her thin brows drawn together. "You're not yourself today," she said, batting her long lashes playfully. "I've never seen you so gay."

"It shouldn't surprise you. On a day like this the sun drives away even the darkest shadows."

"Then why are you so neglectful?"

"I?"

"You talk of composing sonnets to me but you're holding my hand and haven't made a move to kiss it. A woman can never forgive such an omission . . . or is it that you're ashamed in front of my mother?"

"Oh, a thousand pardons!" He kissed both her hands. "I nearly inflicted a terrible punishment upon myself. Is this your mother? I'd sooner say it was your sister." He bowed deeply to Aunt Liba. "Your mother takes very much after you." He laughed at his own joke, excused himself again for barging in, and silently closed the door behind him.

Aunt Liba knew at once who this was—Avner, Shifra's intended, who would introduce her daughter to the world of wealth, comfort, and position. She liked him. He was polite without being snobbish, and quite obviously clever. True, he was too short for Shifra, who towered over him by a full head, but to make up for it he was as broad-shouldered as a porter, had very nice teeth, a fine, noble face and a handsome, curly blond beard. She had feared—she had been almost convinced—that he would turn out to be a cripple or,

God forbid, an epileptic or even an imbecile. But he seemed to be a perfectly normal man. The fact that he had a slight squint in his left eye merely enhanced his appeal.

After Avner's abrupt entrance and departure had eased her mind and left her aglow with gratitude to God for this unexpected gift, Aunt Liba discarded all the questions that had been tormenting her. Her mother's heart filled with joy and with pride. After so many years of toil and hardship, her child, with God's help only, had attained such a worthy goal. And the nausea that had been plaguing her all morning suddenly became very dear to Aunt Liba. She was thrilled that another child was coming. Children meant good luck. True, her children had sprouted up in heat and in cold like trees in a field, but apparently a tree could not develop otherwise. There stood her pretty daughter by the window, bathed in sunlight like a handsome, straight pine.

Aunt Liba crossed her arms over her bosom. "I can't feast my eyes enough on you, Daughter. I haven't seen you in nearly two years. Come, sit here next to me. I've seen enough of trouble in the past few days. Yesterday, on the road with Itzhok, last night with Yeva—and my own in addition. One does not have to borrow trouble from others, thank God. . . . Do you know why I've come?"

"I'm beginning to guess."

"You're guessing?" Aunt Liba said smilingly. "Come, give my heart reason to rejoice. Don't deny me this pleasure, Daughter. Fill my heart with joy. Pour it on, pour it on. Each corner of it is as empty as a poor peasant's potato cellar in the springtime. It's high time we knew the taste of pleasure, of pride and happiness like other people do. Tell me all about it, Daughter. How did it start? How did you meet? How did it come to be said? What were his exact words?"

Her mother's artlessness and curiosity amused Shifra. She drew her brows together, started to redo her braids, and assuming her mother's naïve tone began: "A fated thing. He said that at first he never even noticed me. But once I went to the theatre in one of Yeva's dresses. I didn't have a black dress of my own at that time. That was the first time he noticed me. And, as he tells me now, he was stunned. His sister, Judis, who was with me that night, said to him: 'Put the same dress on Shifra and you have an even more beautiful woman in the house—and without any of that one's caprices and high and mighty airs. Yeva's is an icy beauty but Shifra is full of fire.' "

"And you stood by and listened to all of this, Daughter?"

"I made believe I didn't hear."

"Is that the way an older sister who has children herself talks to a brother?"

"I'm telling you how it happened. It all started that evening."

"And have the parents spoken to you about it already?"

"The father—no. She—yes. True, not directly, but in a kind of veiled way. She took my measure like a shopkeeper, you might say. I was furious over this—this appraisal. But his mother is like a right hand to him. But between me and you, it's all settled already."

"Did he ever say it to you in so many words? Don't laugh at me, Daughter, your silly mother wants to know every detail."

But seeing Shifra's eyes shift uneasily, Aunt Liba mistook her reticence for maidenly modesty and added with her good smile: "Wherever you see a tree stump or a pitfall, jump over it, Daughter." And in order to lend Shifra support she told her a story: "When your father first came to look me over I almost sank into the ground from embarrassment. When he fixed me with those liquid, black eyes I nearly turned to stone. He stood there in front of me and carried to me the smell of wind . . . a man *should* smell of the wind. I hate stay-at-homes. He asked me: 'What are you sewing?' I was sitting by a window, sewing a phylactery bag. My mother, may she rest in peace, had arranged it that way. He

228

spoke to me because he was anxious to hear my voice, to make sure I wasn't a stammerer or a mute, God forbid. But I had lost my voice. I had grown tongue-tied. I turned red. 'Why don't you speak up, Liba?' my mother asked with a smile. When your grandmother, Miriam, smiled that way—may my words not cause her harm up there—it was a sign that you could expect to catch it good from her later on. But what was the outcome? I jabbed a needle into my finger and it started to burn like it should happen to my enemies. But even when I bit down on my tongue it wouldn't start wagging. Besides, my teeth began to set on edge as if I had eaten prune jelly. Seeing that the bridegroom was already turning up his nose, my mother got scared and said: 'Why don't you two take a little walk? It's a fine day.' But you think she'd let us go just like that? God forbid. She tied the large water bucket to the yoke and sent us to the well for water. And she walked behind us, supposedly to check on the cattle that grazed in the pasture. . . . I held one end of the yoke, he held the other, and the empty bucket swung between us. That empty bucket has been swinging before my eyes all my life, daughter. I walked along slowly as if I had just gotten out of sickbed. 'Have you been sick?' he asked, sure enough. This irked me already. I thought: *You've got a nice, shiny pair of peepers, but you're not too smart, are you?* When we reached the well I grabbed the bucket, hung it on the hook, lowered it, and brought it up full. He leaned over the well and his face reflected in the water. His two eyes shone back at me not like human eyes, but like those of a devil. When I was ready to take down the bucket, he jumped in to help, but his hand didn't reach for the bucket handle but for my hand. I pulled it away as if from a hot coal. Apparently I twisted something doing this and I fell. And I fell very hard. Laugh, laugh all you want, Daughter. In those days a girl wasn't so free and easy with her betrothed. The bridegroom wouldn't kiss a girl's hand as if she would be, beg the comparison, the village priest. Your father kissed

229

me for the first time under the wedding canopy although we were betrothed from the Pentecost until Hannukah. Today, you laugh at us. Some day, your children will laugh at you. It seems, this is the way of the world. And who knows? Maybe your children will laugh at you even more than ours do at us?"

"I care less about what others say than about anything else," Shifra said, pulling back her sleeve to look at her watch. "That's for the weak and the frightened. They may laugh at me today, from envy, you understand, but tomorrow they'll kneel before me and tip their caps."

Aunt Liba was confused by Shifra's remark but took it at face value. What she probably meant was that she didn't care if her future children would laugh at her. She could very well have been right. No one laughed at a mother who was rich. It was just as she had said—old Madam Lande was like a right hand to her children, their spokesman and advisor. "You may be right, Daughter. Gold covers everything." She took Shifra's hand and looked at the watch that she had not noticed before. "Is it gold? Did he give it to you as a present?"

Her innocence and simplicity began to irritate Shifra. Besides, she could not tarry here. It was time to stop the idle chatter and get to the point. Her mother had to be told why she had been summoned. Actually, she, Shifra, had been opposed to this move. "Yes, Mama, it's pure gold and it is a present from him. . . ." And suddenly she asked: "What does Yeva think? I don't mean about me. I mean what does she intend doing? How does she plan to go on living? You see for yourself what goes on in this house. She lives here like an outsider. Actually, she is a stranger here. What a pity on her! Why should she waste her life here? She is so beautiful and clever."

"No one has the right to mix in between a husband and wife, unless it's to help them make up. I haven't discussed it with her yet. Her poor heart is broken. It's too soon to bring it up. Daniel's death, his funeral, and Neha—all these things have upset her terribly. She must be allowed to come back to herself. Her heart has been broken, may it never happen to you. I don't find such things laughable. She still can't forget him. May God spare you such grief."

"Yes, God has spared me from that particular ailment. To play at love with some handsome pauper with long hair whose pockets are stuffed with books, who counts the stars and goes into raptures over the moon while his stomach growls from hunger and the mud soaks in through his torn shoes. . . . No, thank you. My father didn't whip me in front of thousands of people so that my own Shmarya could one day whip my children. I don't want any empty buckets swaying in front of my eyes. One of those romantic beggars courted me in Zvihil. It's true he wouldn't have whipped our children, but they would have starved to death. A very handsome boy he was too. He almost killed himself on account of me. They barely saved him in time."

"Did you love him?"

"Even if I did, what of it?"

"You don't live with money, my daughter, but with a human being."

"That's how paupers console themselves. I guard myself against this kind of sickness as I would from a fire. Just about everybody I know gets drowned in this kind of honey."

"But are you in love with your rich groom now?"

"No, Mama. I'm not marrying for love."

"But at least he appeals to you?"

Shifra, who had been pacing through the room with her hands on her hips and her head thrown back, wheeled suddenly. The rapid motion caused her corset to squeak and the folds of her dress to ripple. "Who appeals to me?"

"What do you mean, who? The bridegroom, of course. Avner. What's wrong with you today, Daughter?"

Shifra's habit of screwing up her brows had always irritated Aunt Liba. It reminded her too much of Gavril. She

231

studied her daughter's face intently. It looked somehow tense and calculating. "What is it, Daughter?"

Shifra strolled to the window and pulled down the shade. But soon she decided that the shade did not inhibit her and she rolled it up again. She resumed pacing with her hands on her swaying hips. "To tell the truth, I never thought I'd find it so hard to talk to you, Mama. You ask if Avner appeals to me? I've told you already that young people, especially young men, leave me cold. They may even have a lot of fire in them, but they use it only to boil water. Avner searched through the whole world for the secret of life and he had to come back to his father who is an impractical dreamer himself. Now they pray together every morning and night. What did he waste his youth on? On nothing! Herut wants to overthrow the Tsar and she can't even stay out of jail. She's ruining her own life and her child's as well."

"Does she have a child then?" asked Aunt Liba, who sat listening to her daughter with fascination.

"She had the child while she was still in Siberia. Another one who used her fire to boil water. And Yeva goes around mooning about love. Do you think she would have been happier with that loafer Daniel? Nonsense! They fly like moths into a candle. Avner sits around with a singed soul and wings, and sobs: 'There was a great truth in the world, but people crumbled it, each one took away a crumb, wrapped it in a candy wrapper, and cried that *he* had the truth.' Besides, he is stone broke. Maybe one day he'll end up with a small piece of the inheritance."

"Then what do you need him for, Daughter? If his soul is singed as you say, let him go his own way. After all, you're a healthy, pretty girl, may the evil eye spare you."

"Mama, how old were you when you married?"

"Seventeen. Are you worried about becoming an old maid?"

"I'm almost twenty."

"Is that the only reason you said yes to him?"

232

"To whom?"

"What's the matter with you, Shifra? Why do you ask me 'who'? Didn't you give Avner your word?"

"I never gave Avner my word."

"And old Nossan Lande didn't speak to you either?"

"No."

"Then who sent Abushl to us? He told me and your father very distinctly: 'Old Nossan Lande wants your daughter for his youngest son.'"

"Abushl lied. The old man didn't send him."

"Is the whole story a lie then?"

"No, Mama, it's partly true."

"Did you send him yourself?"

"No, I didn't send him either."

"Then who—?"

"Alexander," Shifra said, and breathed relief. That most difficult of words had finally been said. Now her wise mother would quickly gather the rest.

But the wise Aunt Liba did not understand at all. She was only bewildered by how freely and easily her daughter behaved in Alexander's study, how she dared half-sit, half-lounge in the easy chair.

"Doesn't Alexander have other things on his mind now besides arranging matches?" Aunt Liba asked. "And how can he be so sure that his father will approve?"

Shifra crossed her legs, faced the sun, and with trembling lids said very casually: "No one is asking him."

"So? You dance to your own tune, do you? Well, all right. Let it be this way. But you mentioned before that it was all arranged between you. You've even accepted an expensive gift from him."

"Yes, Mama, it is all arranged and I've accepted an expensive gift from him."

"And then you say that you didn't give him your word. And you also say that he is penniless. Then where did he get the money for such a gold watch with a gold band?"

"I've already told you, Mama. I gave my word to Alexander, not to Avner."

"And Avner knows about this?"

"What concern is it of his?"

"What do you mean—what concern is it of his? Isn't it customary to settle these things with the bridegroom himself rather than with his brother?"

"I did discuss it with the bridegroom."

"So you *did* talk to Avner."

"I had nothing to say to Avner."

"Is he such a ninny that Alexander has to speak for him?"

"Alexander did not speak for him. He spoke for himself. . . ."

Aunt Liba's mouth dropped and the nausea that had been assailing her all morning rushed through her whole body along with a kind of fever. She gaped at her daughter, who sat bathed in sunshine with a serene, unruffled expression.

"Shifra?"

Aunt Liba contained her anger but she could no longer remain seated. That her Shifra could do such a thing—to worm her way into a cousin's house and to steal her husband! It didn't matter that the couple had been living apart for years. There was a child, after all! And although she was terribly distressed by Daniel's death, Yeva would simply have to accept her lot. Time eroded all resistance and defiance. "Shifra, why did you bring me here?"

"So that for once in my life my mother could help me, not with kind words and parables but with action."

"What is it you want me to do?"

"Not much, Mama. Just to help persuade Yeva to get a divorce. Alexander is willing to make a generous settlement on her and the child."

"Me? . . . Me? . . . You want me to help you drive

Yeva from her own house so that you could take her place?"

"First of all, the place is already empty. I wouldn't be taking anyone's place."

"Shifra, I won't allow this to happen!"

Shifra closed her eyes wearily. Who was it had perpetuated the fiction that her mother was so wise? As if she would let anyone hinder her plans . . .

"Do you hear me, Shifra?"

"I hear you, Mama."

"Just like Haman hears the Purim *grogger,* is that what you mean?"

Shifra looked up. "Let's not speak anymore about it, Mama."

"No, Daughter. I've been listening and now it's my turn to speak. Tell me, who gave you such ideas? Are you trying to capitalize on your beauty?"

Shifra smiled. "What else have I besides my beauty? And it doesn't matter whether you allow it or not, Mama. It's too late already."

"Shifra! Shifra!"

Shifra stood up and smoothed the folds in her dress. "Don't raise your voice, Mama, and don't be afraid. I'm not so foolish as to do anything rash. First he will have to divorce her, then he'll have to make a big wedding for me—"

"Woe is me—how can you discuss it so calmly? Without any shame? Don't you people fear God anymore?"

"Shame . . . God." Her daughter grimaced. "Pretty words. God looked on when the pious Shmarya whipped his twelve-year-old daughter and He didn't dim the sun."

"God cannot repay everyone on the spot. Your father didn't do it out of meanness. He lost his head because of all his troubles and he didn't know what he was doing. But what you propose is a cold-blooded sin, committed in full possession of your senses. You want to sell your beauty for luxury and comfort. Alexander is old enough to be your father. He

235

has twenty years on you. Besides, he is a sick man too. He has some kind of serious stomach trouble, it shouldn't happen to us."

"That happens to be one of his lesser faults."

Aunt Liba lost her temper. "Is nothing sacred to you anymore? Can you live such a life without shame? Without God? Is a rich home the only—"

From the room next door came the dry report of a gunshot. Mother and daughter both trembled. At first they thought that the maid had caused something to fall. But soon two more shots followed in quick succession, those even closer and more resounding. They leaped to their feet and ran to investigate. In the center of the sunny room Avner lay on his side, twisted up as if with cramps, his breath rattling, his hands clutching at his breast from which the blood was gushing. Nearby, lay a revolver. Shifra bent down and pulled the shirt away from the wound. Aunt Liba began to scream for help. The silence in the four-story white house of the Landes was shattered forever.

7

Alone in his room, surrounded by his holy books, Nossan Lande did not hear the commotion that had erupted in the house. Isolated from the material world and thrilled by the spiritual regeneration of his penitent son, he sat hunched over the table, and in a state of exaltation scribbled with the goose quill in his *Sanctity of the Godhead.*

His ear was in general closed to the affairs of the household. He did not involve himself in his wife's business matters nor in the activities of his children and their mates. He merely made an occasional kind remark about Yeva to help keep peace in the family. And his comments, rare as they were, were received with exaggerated reverence, particularly since his brief rebellion. His family was constantly on the alert for some new impropriety, and every effort was made to keep him content. This task had been assigned by mutual consent to his son-in-law, the lawyer, since the old man's name and position were still a force to be reckoned with in the city, particularly among the working classes. He, the son-in-law, therefore spoke highly of his father-in-law in public and lauded him as a true model of traditional Judaism. What was more important, for all his mohair gaberdine, high woolen stockings and slippers, old Nossan Lande was still the only member of the Jewish community with access to the Governor-General himself.

In times of crisis, whenever the security of the Jews was threatened, he put aside his books and commentaries and strove to do all that was expected of him, which was to go to the representative of God's Anointed and to present him with an offering from the loyal and obedient Jewish population in exchange for his providential protection and mercy.

Recently, with the approach of Easter, the local reactionary sheet had made frequent allusions to pogroms. The terrible slaughterer's knife that had descended upon Kishinev was being whetted again and the Jews began to take countermeasures. They fasted, they visited their parents' graves, but above all—they began collecting money.

Soon after his arrival in the city, the most honored leaders of the Jewish community had gone to pay their respects to the new Governor-General. He, a tall, heavy-set, grayhaired individual, lacking eyebrows and eyelashes, and with a fleshy red nose, promptly turned his back on them. Behind him on the wall hung a huge portrait of His Majesty the Tsar, Nicholas II himself. In the new Governor-General's lapel the Jews quickly spotted the pin of the ultrareactionary Union of the Russian People. The new ruler of the province barely let Nossan Lande finish his blessing before he burst out in a deep voice that seemed to emanate from his belly: "You Jews raise your children badly. The parents have lost control over the younger generation. You've begun to spare the rod too much. Your rabbis no longer lead your people in the ways of your God. You cry to the outside world how cruel Russia is to you, but who forces you to stay here? It is too crowded for you inside the Pale? Then why don't you leave? The western border isn't closed to you!"

He dropped into a chair and lit a cigar. "The truth is that you've grown so fat and sassy here that the passageway has become too narrow for you . . . just like that fox that invaded the vineyard and couldn't get out after gorging on the grapes."

He waved his hand to indicate that the subject was finished. He was tired. The Jews shuffled toward the exit. The badge of the Union of the Russian People boded no good, and they were anxious to leave. The former Governor-General had accepted bribes. Would this one? The danger was terribly real and Nossan Lande trembled. But just as he reached the door someone stopped him. The old man prepared to give up his soul to God. He was sure that he would be thrown in prison. Despite being frightened, the others waited in the street. They stayed there for a long time, completely bewildered. Nossan Lande had done nothing apparent to offend the Governor-General. On the contrary, it had seemed that the new ruler had studied the old man with special interest and that Nossan Lande had somehow found favor in his eyes. And then—this! They were ready to send for his son-in-law, the lawyer, when suddenly the old man emerged, his face shining.

"Come, let us give thanks to the Almighty! He 'takes,' my friends, he 'takes'! Everything is as it should be. He 'takes'—but in a strange fashion!"

And this is how it happened. Late at night, old Nossan Lande was escorted through back alleys to a certain address. And from there, making slow progress with his old man's gait, crunching the dry snow beneath his shoes, praying to the God of Abraham, Isaac, and Jacob to guide him, he went the rest of the way alone. And as soon as his three escorts saw him enter the gate of the brightly lit palace, they went to a pre-arranged meeting place to wait for him to tap on the window and announce that the errand had been successful.

Once inside, Nossan Lande was led to a dim room where before a table lit by a single candle the Governor-General sat in his dressing robe over a glass of wine. The old man wasn't invited to sit but was left quaking by the door in his skunk fur coat. His blood ran cold when he reminded himself that the fate of thousands depended upon him. He bared his head and the cap slipped from his trembling fingers. He leaned with both hands on his cane. Bowing humbly, his face even paler than his beard, he waited for the proper signal.

But the representative of God's Anointed was in no hurry. With a rare sense of relish he savored the old Jew's discomfiture and obvious apprehension as he swayed before him like a shadow. It took all of the Governor-General's self-control to keep from ordering the silly-looking creature to dance.

He, the absolute ruler of an entire province, was the withered twig of an ancient, princely family. His grandfather had drunk, gambled, and wenched away most of the money that had accrued from the vast family holdings. His father had squandered what was left before committing suicide in a Paris garret. All that his mother had been left with had been the noble name and a mountain of debts. She had spent her entire life defending herself in courts against her husband's creditors. And try as she might she hadn't been able to win a place for her son in high society. This he had later managed by himself with flattery, self-degradation, and calculated bootlicking. As a cornet, he had toadied to the major. As a major, he had pandered to the generals. And so on up the line. In the process, his title had proven advantageous and he had finally made it to the royal court itself. There, he had been tolerated as a clown, a jester, a dancing companion for old maids. He had amused the Tsarevnas by donning a fur skin and imitating a drunken bear. The royal ladies had been delighted by his capers and deep basso. For Alexander II he had worn mutton chops; for Alexander III, a great wide beard; for Nicholas II, a spade beard tapering to a point. And finally, in the twilight of his life, he had been rewarded by being appointed Governor-General over the Pale of Settlement. And here he had come into his own. Drunk with power, he had launched a succession of banquets, balls, and hunts just as his ancestors had enjoyed before their estates had been plundered. And this kind of entertainment required money—a great deal of money.

And Nossan Lande stood there in the nearly dark room,

leaned on his cane, bowed his head humbly, and murmured a prayer while large beads of sweat formed on his forehead.

The table glowed redly as if a flame was burning in the cup of wine. From somewhere a piano was heard. Finally, the Governor-General uttered the appropriate words: "Difficult . . . very difficult . . . the people are dead-set against you sheenies."

And he brought the glass of wine to his lips. Old Nossan Lande trembled for the last time, picked up his cap, hooked the cane on his elbow, and prepared for the frightening bargaining that would begin now.

The Governor-General drank a quarter of the wine, put the cup on the table, and promptly became "drunk." His legs stretched forward, his nose wheezed—His Excellency was "asleep." Now, Nossan Lande did not hesitate for a moment. He knew precisely what to do. From a side pocket he took out a thick packet of money, laid it on the table, then quickly left the room. Through the partly ajar door he watched His Excellency count the money and held his breath. Would the thousands of blamelesss souls be saved from a massacre? The whole province had been under martial law for months; the Cossacks were on a rampage—destroying villages, whipping peasants to death, and ravishing their wives and daughters. And if the cedars themselves were already burning, what would happen to the moss on the wall?

His Excellency counted the thick sheaf of hundreds, grimaced, and shoved them aside. His legs stretched out again, his eyes closed, his head rolled to the side, his nose wheezed—he was "sleeping." Nossan Lande came in, put down another bundle of money, and waited once more. The procedure was repeated again and again until all the money vanished from the table. Then the old man came in and said: "Good evening," and His Excellency, as if seeing the old Jew for the first time, asked: "What does the community want?"

Nossan Lande handed him the petition from the loyal

and obedient servants of the Tsar, drawn up by his son-in-law, the lawyer. Without even glancing at the paper His Excellency threw it aside and said: "You can tell all the Jews in the city that I won't allow any violence and disorder here."

Nossan Lande was eager to plead protection for the Jews in the other parts of the Pale as well, but His Excellency stood up, indicating an end to the audience.

The old man barely made it back to the house where his escorts waited. He greeted them with loud lamentations of woe: "We've saved the city but what will happen to the other communities? Can one redeem one's life and leave others in danger?" He swore to leave the city and to go out among the village Jews to be with them when the knife blade descended. . . . But the others half carried him home, where he lay sick for a long time afterward. And after getting up, he isolated himself even further and resumed his old ways.

And on that particular morning, thrilled and grateful for getting his son back, he strode alongside the great Baal Shem Tov himself, across the mountains and up to the very gates of heaven. . . .

But suddenly, he was rudely brought down to earth as the tumult finally penetrated his ears. The shawl thrown over his back and the goose quill clutched in his left hand, he looked at the multitude that crowded the hall and demanded: "What's happened in the house?"

No one wanted to break the bad news to him, but looking at their faces he surmised that a tragedy had occurred. He raced up the stairs just in time to see his penitent son, Avner, being lifted from the floor, covered with blood. "Is he dead?" he asked. "Why doesn't someone answer?"

But no one spoke.

"Lord of the Universe!" he cried. "Why do You punish me this way? Tell me why so that everyone can hear! What was my crime? . . . What was my sin? . . ." Suddenly he straightened. The shawl slid off his rounded back and the left hand still clutching the goose quill rose high. "There never has been nor is there now a God! I, Nossan Ber the son of Esther, proclaim this for all to hear! There is no, there is no, there is no God! I want . . . you . . . to . . . bring me pork . . . so that . . . I can . . . bite into it . . . right here before everyone's eyes. . . ." His voice grew weaker, the goose quill dropped from his fingers, and he was borne to his room, unconscious.

The old mystic's denial of God swept like a fire through the house and out into the street. From there, the winds carried it to all the workshops, stores, and homes in the city. It passed from mouth to mouth and at each stop grew more elaborate and embellished. Soon, everyone swore on the coming of the Messiah to have been present when the old man had publicly bitten into a piece of pork. And the people began to converge on the four-story white building from all sides. Abushl ran to transmit the tidings to the spiritual leaders of the community and whipped them into a terrible frenzy. Nossan Lande a blasphemer? They tottered toward the house, canes in hand, and tips of beards in their mouths to offer condolences to a friend and fellow scholar and to investigate the frightful rumor in person. It grew more and more congested inside. The spotless floors turned black and grimy. The people gathered around the spot where the corpse had lain and the only one to dare tread there was Abushl, who sifted sand over the blood and began the ritual of burial right there and then. Through the opened windows streamed the bright sunshine, the scent of wet soil, and the twitter of sparrows bickering on the bare tree branches in the garden. Women sobbed. Girls silently dabbed at their eyes. Avner had undoubtedly shot himself because of unrequited love. Bearded Jews pressed against Nossan Lande's room to catch a word of what was being said between the old mystic and the rabbis. The occupants of the house were locked behind closed doors where the body had been taken. There were doctors there, the police and—Aunt Liba. Shifra, after exchanging a few words with Alexander, had vanished. But where? And would she be back soon? Aunt Liba stood there feeling lost. She could not understand why she had been brought here, but the reason soon became apparent. She was summoned to the table at which a uniformed official sat writing. She recognized him at once. It was the same gendarme colonel who had been at the Inn on the night Daniel had died. When he fixed his cold blue eyes on her, her heart lurched. She had been the first to raise the alarm and now she must tell everything that had occurred and precisely as it had happened.

"What do I know? What do you want of me? I only came to see my daughter. We sat and talked. While we were talking I heard a shot, then two more. So we ran out and saw— You know already what we saw."

"Never mind what *we* know. We want you to tell us exactly what he said before he died."

"I didn't hear . . . I don't remember. . . ."

"S . . . so we'll wait until you d . . . do remember."

Aunt Liba spied Alexander lurking in the corner and biting his fingernails anxiously behind a bookcase, and she went up to him.

"Why did you call me here?"

"Who are you? Who called you here? Why are you dragging around underfoot?"

"I'm not dragging around, I'm being dragged. . . ."

"What do you want here? Why isn't the house cleared of strangers?"

"I'm Shifra's mother. You still don't recognize me?"

He stopped chewing his nails and looked up at her in confusion. "Oh? . . . Don't bear us any grudges. No one here is at fault. You saw for yourself what happened. Who could figure on such a thing? My brother has spoiled all my plans. After all, you are supposed to be a wise woman. That's why I called you here."

"Wise or foolish, I won't allow what you have in mind. Where did Shifra go?"

"She mustn't be here. You came at a bad time and the fact that you say that you won't allow it—" He thrust his hand into his pocket. "Go home with my blessings."

Aunt Liba heard paper rustling as he counted the money in his pocket, and she took a step backward and held up her arms as if a stick had been raised to her. The thought of Alexander attempting to bribe her made her blush until tears came. From rage and humiliation she mumbled, "God save me!" and fled from him. She wanted to run to Yeva's room, to put on Shmarya's boots, pick up her bundle, and beg Itzhok to take her home. But the towering gendarme with the two pits of ice for eyes blocked her path. "We're not finished with you yet. You confirm that—"

Just then Yeva came in, a handkerchief pressed to her mouth. Seeing the gendarme badgering Aunt Liba, she came up and very politely but firmly said: "My husband will answer all your questions." And she led Aunt Liba to her own room.

"Yeva!" Aunt Liba cried, falling on the unmade bed, "did all this actually happen or did I dream it? And even if it was a dream, such a dream can cut your life in half. You should have seen him lying there with the blood pouring out from between his fingers! May neither of us live to see such a sight again. A person actually must be stronger than iron! I thought that your father-in-law would succumb right there and then. When I heard him cry out it made me feel better already. When he screamed, 'There is no God!' I repeated after him, 'There isn't! There isn't!' Woe is me, may the Eternal One punish me for my sinful words. But did I know what I was saying? But He will certainly forgive an old father. Who else can see better into a human heart? Oh, oh, the world is so full of sadness! There isn't a house where God's anger hasn't spilled. When you sit in your own

245

shack you think your troubles are the worst. . . . But why do you look at me this way, Yeva?"

"When I look at you or at Itzhok I feel the ground grow more solid beneath me."

"I don't know what you mean by that, Yiveniu."

"I can't explain it in a few words either."

Aunt Liba took off her shoes and reached for Shmarya's patched boots under the bed. "It's beyond me! First the ground grows harder for you people, then it grows softer. It's more than my foolish brain can grasp. You stumble around like drunks. . . . God take pity on you! Either you see the frost patterns forming in the forest in the dead of night or you can't see the sun in the sky in midday."

The noise in the house abated. The sound of feet scraping gingerly could be heard, then the footsteps quickened as if people were walking past something that frightened them, then rushing to get away from it. Soon the sound of departing footsteps could be heard and the strong odor of iodoform spread through the house.

"What a dreadful thing," Yeva said. "Was the sand used to cover the blood spot?"

Aunt Liba nodded.

"What a pity on the old man," Yeva said, handing Aunt Liba the other boot. "He'll never live through it! Of all his children, Avner was the only one to turn out a human being. He searched for something in the world, but he found nothing."

Aunt Liba finished putting on her second boot and stood up—tall, solid, her arms folded across her chest. "What was he looking for, I ask you? Before one goes searching one must have a goal. Why look for a paradise apple on a water-elder? Dearest God, they chase after a hare's shadow, then end up by shooting themselves. . . ."

Yeva looked at Aunt Liba, at her wide-sleeved dress and patched boots, above all, at the handsome, flushed face and stubborn lips—and was forced to smile.

"How can a person speak and laugh one minute, then take his life the next?" Aunt Liba asked angrily. "He searched for something—well, what of it? And who lives like a cow, beg the comparison, and doesn't search for something? What would you think of a tailor who killed himself just because his thread got tangled? But that a person should serve as his own Angel of Death! That a person should blot out his own sun! God have mercy on him!"

"We all have to die someday."

"Of course we do—no one lives forever. But who is so anxious to die? Only a fool wants to give up his life. Dear God, just to have a piece of bread each day and to walk barefoot through the garden in the summer . . ."

"What a beautiful soul you have, Auntie," Yeva said.

"Only I? Do you think your great-grandmother's soul was ugly? When she was long past ninety she used to go out into the garden by a beehive to hear the bees buzzing around her. And your great-grandfather Zorechl, who was already approaching his second Bar Mitzvah, used to roll up his sleeves, reach inside the hive and take out a piece of honeycomb for her. 'Here, Brocha dearest,' he'd say, 'for you. You have a sweet tooth, after all.' "

"Talk to me, Auntie, keep talking to me. You and Itzhok make so much sense when you speak."

"Don't compare me with Itzhok. Maybe I've gone beyond being a fool, but I'm far from being a sage. My head aches from all the trouble and cares but certainly not from an excess of wisdom. They call me Aunt Liba in the family, but what kind of an aunt am I to them? If I was rich Liba I'd be not only an aunt but a mother too. But this way, how can I be of help to anyone?" People come to cry on my shoulder and after they leave I cry to myself. A woe on my wisdom! I've been in this house twenty-four hours already and I'm still not sure if I'm asleep or awake. I feel like I'm having a nightmare. Do you think I didn't hear what you told me last night? But I'm so confused by all that's happened! A young, healthy man takes his life, and his pious old father cries out that there is no God. Doesn't this sound like a nightmare? Did I actually hear my own daughter tell me that she called me here to help make pork kosher? If all this isn't a nightmare then the world is about to be flooded again. You are asleep, too, Yeva. . . . Wake up, Yeva, your house is on fire! Don't you see how Shifra and Alexander —woe is me, I don't even know how to tell you this. . . .''

She deliberated whether to go on. Yeva was troubled enough, and hadn't Alexander said, "My brother has spoiled my plans"? Maybe she had said enough already. After all, she had mentioned their names together, she had warned Yeva that her house was on fire . . . still, she couldn't drop it completely, and continued to expound further, but in pantomime. Her eyes, her hands and shoulders seemed to say, "Yeva, don't you see? Shifra wants to steal your husband, to usurp your position and abandon you and your child to the fates."

Yeva felt warm and as if closed in. She unbuttoned her coat, folded her hands in back, and began to pace through the room. Her feet, slimmed by her sickness, were loose inside the shoes and made it difficult for her to walk. She kept stopping. "Don't say another word, Auntie. I know everything already. Tell me instead if there is a life for me somewhere? Can I find a house and a garden where I can walk barefoot in the summer?"

"What nonsense! Of course you can. You have a husband, a home, a child. Yes, Yeva, you have a child. And may they live to a hundred and twenty, you still have a mother and father and four brothers."

"No, Auntie, I have no husband nor did I ever have one. I can't live with him under one roof anymore. I do have a child. Indeed I do, Auntie. Some things are beyond belief and I am amazed myself why I don't hate this child. But I don't. I love her. She is so full of life—her skin actually glows with it. But where can one take such a child? I won't give her up to him! One day she will pay him back for all that he did to me! Can I go with her to my brothers and sisters-in-law? They are like strangers to me. You've been in my house for twenty-four hours and you haven't even mentioned my family. Nor have I asked you about them. Itzhok did mumble that everything there was 'the same as usual.' What a terrible 'same as usual' that is. It means that my mother is still sitting there with the buck in her arms and with that awful shorn head. Oh, Aunt Liba, those terrible 'steps' on her head!"

And Yeva put the handkerchief to her mouth and her eyelashes dipped in tears. "Where does one go, Auntie? Where does one go?"

"Yeva, make up with your husband. Don't make a living orphan of your child. Who lives as he pleases, my dear? Even if the things you told me last night were true—oh, I believe you! I believe you! You really bear a terrible wound in your heart. But in a way, Yiveniu, that is more your fault than his. *You* stood with him under the wedding canopy. *You* let him put the ring on your finger before God and man. The fact that you were dragged to the canopy by force is your parents' fault. And what about him, you'll ask? Let us not speak of decency here. He came like a merchant, the goods were placed before him, and he bought them according to law and to his own rules. Legally speaking, you became his wife. Then he took you home and what did you do? The whole city knew that Alexander Lande had taken a bride, arranged a wedding supper and a reception. All his friends and relatives came to meet you and you didn't even come out to see them. He had to make up some cock-and-bull story—the bride was indisposed. Do you think people are such fools that they don't catch on? It really was something to laugh at. A man brings home a bride who locks herself in a separate room and won't come out. You did stand under the canopy with him, after all. He did take you as his wife."

Yeva could not bear anymore and yanked the handker-

249

chief from her mouth. "Don't you defend him! Your eyes belie what your lips are saying. You cannot lie to me. Make up with him? Resign myself to such a life? I'd rather do what Avner did."

She ran to the window, her feet sliding in the too-large shoes, tore down the curtain with all her might, and yanked at the window that had been locked and sealed for the winter. A pane cracked as the inner window opened with a groan and yellowed strips of paper were left dangling from the frame. A cloud of dust rose up. Yeva caught her breath, then hammered and pushed with both hands, exerting her waning powers to force open the outer window. A sweet, balmy breeze came drifting into the room. Glittering sparks dripped from the roof. The scent of wet bark filled the air. Sparrows hopped noisily from branch to branch with wings outstretched.

"I'll go out into the world," Yeva said.

"God keep you!" Aunt Liba said, looking at Yeva who leaned on the windowsill breathing heavily, her face still drained of blood. "God pity you, where will you go? Will you wander like a gypsy from fair to fair?" She came up to Yeva and smoothed her hair. "Listen to me, Yiveniu. Come stay with me for a while. I'll make you the kind of groat pancakes that you like so much. Your father will come and we'll take everything under consideration at the same time."

"No, no, Auntie dear, I must stay here. Tell my father to come for me in a day or two. He must help me finish up here." Suddenly she wheeled. "I've known right along about Alexander and Shifra."

"You knew and you kept quiet?"

"Only today my eyes were opened to what a big fool I've been."

"If you know what a big fool you've been then there is still some hope for you. Well, what do you say to this thing?"

"What can I say? No, Auntie, don't cry. We're living at

250

a time when everyone's soles are on fire from treading on hot coals. Who can have complaints against anyone else these days? Can I tell Shifra that what she is doing isn't nice? Let it be the way it is, Auntie. To me, it's all the same whom he marries. They'll get along well together. Unless I'm wrong, they're pretty much alike. No, don't cry, Auntie, I'll come to see you this summer and we'll walk barefoot through the garden together. . . ."

Aunt Liba smiled her good but sad smile and thought: *We certainly will walk barefoot. Will I have any choice? By then, I'll be too far gone to wear shoes already. . . .*

"Yes, come to me, Yiveniu, and we'll walk barefoot through the garden. We'll sit in the sun with our eyes closed. In the evening we'll take the children down to the river to bathe under the willows. Oh, Yiveniu, how beautiful the world is and how bitter are our lives!"

She rose to go in her cracked boots, the moth-eaten burnoose, the gray, borrowed shawl over her head, and the basket in hand, but she still could not bring herself to leave. She kept turning her head hopefully toward the door. Maybe Shifra would still come back? How could she abandon a child forced by her unhappiness to leap headlong into the fire itself? To whom would Shifra turn for help and advice now? The hearse was already waiting in the courtyard below, and a kind of yellow-black stillness mingled with a sharp, bitter odor had settled over the house.

8

Yeva accompanied Aunt Liba partway outside, explaining in great detail how to get to the coachman's house. She kissed her goodbye and left her alone in the bright, sunny street. The great fair had filled the city with a variety of sounds and smells. Greasy, shiny puddles floated in the pitted, dug-up streets. Silvery smoke curled up into the clear, azure skies. As soon as Yeva had vanished from sight, Aunt Liba stepped behind a fence post and had herself a quiet little cry to keep her heart from drowning.

When she came to Ashmedai's house the mare was already harnessed to the sleigh. Avrom, beardless now but wearing a dashing mustache, sat in the sleigh fingering a coral necklace and trying to catch the sunlight in it as he mumbled to himself. Hearing footsteps, he looked up. When he saw that it was Aunt Liba he quickly hid the necklace inside his breast pocket, but just as he did this a round mirror in a gilt frame fell to the ground as if from sheer spite. He flushed in embarrassment, but his eyes sparkled with happiness. Aunt Liba smiled. A young man in love. He was bringing gifts from the city for Dobche.

"Never mind, Avrom, never you mind. Believe me, there's nothing to be ashamed of. Dobche deserves only the best. When will you invite me to the engagement party?"

"If it was up to me, you'd have been invited a long time ago. But I don't even know if she'll accept my presents. I talk and I talk, but she remains silent."

"You foolish boy, when a girl says nothing it's often more

252

than if she would speak. That is the golden silence, Avrom."

"Do you think she'll accept my presents?"

"Why wouldn't she? Are you, God forbid, a bad fellow? I should have such a good year. Why do you show me your cane? With God's help your leg will heal completely and even if you should limp a little, what of it? Jacob was a bigger man than you and he also limped. Still, didn't Rachel stand under the wedding canopy with him?" She put her basket in the sleigh and started to ask about his father. She was very anxious to talk things over with Itzhok. But just then she saw him coming out of the house carrying a child. Akiva was walking behind him, and Ashmedai and his wife stood in the doorway.

In the short time since she had last seen him Itzhok seemed to have grown even grayer. He walked quickly to the sleigh. "Liba, I thought I'd have to leave you behind already," he said. "No, no, don't bother to explain. I heard what happened at the Landes'. What a tragedy! What a curse! Yes, I know, Liba, I know everything. There is nothing you can tell me. They're running from us, Liba, our children are running from us. They run wherever their legs will take them . . . whichever of them can—runs. They run even to the grave. Don't stand there, Liba, get in the sleigh. What do you think? Will the child be warm enough? Are you all settled in there? Good, take the child." He turned to the coachman and his wife. "A good day to you, my friends, and many thanks. May God reward you for your hospitality and your goodness. Stay well, dear people . . . and you, Friend Akiva, don't forget the way to the Inn. Drop in on us some fine day even though Daniel is no longer there. Well, let's go, Avrom, my son. The day does not stand still. Don't plead with her—here, give me the whip. She would stand there and wiggle her ears for another three hours if you'd let her. Everything she has to hear and know."

Itzhok Boyar walked silently behind the sleigh as it plowed through the grimy, nearly melted snow of the narrow streets on the edge of the city. The metal runners often scraped against the cobblestones. Wagons coming from opposite directions made way for each other as the coachmen brandished their whips and cursed foully. Half-naked children—flushed, bareheaded, and deeply absorbed—whistled shrilly to pigeons racing overhead. The first streams of the spring thaw came trickling down from out of the hills. Crows cawed, fluttered their wings, and fanned out their tails. Magpies cried as they settled in flocks on the fences. Swifts clung to chimneys, scouting likely places for nests. The air smelled of willows bursting with sap and of freshly baked bread.

"Liba, once we get out of the city we'll have a bite to eat. I can tell from looking at you that you haven't eaten anything today yet. Don't neglect yourself. Troubles here, troubles there, a person still has to eat. No point in taking it out on yourself. You especially have to guard your health, Liba."

She lowered her lashes and nodded. It was true. A life was growing within her. And she had made a promise to Itzhok. "I'll keep my word, Reb Itzhok," she assured him.

"It should only come true. . . ."

Coming out into the broad, sparkling-white field, Itzhok pulled out a bag from under the hay. "Let's see what Mother prepared for us? Oatmeal pancakes, roast veal . . . why the long face, my son? Don't these things appeal to you?"

"Who said they don't? But out here in the middle of the field? In the cold?"

"Ah, so you think a little whisky would go nicely, do you? In that case, get up and look there in the box of chaff. There should be something—"

Avrom twirled his mustache with satisfaction. "That's something else altogether. Cold meat with cold whisky can keep a soldier going already!"

"Wait, don't sit down yet, Avrom. There should be a cup there also. What do you say, Liba, should we give you a sip too?"

"No, I won't drink. But I'll dip a piece of the pancake."

"Better have a drink. There isn't enough there for dunking. We'll give you the first drink, Avrom. The Torah says: 'A father must have pity on his children.' Look at that, will you? She's stopping to look around already! Give her a taste of the whip, Avrom, or else we'll have to give her a drink too. No, not so hard, my son; after all, she's one of God's creatures. Giddy up now, you! Giddy up!"

The wind blew in stronger from the field. The snow crusted over and the air grew drier and more transparent. The alders lining the road rustled beneath the westbound sun. Long shadows formed across the snow. Somewhere deep within the primeval forest the frosty night lurked with its late-rising moon. Itzhok Boyar squinted at the child as he finished his second cup of whisky. The innkeeper's drinking and brave talk did not deceive Liba. She had noticed his right eyebrow cocked high and his hairy, chapped hand twitching. She sensed that this was somehow connected with the child and she was consumed with curiosity about the little girl. Was it the one Shifra had mentioned? But she could not believe that the devout Itzhok, who had ruthlessly disposed of all reminders of Herut, would accept the child of a convert into his house. Since Herut had run away from home leaving a note in her father's phylactery bag saying that she could not live like her mother, no one had heard that she had borne a child. At first she had gone to Petersburg to study, and had written an occasional letter home. Although she had never requested help, Itzhok had sent whatever he could afford and even Gavril had sent twenty-five rubles one time. A girl who was studying needed help, and the Boyars could use a doctor in the family.

Her leaving had been considered a serious tragedy and the blame had been laid upon Daniel, and even more upon Akiva, who had brought her worldly books and filled her head with wanton thoughts. The upshot had been that the Boyars had commenced to pay stricter attention to their sons and daughters and married them off in a hurry to avoid complications. Itzhok had consoled himself that it had been merely a matter of luck. As suddenly as she had left, so suddenly was she likely to return. But one day, Abushl had brought the terrible news that Herut had converted. The reaction had been chaotic. Bearer of evil tidings that he was, Abushl was not considered to be a liar, and it had become terribly clear why she had ceased writing altogether and why Daniel's letters and the money he had sent her had come back unopened. Itzhok and Rivka had observed the suitable period of mourning over her, and later the family had heard that she had been sent to Siberia. And from then on, her name was never mentioned again. If someone did refer to her, it was not by name but as "the one who stood under the church-bell."

The sun moved farther west while the sleigh continued its northward direction. Itzhok sat with legs dangling over the side, his bare hands resting on his knees and his eyes closed as he recited the prayer offered after eating. Avrom held the reins and sang quietly to himself:

"What did you do to me, dear life of mine,
That I am so drawn to you?"

His cup was running over with happiness. He had come out of the war whole and she was waiting for him back there, his Dobche. . . .

The big-bellied mare snorted, twitched her split ear, and blew white clouds of vapor through her nostrils. She trotted along the rolling road past dark pine woods and over frozen streams where the ice rang echoingly beneath her hoofs. In the center of a field an isolated windmill spun its blades as if straining but unable to lift itself from the ground. Two young birches at its base glowed with a flickering, golden glitter.

Aunt Liba stared at the child that sat wrapped in its fur coat without making a sound. It was obviously accustomed to being with strangers. She couldn't have been more than five or six, yet wrinkles had already formed in her forehead. She seemed to be thinking about something very intensely, as if wondering what was happening to her. Her eyes reflected fear and unhappiness. Children who had had no chance to be children often bore this look and Aunt Liba, to whom it was all too familiar, shuddered to see it. She made an opening in the fur coat to let the child breathe. The little girl thrust out her head. "Is it still far to my mama's?"

Itzhok Boyar seemed to shake awake. "What? . . . To your mama? . . . Soon as we cross those woods."

"And my mama is there?"

"Yes, my child . . . somewhere there . . . now sit back and don't talk."

He threw one leg inside the sleigh. "Go ahead, Liba, ask me already! Don't you want to know whose child this is? It's hers. Can't you recognize the big gray eyes? The child's eyes take up half of her face, just like her mother's. When I first saw her, I started to shake. For eight years those eyes have been haunting me. And then I saw her. I didn't have to ask anybody—I knew right away why the coachman rode out in the middle of the night to intercept us. This whole business of calling me here was all a pretext. Avrom could have come home by himself. But they figured right. Akiva knows me. I won't keep you in suspense too long. I'll shake the whole tree down at once. . . ."

Aunt Liba forgot everything else and sat up straighter on the sack of straw, straining forward in order not to miss a single word. Wagons and sleighs kept passing from both directions and shattering the stillness of dusk. Itzhok exchanged greetings with the peasants but instead of "shaking down the whole tree at once," as he had promised, he filled his pipe and began to speak about the coachman's wife, of all things.

"We rode to the coachman's courtyard, unhitched the mare, fed and watered her. Do you think that we went straight into the house then? Far from it! We spent over an hour waiting outside in the cold. His wife wouldn't open the door. I stood there and looked at him in amazement. Where does a person get so much patience? He kept tapping gently on the window and whispering: 'Machlie, open up . . . Machlie, a stranger is at the door.' But no one came. It was as if everyone inside had died. He tapped and tapped. Machlie here, Machlie there . . . To make a long story short, finally a voice was heard inside. 'Who is it?' 'It's me, Machlie.' 'Oy, woe is me, is it you, Lazar? You're standing out there in the cold?' Now I was sure she'd come running out to open the door. . . . But after a while, it grew so quiet again inside that you could hear a pin drop."

"And the coachman?" Aunt Liba asked with indignation—"he didn't bust in the panes?"

"That's what's so puzzling," Itzhok said, finishing his pipe. "I, in his place, would have smashed in the door, but this brute who could tear an oak out of the ground with his bare hands stood there like a dunce and kept tapping and begging. 'Machlie, open up. . . .' Still, no one came. It was like a voice crying out in the wilderness. He tapped and tapped and tapped. Finally we heard again: 'Oy, in such a terrible frost he stands outside. Sarele, Sare-le! Go open the door for your poor father!' So you think this Sarele would run to open the door? Not at all! Didn't even make a move to get up. It got quiet in the house again. But the giant still didn't get angry. He even apologized for her. 'It's not that she is mean, God forbid. She has a good heart, but after a hard day's work she can hardly lift her head. It's such a shame to wake her.' I looked at him and I thought: How much compassion like this is there in the world? What does a 'woe is me!' mean when you're standing outside freezing?"

He grew silent. The wind grew stronger and criss-crossed the whiteness of the field with green and blue shadows. Aunt Liba sat with her hands drawn inside of her sleeves and her lips pressed tightly together. Itzhok's abrupt silence horrified her for some strange reason. It would have been better if he hadn't said anything at all. He found it so difficult to come to the point. She knew that it wasn't easy to discuss one's troubles with others. It only served to revive the tragedy and to bring it out into the open. Only then could one conceive of it in all its enormity, and the solace offered by others only emphasized how alone one was and how little others understood. No, it was much easier to let trouble nestle within one's heart where it was muffled and finally completely smothered.

Suddenly, she heard him say: "Liba, is the child asleep?"

"No, Reb Itzhok. She's sitting up looking around. She seems to be accustomed to being with strangers."

"Yes, she knows already what a pound of trouble is worth, the poor thing." And he flung his other leg inside of the sleigh, straightened his back and clasped his long, narrow beard between his fingers.

"Anyhow, Machlie finally opened the door. I lay down on the floor and had a nice snooze. But the minute it got light I went out to find a House of Worship. I wanted to say the mourner's prayer for my dead children. . . ."

His chapped, shaggy hands fell to his knees again, where the fingers began to clench and unclench.

"Don't say any more, Reb Itzhok," Aunt Liba urged, "why stir up old wounds?"

But he was determined to go on. It seemed as if not his voice were speaking but rather his anger. He shouted as if wanting the whole world to know that he, Itzhok Boyar, had not been allowed near the Holy Scroll. "When I left the House of Worship I couldn't find my way back to Ashmedai's. I didn't know if I was in this world or in some other. I stood on the river bank and though the sun was shining everything looked black to me. Everything! Did you ever see black snow? Liba, I swear to you on my poor orphaned grandchildren that I'm telling you the absolute truth! Wherever I looked the snow was black! Akiva led me out of there by the hand and I followed him like a blind man to the Doctor's. He is my worst enemy!"

"Who, Reb Itzhok?"

"Akiva. He is the one responsible for my greatest tragedy. No, don't say anything, Liba. What do you know about it? It wasn't Daniel, may he rest in peace, who led her astray. He used to talk to her like to a child. For that's what she actually was then—a child. What was she—not quite sixteen? But Akiva, who makes fun out of everything in the world, he talked to her as if she were a grownup. Even then my heart told me that no good would come of it. I tried to keep her away from him and watched over her the whole summer. But what good did it do? One cannot hide from calamity. He was my executioner. This 'Friend Akiva' was actually the one who convinced her to run away from home. Yes, Liba, he once confessed it to me himself. He tried to justify it by saying that he hadn't intended for it to turn out this way. The most important thing for these people is to find excuses. It's true that she ruined his life as well. Why do you think he never married? He can't find a place for himself either, so he wanders from town to town in that wagon and plays his fiddle. . . . Ask him why he lives this kind of life. He'll answer you with a joke or some flippant remark. He claims to be forever riding to some golden land. As if golden lands could be reached so easily. But he doesn't fool me. I know that he is still waiting and hoping for her to come back to him. Nothing surprises me anymore, Liba. But what can we do if He Who is eternal sits in heaven and keeps His feet on us?"

He grew silent again, but only with his mouth. The rest of him kept talking and expressing itself.

The sun was setting. The blackness of the forest drew nearer. They seldom passed a village now, only an occasional farmhouse isolated from life and the world and squatting on some knoll with windows glowing golden-red from out among the green firs.

Itzhok bent toward the child. "It seems to be sleeping."

"Yes, she finally fell asleep."

"It shouldn't catch cold, God forbid. Let's keep moving, Avrom. Let's hurry right along, my son. There is a strong frost coming." He suddenly seized Aunt Liba's elbows. "Tell me, Liba, what should I have answered the Doctor? Every word he spoke pierced my brain! My heart overflowed and he kept slashing and slashing away at me like some murderer! And 'Friend Akiva' stood there playing with a human skull and smiling that rusty smile of his. Everything that the Doctor said I knew myself already. Can there be any justification for what she did? Any excuse? But the one thing I hadn't known was the real reason for her conversion. I didn't want to know it. As if there could be a reason for such a thing! But since I was already trapped in this *Gehenna* I sat there and I listened. It seems that when she was in Petersburg she wanted to study. So in order to get a place to eat and sleep she took a job as a maid. Everything seemed to be alright already but she didn't have the right of residence and the police were all set to ship her out unless she brought them that little book."

"What book? Which book?" Aunt Liba asked, staring at him.

"What book, which book?" Itzhok mimicked her angrily. But he quickly reminded himself that he had no right to vent his rage on her and recalled that he had used the very same phrase when the Doctor had told him the story. He leaned forward and barely whispered: "The one that said that she was a whore . . ." *

Aunt Liba wrung her hands and moaned loudly.

"Yes, under Nicolai, a whore enjoys all the privileges. There she was, a child of sixteen . . . all alone . . ." He closed his eyes and his face twisted with bitterness.

---

* Translator's note: In Tsarist Russia, a Jewish woman would register herself as a prostitute to be permitted free and unrestricted residence throughout the empire. Otherwise, all Jews and Jewesses were confined to the Pale of Settlement.

"Reb Itzhok!" Aunt Liba cried, "God be with you!"

"Don't shout, Liba, don't shout," he said, his eyes still shut. He shook his head. "We sit by the rivers of Babylon and we must repeat every day: 'How good are thy tents, Jacob . . .'" He tapped his pipe against the side of the sleigh. "They tell me in the city that when old Nossan Lande saw his son's body covered with blood he cried out that there is no God. I know just how he felt. I must confess, Liba, that if the Eternal One wasn't so high up in heaven I would smash all His windows. . . ."

He glanced up at the sky fearfully, then seized her elbows again. "Tell me, Liba, what should I have answered the Doctor? His words made my heart stop, and the hair stand up on my head. And he kept slashing and slashing away. He told me how they beat her in prison and trample on her. Then they pour cold water over her and begin all over again. They wanted to know the names of her confederates but she wouldn't tell them. Liba, Liba, how strong can a person be? I was ready to run to that prison and to go to the gallows in her place; to throw myself in the fire to save her, but in my ears kept ringing the cry of the Jews in the House of Worship. 'She brought misfortune down upon us!' And I sat there and didn't do anything. I told myself: 'Itzhok, you dare not! Not even if the Doctor is right in saying that the Black Hundred would make up another excuse. If not Herut, they would find some other reason to kill Jews. Still, I asked myself, 'Why should the police parole her only to me? Why couldn't she be released to her Christian family? After all, her name is now Christia Vasilevna.' No, Liba, I refused to be a party to putting a burning torch in a haystack. I wouldn't want, not even by the thousandth of a thousand to be responsible for a false accusation against our people. One who does such a thing deserves to be stoned to death and his name to be cursed for generations."

The mare stopped, turned her muzzle toward the sleigh, dangled her lower lip, and twitched her notched ear. The sun hung like a huge, fiery wheel on the horizon. Avrom, his face turned toward his father, had not noticed how long they had been standing still. Aunt Liba was surely unaware of it. Itzhok's words had cast an icy pall over her heart.

"Hey now!" Itzhok suddenly shouted, "we're not moving. Let's get going, Avrom!"

But seeing that his son wasn't about to do anything he got out, tightened the mare's bit, and untangled the reins. He climbed back into the sleigh and let his feet hang over the side again.

"Giddy up! Giddy up, you! . . . It's easy for me to discuss these things with you, Liba. We both share a heap of trouble. But I can't talk to those driveling prophets. I lose my tongue when I'm around them. What can a simple village Jew like me have to say to a lawyer? His tongue has been dipped in gold, his livelihood depends on it. So I told them about Yontel the Martyr. Let them gather from it what they want. . . . I grabbed Avrom and asked Yeva to tell you that we're leaving. I was itching to get out of there as fast as possible. Rivka and Malka are home alone with the orphans and Rivka is dying to see Avrom. Giddy up! Gee up there! When we got to the coachman's house he wasn't home. His wife, the one I thought was such a witch for not letting us in last night, was sitting at the table and feeding this child. As soon as I saw those huge, gray eyes the blood rushed to my brain. I felt as if my legs had been chopped out from under me. I sat down and told Avrom to hitch up the mare. I tried to calm down. Aren't there many children in the world with eyes like that? I told myself. And the woman began complaining to me that the neighbors had beaten up her daughter again. Her Sarele is a queer child. She has this urge to play with fire. She finds matches somewhere and lights them. So she isn't allowed near anyone's house. But all the time that the woman was talking the child's eyes kept burning into me. I asked the woman: 'Tell me, I beg you, whose child is this?' She answered me as if I had insulted her.

'Where would such a little chick come to me? My youngest is eleven. No, Akiva brought me this one for a present. She's been with us for nearly five months now. As if I didn't have enough troubles of my own . . .' I couldn't listen to any more, Liba. I ran outside to Avrom and asked him: 'You didn't hear whose child this is? Akiva didn't tell you?' He didn't answer. 'Speak up!' I yelled. He kept harnessing the horse and without looking up he said: 'It's Herut's, Father!' ''

Avrom nodded. That was just what had happened. He turned to his father. "Should I have denied it?"

"God forbid!" Itzhok said. "Am I finding fault with you? If they had told me about the child from the beginning . . . Giddy up you, the wolves should devour you! Giddy up! . . . If it concerned a child—is it asleep, Liba? God forbid it shouldn't catch cold. Maybe you'll cover it with something else?"

Liba dabbed at her eyes. "No, Reb Itzhok, it's not necessary. She's well covered."

Itzhok Boyar sat with his back bowed, his head tilted toward the uplifted shoulder, and his ear listening to the sound of train wheels clacking over rails in the distance. Somewhere nearby, there was a little-used way-station, and a verst and a half farther—a compound for convicts in transit. Soon, the wind carried to them the sound of a locomotive's whistle and a white puff of steam appeared on the horizon.

Itzhok moaned softly. Aunt Liba, her own cares forgotten, tried to think of some way to console him. Avrom, huddled in his greatcoat, his legs crossed beneath his body, the soldier's fur cap with the cockade on his head—Itzhok felt that it would be wise to wear it in such troubled times—leaned his back against his father's and thoughtfully puffed on a cigar butt.

The day was coming to an end. The sun was sinking fast. The earring-like appendages dangling from the alders glowed scarlet against the white snow. The birds that had gathered on the tree boughs to watch the flaming sun go down, launched their hymn to spring—a melody of passionate love and unrest.

The moment the occupants of the sleigh grew silent the mare began to trot happily, even to prance, as the spleen gurgled noisily within her ponderous belly. They were almost upon the paved government highway. They would have to cross it and continue on through the woods. The wind there would not be as biting and the deep, hard-packed snow would provide easier passage for the runners.

Itzhok Boyar still sat in the same position, his eyes shut and the beard clasped between his fingers. His eyebrow shot up even higher as the faint echo of a sad, haunting chant came drifting in from the fields. At first, he thought that it was his imagination, but after a while there was no mistaking it. From the valley below, in which half of the sun had already immersed itself, the chorus of a multitude of voices rose and expanded, growing ever louder and nearer.

He pulled at the reins. "Avrom, Liba—do you hear it too?"

They did and were astounded. Who could be singing in that stretch of wilderness far from any known settlement?

Terror consumed them. In a Russia of prisons, floggings, and gallows, any departure from the ordinary produced fear. These were extraordinary times. One could be stopped, searched, and arrested anywhere and at any time, without ever learning the reason. It was not unusual to be deported in chains or even executed without leaving a trace—and the occupants of the sleigh trembled with fear. But coming closer to the wide and elevated Kazionem Tract, with its telegraph poles and striped road markers, they suddenly saw a troop of mounted Cossacks driving a horde of people down from the winding, hilly path onto the highway. At the end of the procession of marching men rolled three green, high-sided wagons full of women pressed closely together. Aunt Liba's mouth grew suddenly dry and she was overcome with nausea again. Her fear made her hug the sleeping child closer to her bosom. Avrom knelt in the sleigh to better display his military greatcoat and fur cap with cockade.

Itzhok Boyar, his face whiter than the snow, tugged at the reins and jumped down from the sleigh. He stood erect at the edge of the highway, his hands folded behind his back and his head high, looking intently at the approaching mob.

"Father," Avrom said, "let's get away from here. Those are convicts. . . ."

But Itzhok Boyar stood there while his eyes roamed over the highway—searching, searching.

Several more sleighs pulled up alongside the road. Seeing the free people, the convicts began to sing louder. The Cossacks rode back and forth along the line with sabers bared but the mighty song swelled lustily across the red-tinted wastes.

> "Enemy winds blow overhead,
> The powers of darkness oppress us . . ."

Itzhok's staring eyes darted from face to face. No! Not there! Only men here . . . mostly peasants and of all ages— even graybeards. Suddenly, he turned around. "Avrom, give me your hand!"

"Father, what's wrong? Here is my hand. . . ."

Itzhok took his son's hand but he did not speak. His eyes had met someone else's on the highway. "Avrom," he barely whispered, "it's she. . . ."

"Where, Father, where?"

"The last wagon . . . in front . . . the third one . . . I knew that she'd be here. She's seen me too . . . there, you see, Avrom? She's torn the kerchief from her head."

Herut had recognized her father. She tried to rise but her legs would not support her and she fell backwards. Her comrades caught her and held her up firmly. She swayed in their arms in the rapidly moving wagon and waved her kerchief at her father. She was saying something to him too, but even Itzhok's keen ears could not make it out against the booming sound of the song and the angry cries of the Cossacks.

He moved closer to the highway, but two Cossacks came riding up swiftly and he stopped. It wasn't fear that held him back but a sudden reminder that there was something he had intended to do. But what was it? The frustration made his senses reel and the snow grew black before his eyes again.

Seeing the Cossacks riding toward his father, Avrom leaped from the sleigh and began to pull him away. "What are you trying to do, get those dogs started on you too? They'd kill you right here without a second thought, and get a St. George's Cross for doing it."

Only after he had been dragged back to the sleigh did Itzhok remember what he had wanted to do, and seizing the child he held it high in the air. Sleepy and frightened, she began to scream.

"Never mind, Liba, never you mind! What if it cries? Let Herut see her child and hear its voice!"

The song stopped abruptly, as if it had been axed, and a brooding silence descended over the fields as the convicts recognized the significance of the gruesome confrontation. Even the Cossacks turned aside. Herut, supported by her comrades, rose high in the wagon, one hand on her wind-whipped hair, the other gripping the kerchief. She did not call out, nor strain toward the child but her head nodded. She saw, she saw everything. . . . The wagon increased its speed and the Cossacks raised an even louder clamor but the quickly darkening fields again resounded to a stirring chorus.

> "The fateful struggle with our foes we have launched,
> We know not what our future holds—"

And Itzhok Boyar, holding the screaming child aloft against the light of the dying sun, locked his eyes for one final second with the two huge, gray, shining ones as they quickly swept past and were lost. But one word drifted back to him clearly in the twilight: "Father! . . ."

It took Aunt Liba a long time to quiet the child. She cradled it in her arms and whispered, without knowing what her lips were saying. Finally, sucking on a piece of the candy that Avrom was bringing for Dobche, the child dozed off. But it kept tossing in its sleep and whimpering. The sleigh moved along silently. The hearts of its three occupants were filled with grief and a helpless rage.

"Giddy up!" Itzhok shouted at the mare pounding the whiphandle against the side of the sleigh. "Get along with you, damn it!"

Halfway in the night the wind carried the smell of smoke into the forest. In the distance, as if issuing from the earth itself, they saw flames spurting into the sky. The fire appeared, then vanished as if something had smothered it. Gray-black clouds of smoke curled upward. But soon fire broke out in another spot and the flames shot up ever higher and higher until they seemed to have ignited the moon itself.

"Reb Itzhok!" Aunt Liba cried, unable to hold out any longer. "The woods are burning!"

"Let them burn, Liba, let them burn. But it's too far away to be the forest. That's Squire Bogushevski burning there. . . . Gee-up!"

Red shadows licked the black tree-trunks. The mare snorted and strained to leave the road. The air grew foul with the stench of charred wool and burned chickpeas. Sparks leaped into the heavens and the half moon hung over the earth like a gleaming, sharpened, bloody axe. . . .